BLOOD AND FIRE

Also by Nick Brownlee

Bait

BLOOD AND FIRE

Nick Brownlee

MINOTAUR BOOKS

A Thomas Dunne Book
New York

A THOMAS DUNNE BOOK FOR MINOTAUR BOOKS.
An imprint of St. Martin's Publishing Group.

www.thomasdunnebooks.com
www.minotaurbooks.com

Library of Congress Cataloging-in-Publication Data

Brownlee, Nick.
　　[Burn]
　　Blood and fire / Nick Brownlee.—1st U.S. ed.
　　　　p. cm.
　　"A Thomas Dunne book."
　　ISBN 978-0-312-55024-0
　　1. Police—Kenya—Fiction. 2. Detective and mystery stories.
3. Mombasa (Kenya)—Fiction. I. Title.
　PR6102.R73B87 2010
　823'.92—dc22

　　　　　　　　　　　　　　　　　　　　　　2010032673

First published in Great Britain as *Burn* by Piatkus

First U.S. Edition: November 2010

10　9　8　7　6　5　4　3　2　1

For Geoff and Jane and Candace and Lucie

Acknowledgements

Respect is due to the homies of the Collingwood Massive, especially Dave, Helen, Bez, Carole and Jo, who have been waiting patiently for me to deliver for the best part of 20 years and whose collective goodwill has been an inspiration. Thanks also to my brilliant editor Emma Beswetherick, my equally brilliant agent Jane Gregory, and the formidable team at Piatkus. Of course none of it would have been possible without the wonderful and ever-supportive Janey, and little Georgia Isabella Brownlee who makes me laugh every day.

BLOOD AND FIRE

Day One

1

When she opened the door to her apartment there was a month's mail on the mat, forty-one messages on her answering service, and her killer was in the kitchen, a stiletto knife held lightly in the gloved fingers of one hand.

She ignored the mail and pressed the play button on the machine in the hallway. By the time she had emptied her suitcase on the bed, stripped out of her travelling clothes, showered and changed into jogging pants and a T-shirt, there was only one message left to hear.

A man's voice said, 'This is FBI Special Agent Clarence Bryson. Please give me a call when you get this.'

Agent Bryson gave his number. Then there was a beep and a robot voice said, '*There are no more messages.*'

Yeah, yeah, she thought as she towel-dried her hair and dragged it back into a ponytail in front of the bedroom mirror. *For now.*

She went back into the hallway and, two-handed,

scooped up as much mail as she could. Bills and junk. Nobody ever sent anything interesting through the post any more. Nobody ever sent *letters*. She sorted it into two piles on the hall table, one on each side of the telephone. The junk towered above the bills, which was the only good thing to report.

The phone rang. She stared at it just long enough for the answering service to kick in.

'This is FBI Special Agent Clarence Bryson again. Please call me urgently when you get this message.'

As he gave the number her hand hovered momentarily over the receiver.

But she knew what Agent Bryson wanted to talk about. And right now she just wasn't ready. Things had happened too fast. She needed to get her head together.

She grabbed the bills, went through to the living room and tossed them on the coffee table. Then she pulled the blinds covering the windows. Weak sunlight filtered through three large panes of grimy glass. The panes needed scouring. But then after what had happened so did the whole apartment. She could still smell his expensive cologne clinging to the furniture. She could see the indentations in the sofa cushions where he used to sit. She knew she would find his suits hanging in the bedroom wardrobe and his toothbrush in the mug on top of the bathroom medicine cabinet. Everything needed to be tossed into a big pile in the middle of the room and set alight.

In the kitchen, her killer watched through a crack in the connecting hatch door.

The door buzzer sounded.

She grimaced. *Special Agent Clarence Bryson, by any chance?*

She retraced her steps down the hallway and opened the door. Something fast and sinuous shot past her ankles into the living room and she let out an exclamation of surprise and delight.

A fat woman in a kaftan was standing in the corridor outside.

'We thought we heard you,' she said. 'He's been *sooo* excited.'

'Mrs Liebnitz – what can I say?'

The fat woman shook her head solemnly and backed away towards the apartment door behind her. 'Don't say a word, dear. I'll leave you two to get reacquainted.'

Having shut the door, she returned to the living room.

'Chico?'

There was a noise from the kitchen and she smiled, not knowing that it was the sound of her cat's neck being snapped with a single twist.

'Chico?'

She entered the kitchen. She saw the cat lying on the breakfast bar with its eyes open and blood on its teeth. She drew breath to scream but a gloved hand closed around her mouth. The killer pressed the tip of the stiletto against the base of her skull and, with one smooth upward movement, pushed the blade in as far as the hilt.

Ten minutes later there was a hammering at the door. Seconds after that the door smashed open on its hinges and a dozen armed men in protective vests and helmets streamed into the hallway. By the time

FBI Special Agent Clarence Bryson entered the apartment it had been cleared and locked down, and one of the armed men was standing guard over the dead woman and her cat lying in the kitchen.

2

The two men had dined that night at an Algerian café just off Government Square in Mombasa Old Town, near enough to the dhow harbour to hear the shouts of the stevedores unloading sacks of sorghum from the night freighters, but far enough from it to escape the stink of rotting fish and sump oil. And later – much later – they would reflect that, until Lol Quarrie plummeted a hundred feet from the ramparts of Fort Jesus and landed at their feet with a sound like breaking eggs, it had been a most convivial evening.

Detective Inspector Daniel Jouma, as befitted a man with the wiry build of a jockey and the abstemiousness of a saint, chose a small dish of chickpeas and a pot of mint tea. Jake Moore, six foot tall and with the appetite of a horse, ordered a slab of bloody steak and a schooner of ice-cold Tusker beer. They sat at a table by the open doorway and talked and laughed, and occasionally, lost in thought, gazed up at the glow of the city lights reflected on the high scudding cloud and wondered just how a fifty-one-year-old Kenyan policeman and an English fishing-boat skipper fifteen years his junior should have ended up as friends.

A month ago they had never met. Jake was an ex-Flying Squad cop whose dreams of running a charter business were sinking faster than a lead marlin weight. Jouma, meanwhile, had reached the conclusion that his thirty years in Kenya Police had been a waste of time and that the country of his birth was deservedly going to hell.

Then a thirty-foot fishing boat called *Martha B* had blown up six miles off the coast along with its skipper Dennis Bentley, and Jake and Jouma had been plunged into a deadly game of cat and mouse with an organisation whose trade was human lives. Patrick Noonan, the man who had controlled the organisation's east African supply network, had died in the blades of a five-hundred horsepower outboard motor after a desperate struggle with Jake and was buried in an unmarked grave because nobody knew who he actually was – not even the woman who had once been his lover.

'Have you heard from Martha since she returned to New York?' Jouma asked as the café proprietor cleared the plates with a peevish glance at the half-eaten chickpeas.

Jake lit a cigarette and ordered a glass of *boukha*, a potent Algerian fig brandy. 'I expect she's got more important things to think about,' he said.

Martha Bentley clearly meant a lot to the Englishman – certainly more than the money she planned to invest in his ailing business. Her return to New York, where she worked as a high-flying lawyer, was only temporary while she sorted her dead father's affairs and finalised the transfer of his insurance money. But while Jake was a man who did not show his feelings, Jouma could sense that he missed her more than he would ever admit.

They paid and walked along Mbaraki Road in the direction of the sixteenth-century fort. Lights were burning in the shops and cafés and the thick night air was laden with the smell of strong coffee and hookah smoke.

'How is life under the new regime at Mama Ngina Drive?' Jake asked.

'Superintendent Simba has yet to show her colours.'

'Or her claws?'

Jouma frowned. 'I am of the opinion that anyone will be an improvement on Superintendent Teshete.'

'I hope so, Inspector. For your sake.'

So did Jouma. Having put one corrupt boss behind bars, he had no desire to go through the process again.

They had arrived at the hulking stucco walls of Fort Jesus. It was seven o'clock in the evening. By the entrance were a line of hawkers selling trinkets, and nearby old men were playing kalooki beneath the cashew trees. It was such an utterly mundane scene that what happened next seemed all the more unreal.

Jake saw the body out of the corner of his eye. With one hand he grabbed Jouma by the arm and yanked him clear. It was an instinctive reflex and one which most probably saved the small Mombasa detective's life – because Lol Quarrie weighed in excess of sixteen stone and would have crushed him had he landed on him. Instead the body landed head first on the concrete at the foot of the wall, less than five feet from where they stood.

Later still Jake would find it odd that his abiding impression of that terrible moment was not Lol Quarrie's skull bursting open and spattering him with blood and brains, but how strange it was that the dead man's smart blazer and flannels should be covered in dirt and his fingernails should be torn and bleeding.

Day Two

3

She has lost count of the number of days she has been down here, alone and in the dark. It could be three. Then again it could be ten. Normally hunger and thirst would be a good indication of time; but she has spent her life training herself to be indifferent to food and drink. Both are essential for life, yet so little of both are required for survival. Any more than that is akin to gluttony, and gluttony is a sin.

Sin. Is that why she is here? As punishment for her own mortal transgressions? If so, then it is a fitting place. In the oppressive and total darkness there is nothing else to do but listen to the sound of dripping water and contemplate her failings.

Especially now she can no longer feel the pain. Her hands, tied above her head and suspended from some sort of metal hook, became numb a long time ago. Her knees, scraping against the rough stone surface on which she is kneeling, no longer have any sensation. She is oblivious to the damp chill on her naked skin. The only real discomfort is the dull muscular ache in her neck from keeping her head upright.

'I will lift up my eyes to the hills from whence cometh my help; My help cometh from the Lord who made heaven and earth.'

The words of the 121st Psalm are comforting to her in her hour of need, as are all the Psalms that she has been reciting, from memory and in numerical order, forwards and backwards, over and over, since her incarceration.

'The Lord shall preserve thee from all evil: He shall preserve thy soul.'

But sometimes, in her more pragmatic moments, she cannot help but wonder who is keeping her here against her will – and why. And again she dredges her mind for the sequence of events leading up to the moment she woke up in this inky prison.

She sees herself hurrying through the crowded, narrow streets of the Old Town, a hunched figure in a heavy red and white robe. People acknowledge her with deferential nods and smiles, but she has no time for them. She is late for an appointment. *Yes – that's it!* An important meeting, the last on her busy schedule. She hates to be late for anything. To her, punctuality is the most important thing in the world next to God.

Where is she now? That's right. The busy square in the shadow of the Portuguese fort. *Hurry, hurry.* She crosses the square, weaving through the crowds of tourists. A hundred yards ahead she sees the white stucco minaret of the Mandhry mosque jutting out into Mbaraki Road. Further along is Government Square and the dhow harbour, and it is here that she must get to.

'Sister Gudrun.'

She stops. The voice is a rasping hiss, clearly audible over the hubbub. Did she imagine it?

No – there it is again. Rasping, wheezing.

'Over here, Sister.'

It is coming from a passageway between two buildings at the junction of the square and Mbaraki Road. The passage is so narrow that one blink and you would miss it. Every atom of common sense is screaming at her not to go near it, to keep on walking, to get to her meeting.

But there is something about that harsh voice that is familiar—

'Who is it? Who are you?'

'Closer, Sister.'

As she enters the passageway she sees a figure in the shadows.

'Who is it?'

'A poor sinner. Please, Sister – give me your hand.'

She reaches out and touches something that feels rough, like stitched leather. Then there is a sharp pain in her neck, just beneath her jaw. She cries out with surprise, but her vision has already exploded into exquisite cascades of searing white light and she realises she can no longer feel her legs.

After that there is only darkness.

'Out of the depths I cry unto thee O Lord; Lord hear my voice: let thine ears be attentive to the voice of my supplications.'

She is up to the 130th Psalm now.

'I wait for the Lord, my soul doth wait, and in His word I do hope.'

There are only twenty more before she will have to start again.

But then light suddenly blinds her. She squeezes shut her eyes, but the light penetrates her eyelids and scorches her retinas. She hears the sound of something dragging on stone. Coming nearer. Her mouth works but it is too dry to form words. How she needs water now. She tries to open her eyes, but after so long in the dark it is like sticking needles into them. All she can see are vague shadows.

'Open your eyes, Sister.'

'I can't. It hurts.'

'Open them,'

Tentatively she lifts one eyelid. The light still stings, but not with as much venom as before. Now she opens the other eye.

'Now do you see?'

The blur coalesces. Her captor is beside her, framed in the flickering light of an oil lamp. To her surprise she recognises the face and, for the first time since her ordeal began, she feels angry. 'How dare you do this to me!'

Her captor shuffles out of her line of vision, taking the lamp away. She sees her own shadow cast briefly against a wall of crumbling, uneven brick. Her legs are folded under her body, her hands fastened behind her head. Is she in some sort of tunnel?

'What are you going to do with me?' The anger has been replaced with fear now.

'I think you know the answer to that, Sister.'

She does. But no matter how she steels herself, the first blow against the bare skin of her back is an agony she could never imagine.

4

Lol Quarrie was a fifty-nine-year-old former police sergeant from Antrim and had played in the second row for Ulster in the days when rugby players could get away with smoking sixty cigarettes a day and drinking a gallon of beer the night before a match. But the indestructibility of his youth was long gone. Three months earlier he had undergone quadruple heart bypass surgery, which had hit him hard – almost as hard as when he was pensioned out of the Royal Ulster Constabulary on his fiftieth birthday.

According to friends who saw him at the Constabulary Club on the day he died, he seemed cheerful enough, but was lacking his usual sparkle. They put it down to the fact he was eating a modest lunch of poached fish washed down with mineral water. Until his operation old Lol had always been a confirmed roast beef and Guinness man.

Quarrie left the club shortly after three in the afternoon and was last seen walking in the direction of a taxi rank on the south-west corner of Jamhuri Park in central Mombasa. Why he should have plunged to his death from the walls of Fort Jesus four hours later was anybody's guess. For a start, how did he get in there? The fort had been closed to the general public for nearly a week while urgent work was carried out to strengthen its crumbling bastions. The sturdy main gate was bolted shut.

The last person to see him alive was an Old Town whore known as Dutch Alice; and if she hadn't been on her knees, performing fellatio on a Moroccan dockhand in a dank, fenced-off passageway once used for loading munitions and supplies into the fort from the sea, there would have been no witnesses at all to Lol Quarrie's last moments.

Dutch Alice was white and probably in her late forties and had been working the Old Town for twenty years. She had only come forward because she thought there might be a few dollars in it for her. Indeed, as she arranged herself at a table in the interview room of Mombasa's central police station, there was an irritation in her manner that suggested the official interrogation was going on rather longer than she'd expected.

'How much longer is this going to take, Inspector?' she snapped, blowing cigarette smoke at the defunct ceiling fan and scratching absently at a scab of dried make-up below her left ear. 'I hope you realise that all this is costing me money.'

Jouma regarded her across the scuffed wooden surface of the table. 'A man is dead, madam,' he said.

Dutch Alice rolled her eyes. 'Well, *I* didn't push him!'

'No – but you saw him fall.'

'Well, I now wish I'd turned the other cheek. So

18

much for being public spirited. I feel like a criminal.'

'Please, madam. Tell me again what you saw.'

The whore snorted and sucked on her cigarette, and Jouma wondered precisely how much of a handout she had been expecting for her public spiritedness.

'I looked up and he was just *up there*. On the top of the wall, I mean. I don't know where he came from.'

'Did you mention this to your . . . client?'

Dutch Alice smiled lasciviously. 'My mouth was full, Inspector.'

Jouma tried not to picture the scene. 'You said earlier that Mr Quarrie appeared to be unsteady on his feet.'

'Quarrie? That's the stiff, yeah?'

Jouma nodded.

'What sort of name is that? Jewish?'

'If you could answer the question, please, madam.'

'If you ask me he was drunk. Staggering about. Talking to himself – you know, like drunks do.'

'Did you hear what he said?'

'No.'

'Did you see anyone acting suspiciously in the area?'

'Where – in the Old Town?' Dutch Alice looked at him as if he was a simpleton. 'The Old Town is full of men looking to get laid. They all act suspiciously.'

'The man you were with – have you seen him before today?'

'Abdelbassir?' A harsh laugh. 'I know every kink in his filthy Moroccan cock.'

'Why did he run away?'

'Wouldn't you?'

'Do you know where he is now?'

'Telling lies to his wife, I expect.'

'Do you know where he lives?'

'Why should I care where he lives? I don't send him Christmas cards. But don't worry, Inspector. He'll be back. They always come back.' A flickering, rattlesnake tongue darted from her mouth, and the whore cackled again as Jouma recoiled in his chair. 'Sensitive soul, aren't you?' she said. 'I'm surprised. After everything I've heard about you, I mean. *The Man Who Cleaned Up Mombasa!* That's what they call you in the newspapers, isn't it?'

Jouma looked at her expression and felt his heart sinking fast. 'You shouldn't believe everything you read in the newspapers, madam,' he said.

5

Quarrie's body lay on a metal autopsy table in the basement mortuary of Mombasa Hospital.

'Neat, wouldn't you say?' said Christie, the pathologist, running one latex-encased finger along a raw, foot-long scar that ran vertically down the cadaver's chest. 'Straight as a die. And recent too, which saves me a job.' With a sweep of his scalpel blade, Christie opened the wound. A sharp tug and the flesh parted like curtains, exposing the white bone beneath.

From his customary autopsy viewing position – pressed against the tiled wall with his fingers clenched around the nearest bench for support – Jouma watched aghast as Christie began unravelling the stainless-steel wires that secured the two halves of the dead man's sternum. As he worked he hummed a tuneless dirge that seemed entirely in keeping with his bodysnatcher's demeanour. All it needed was a swirl of mist licking around his feet and a vulture perched on his shoulder and the macabre image would be complete.

'I always think it's a shame to undo someone else's

handiwork, especially so soon after it was completed,' the pathologist remarked. 'And especially when the surgeon was clearly an expert in his field. Who did you say this fellow was again, Jouma?'

'A retired officer with the Royal Ulster Constabulary.'

Christie nodded approvingly. 'You can say what you like about the British Police, but they look after their own. If he'd been on your healthcare policy, Jouma, they would have rammed him full of pig valves and sent him out to drop dead before his pension kicked in. This, on the other hand—' he pointed at something in the exposed chest cavity at which Jouma had no intention of looking '—is pure craftsmanship. Made to last. And such a pity.'

His outstretched finger moved upwards, beyond the chest, to where the top of Lol Quarrie's skull was flattened just above his eyebrows.

'If it hadn't been for this,' he said sadly, 'our friend here would have lived another twenty years.'

Superintendent Elizabeth Simba extended a red-painted fingernail and used it to press a button on the intercom console in front of her.

'Wendy – could you bring me a glass of mineral water, please?' She looked across her desk at Jouma. 'Tea, Daniel? English breakfast, am I correct?'

They were in Simba's office in the compound of Coast Province Police Headquarters on Mama Ngina Drive, the sweeping thoroughfare of municipal buildings and state-owned mansions on the south shore of Mombasa island. Behind her a large window overlooking the Indian Ocean rattled in time to the late-evening breeze that ruffled the palm trees on the headland. Simba, a well-built woman in her early fifties, sat back in her chair and put on a pair of narrow-framed spectacles.

'So what do we have?' she said presently.

Jouma cleared his throat and looked at his shoes, uncertain how to begin. Simba had been in her post for a month now, and in that time she had been nothing less than civil to him – but still he felt apprehensive in her presence. Was it because she was the disgraced Superintendent Teshete's replacement from Nairobi? Was it because *he*, Jouma, was directly responsible for his former superior officer's current incarceration in prison awaiting trial for corruption? Surely she would appreciate that he was only doing his job, and that if Teshete had grown rich on bribes from the Mombasa underworld then it was his duty to bring him to justice.

But Jouma knew all too well that certain high-ranking officials in both the police and government, while publicly praising him for what he had done, privately hated his guts for holding Kenya's dirty laundry up to the light. They wanted him pensioned off, or at the very least dispatched to some anonymous backwater where he couldn't cause any more trouble. The fact that he was still at Mama Ngina Drive, that he had steadfastly refused every promotion or lucrative transfer he had been offered, must have irritated them beyond measure.

'The dead man is Lawrence Quarrie, aged fifty-nine years,' he said. He gave an address in Nyali, a genteel suburb on the north coast, and Simba, who had obviously heard of the neighbourhood, looked surprised. 'Mr Quarrie was a uniformed sergeant in the Royal Ulster Constabulary in Belfast until his retirement nine years ago.'

'Married?'

'His wife died in June 2000. He moved to Kenya soon afterwards. I understand the couple regularly came here on safari holidays.'

'What was he doing in Mombasa yesterday?'

'He was having lunch at the Constabulary Club.' Jouma noted Simba's narrowed eyes. 'It is a private club, ma'am, for retired police officers. Mostly ex-pat British, although there are a few Kenyan members.'

Simba sipped her water carefully. 'None of them African, I expect,' she said without looking up. 'So did he jump? Was there any reason he wanted to kill himself?'

'Mr Quarrie had recently undergone heart surgery,' Jouma said. 'Depression is a recognised side effect of such a traumatic operation.'

'What about the whore? According to her statement the victim appeared to be drunk.'

'I am awaiting a blood analysis report from the pathologist, ma'am. But Mr Quarrie was drinking mineral water at lunch.'

'And after lunch?'

Jouma could only shrug. 'We are still trying to ascertain his movements between three and seven o'clock yesterday, ma'am.'

Simba exhaled thoughtfully and ran her fingers across her short-cropped hair. Rather than risk eye contact, Jouma gazed around the room. His new boss had made a few superficial changes − a vase of flowers in the corner, the leather sofa moved against a different wall, a new picture by the metal filing cabinet — but in essence the office was much as Teshete had kept it. The main difference was the smell: instead of acrid cigarette smoke, the room was filled with the anodyne aroma of air freshener. Jouma wasn't sure which he preferred. It was almost a relief when Simba's secretary entered the room with a tray of refreshments. The bone china teacup gave him something to look at.

'Have you found the Moroccan dockhand?' Simba said. 'The one that ran away?'

'His name is Abdelbassir Hossain. We brought him in for questioning an hour ago.'

'And?'

Jouma cleared his throat. 'He was most concerned that his wife did not find out what he had been up to.'

'You do not think he is involved?'

'No ma'am. Of that I am very certain.'

'So what *do* you think, Daniel?'

The question was without apparent menace or hidden meaning, but still Simba did not look up and Jouma had the uneasy sensation that he was somehow being *tested*.

'At this time suicide would seem to be the most *feasible* explanation. Although I am still at a loss as to how he gained access to the fort, and indeed why his clothes were covered in mud.'

Simba looked up with a weary expression. 'Trust me, Daniel, when retired British policemen fall to their deaths in mysterious circumstances the answer is never as simple as suicide.'

'I am aware of that,' Jouma said. The prospect of his

every move being scrutinised by a bunch of ex-cops whose opinion of Kenyan policing was non-existent had already filled him with foreboding. 'I will know more once I have the blood analysis.'

'Good. Until every line of inquiry has been exhausted, I want you to treat Mr Quarrie's death as suspicious.'

Jouma nodded. 'As you wish, ma'am. And the missing nun from Jalawi village?'

She waved a hand. 'Detective Constable Mwangi will take over. I want your full attention on this case.'

'With respect, ma'am, Mwangi is very inexperienced.'

'We were all inexperienced once, Daniel,' Simba said.

It took Jouma a moment to realise that the meeting was at an end.

6

Five miles off the coast of Africa the air was warm and the sea was benign, and on the flying bridge of the game-fishing boat *Yellowfin* Jake had now gone almost two whole minutes without thinking about Lol Quarrie's skull exploding at his feet.

In the scheme of things this was a big improvement, because the image and the sound had kept him awake all the previous night. And while it would take a lot longer to erase the memory than it had taken to swab Lol's brains off his clothes, Jake knew that eventually it would fade away, because even the worst experiences subsided after a while.

Like getting shot.

There was a time when he thought a night would not pass without the white, frightened face of an eighteen-year-old east London hoodlum named Ronnie Cavanagh haunting his dreams. On those nights he saw the loaded pistol just as clearly as that day five years ago, and heard the explosion as Cavanagh pulled the trigger. But now it was almost as if the bullet had torn into someone else.

Sometimes Jake had to run his fingers over the puckered scar on his abdomen to prove to himself that it had really happened.

Days like this helped, of course. The ocean was therapy and *Yellowfin* a confidante. It was why he had quit the Flying Squad and jumped on a plane to Kenya after reading Harry Philliskirk's appeal for a like-minded business partner in the classifieds.

And, if all else failed, there was always the Ernie strapped to the fighting chair to keep him occupied.

'Excuse me,' a plaintive voice called up from the cockpit, 'but I think I've caught a shark.'

'OK.'

Lighting a cigarette, Jake reflected that if he had a dollar for every time he'd heard that line he'd never have a financial worry again. To pasty-skinned Europeans, who spent their lives surrounded by freezing oceans of cod and haddock, even the tug of a sailfish was like that of a Great White. Harry had christened them Ernies. 'Every one of them thinks they're Ernest Hemingway,' he would say, 'and every sprat they pull out of the sea will be a three-hundred-pound marlin by the time they get back to the office on Monday morning.'

'Ah – excuse me . . .'

'Yeah, I'm coming.'

Jake consoled himself with the thought that at least this would be the last Ernie he'd have to chaperone for a while. Tomorrow he was taking *Yellowfin* to Missy Meredith's yard to see what new life a complete overhaul could breathe into an old crate with fifteen years' hard labour under her belt. With two new turbo diesel engines, rewired electrics, purged hydraulics and a flying bridge bristling with VHF radio, GPS navigation and sonar fish-finding equipment – not to mention several hundred dollars' worth of gleaming new tackle in the cockpit – he suspected it would be like being the skipper of a new boat.

Thank you, Martha.

He drew hard on his cigarette, and as he did so he could almost hear Martha Bentley scolding him for smoking. He chuckled to himself as he imagined her face screwed up with self-righteousness. There was no doubt about it: he missed her – and not only because she had agreed to save their bacon by injecting her murdered father's insurance money into their dying charter business.

Not for the first time he wondered what might happen in a few weeks' time when she returned to Africa from New York to supervise her investment. In the short time they had known each other he had felt a definite chemistry between them, and it was true that he had rarely felt as comfortable in the presence of a woman. But did that mean they could ever be anything more than business partners?

'Excuse me – but I *really* think you need to come and look at this.'

'On my way, pal.'

Dah – who was he kidding? At thirty-five Jake was more than ten years older than her, a knuckleheaded Geordie ex-copper with even more than the usual number of failings and fuck-ups to his name. Martha was smart and sassy and beautiful; the kind of girl he only ever saw in the kind of movies about smart, sassy women he always tried to avoid.

Some things were best left to the imagination.

'Mr Jake – I think the boss needs help.'

The shout from Sammy the bait boy brought him back from his reverie and he looked down from his perch on the flying bridge. The Ernie was a balding, middle-aged schoolteacher from England. His wife and daughter had booked him a half-day's fishing with his prospective son-in-law as a bonding exercise. Landing a tuna or a wahoo together might well have done the trick – except the prospective son-in-law had been prostrate in the cabin with acute seasickness ever since they'd left the calm waters of the inner reef.

'OK, Sammy, I'm coming down.'

Jake slammed the throttles into neutral and climbed down the ladder to the cockpit.

'You must be getting tired,' he said to the Ernie, patting him on the shoulder. 'You want me to take over for a while?'

'Like I've been trying to tell you,' the Ernie grimaced through a torrent of sweat pouring down his face, 'I think I've hooked a shark.'

Jake followed the direction of the line and, behind his Ray-Bans, his eyes widened. Fifty yards off the stern rail a huge grey-white shape was twisting and rolling in the swell, the triangular line of its dorsal fin like a calling card.

Jesus—

'I think you're right, mate,' he told the Ernie. 'You've hooked yourself a *zambi*.'

'A what?'

'Bull shark.'

And it was a big bastard as well. There wouldn't be

much change out of 500 lbs from this one. That was damn near half a ton of pure muscle and bad attitude on a rod set up to land a 200 lb tuna. How the line hadn't snapped was a mystery. And how this scrawny schoolteacher had kept reeling without being ripped out of the flying chair and into the shark's maw was little short of miraculous. He didn't look as if he had the strength to pull the skin off a rice pudding.

'Sammy – pass me the rod belt.'

The boy ran to one of the tackle boxes and returned with a leather harness which Jake pulled over his shoulders and belted firmly around his waist.

'OK. Now get up to the bridge.'

As Sammy shinned up the ladder, Jake carefully lifted the butt of the rod from its gimbal cup at the base of the fighting chair and jammed it into the holder in his midriff. As he did so the huge shark shot down beneath the surface. The rod bent almost double as Jake took the strain, bending forward to allow the run-on, then heaving backwards and winding with all his might.

'Come on, Sammy!'

Yellowfin's ageing diesels spluttered to life as the bait boy opened up the throttles. Eyes never leaving the fish, he expertly controlled the boat so that it kept pace.

Down in the cockpit sweat was already pouring off Jake and his arms and thighs were burning. Sure, he'd used the rod belt to help an Ernie in distress many times. But even landing a marlin was nothing compared to tackling this monster.

And yet . . .

Fifteen minutes passed. Then thirty. In the broiling

heat of the cockpit, Jake realised that the shark's resistance was waning. *Was the bastard getting tired?* It hardly seemed possible. But then its dorsal fin burst out of the water and he saw to his astonishment that the great fish was now less than ten feet off the stern.

'My God,' the Ernie said. 'Look at the *size* of it.' He backed away towards the cabin, determined to raise his son-in-law from his deathbed.

It was a big one all right, probably fifteen feet from nose to tail and three feet wide. What Jake hadn't told the Ernie – indeed what he didn't like to think about too much himself – was that of all the species of shark, Great Whites included, Bulls were generally considered to be the most dangerous to humans. You read about a swimmer being attacked a few feet from the shore? Most likely it was a *zambi*. This particular species even liked fresh water, which was why it had a reputation for swimming up rivers and grabbing small children from the shallows.

And right now, Jake thought, he was about to land one with a tuna line.

They would never believe it at Suki Lo's bar back at Flamingo Creek.

'Sammy – get ready.'

But the boy had already scampered back down to the cockpit and was bent over the stern rail, extending the canvas landing stretcher that was used to secure the really big fish until they were either tagged or else transported back to shore for the glamorous photo session on the dock.

The shark was almost touching distance from the boat now, on its side, staring at Jake with one coal-black eye.

'*Smile, you sonofabitch!*' he said.

It was the only line in *Jaws* he'd ever wanted to say.

And it was right then that the line snapped; and Jake, suddenly pulling against thin air, fell on to his backside with the rod still gripped in both hands.

'You lost it.'

He looked up to see the Ernie staring disbelievingly out to sea. Behind him, like a grey-faced wraith, his prospective son-in-law clung to the frame of the cabin door. There was drying vomit down the front of his safari shirt.

'He *lost* it!' the Ernie said. The Ernie was right. Jake had lost the fish. And there was a time when a humiliation like this would have put him in a bad mood for the rest of the day. But, as he picked himself up from the deck, Jake felt only a strange inner calm. It was just a bloody fish after all. Nobody had died. And, after everything he had been through recently, that made a pleasant change.

7

The hippies arrived at Flamingo Creek mid-afternoon, bumping along the dirt road from the Mombasa highway in a battered American schoolbus painted every colour of the rainbow. There were two dozen of them, and their leader was a white Kenyan in her late twenties. Her name was Evie Simenon, a name which struck Harry Philliskirk as strangely alluring and exotic – even if her appearance, all tie-dyed cotton and lank-looking dreadlocks, was not. She wanted directions to a place called Jalawi village, and in return she and her people had some rather potent grass they were more than willing to share – which was why Harry, dozing in the sun outside the workshop of Britannia Fishing Trips Ltd, was more than happy to help.

Trouble was, they were on the wrong side of the river, he told them. Jalawi was on the north bank, near the mouth of the creek. And, apart from a handful of mud huts, a few hundred people and maybe twice as many goats and stray dogs, there wasn't much else to see. Were they sure it was Jalawi they wanted? If they were looking for Zen enlightenment they wouldn't find it round there.

'We're not here for Zen enlightenment,' Evie Simenon said sharply. 'We're here to stop Spurling Developments building a hotel.'

'Ah,' Harry said, as suddenly it all made sense. They were not hippies after all. He should have guessed just from Evie's appearance that she was nothing less than a fully-fledged eco-warrior. Any residual allure evaporated like morning mist.

'Spurling Developments is systematically implementing a slash and burn policy all along the eastern seaboard of Kenya,' she told him. 'Jalawi village is next on the list. They plan to build *another* five-star hotel – as if the coast isn't choked with them already.'

Her followers – mostly gormless-looking kids of student age – nodded in agreement, then looked to Harry for his response. And, as he lounged in his faded canvas director's chair with a king-sized joint between his lips, it was hard not to feel like some wizened old guru from the acid-soaked 1960s, dispensing wisdom to a new generation of dropouts. It was a curious sensation, because back in the days when he commanded a six-figure basic salary in the City of London it was accepted wisdom among the stock-market speculators and hedge-fund managers that anyone who sang Bob Dylan songs in Underground stations or marched for peace or hugged trees was an indolent shirker in need of delousing and a damn good haircut.

He gestured across the water at the gleaming edifice of the Flamingo Creek Yacht Club, its plate-glass windows glaring disapprovingly at the ramshackle boatyard opposite.

'As you can see, Spurling Developments already has influential friends on the planning committee. I suspect if they want to build a hotel then they will go ahead and build one.'

'That's why someone has to stand up to them,' Evie retorted. 'Think of the people who will lose their homes and their livelihoods if this hotel is built on their land.'

Harry drew the acrid smoke deep into his lungs and tried not to cough. 'Is this what you do, Evie?' he said. 'Drive from building site to building site in that bus of yours?'

'We can't just sit back and let rich white developers turn Kenya into one big hotel complex.'

'Bravo. That's the spirit.'

'Why don't you come with us?'

Harry smiled indulgently. 'I'm a bit old to be lying down in front of bulldozers, my dear.'

Through a cloud of pungent hash smoke he was aware of Evie sizing him up.

'Thank you for the directions,' she said. 'But we should go now.'

Harry gestured woozily at the bus. 'Then watch your suspension,' he said. 'There are potholes on that Jalawi road that you might never get out of again.'

When they had gone Harry heaved himself unsteadily out of his chair and plodded back towards the workshop.

It must be nice, he reflected, to be so damned *idealistic*. One of the great regrets of age was the inevitable discovery of how little difference you made to anything without money and power. Spurling Developments had both – which was why Evie Simenon had absolutely no chance of stopping the development at Jalawi or the bulldozers rumbling along the north bank of Flamingo Creek like a Panzer division across France. Like all Spurling Developments shareholders – and Harry had been one since his days in the City – he had seen the plans, knew all about the five-star hotel and knew that Jalawi village was doomed. It was simply a fact of life. And as far as he was concerned it was better to embrace the inevitable and benefit from it than to gain nothing by standing in its way. After all, a hotel on the doorstep could only be good for business.

It was almost four o'clock now and Jake was due back at Flamingo Creek. The little interlude with Evie Simenon had been fun, but now it was time for the managing directors of Britannia Fishing Trips Ltd to discuss the burning issues of the day over a few beers and a bowl of Suki Lo's chilli noodles.

And a healthy dose of man-talk was just what Jake required in Harry's opinion. Ever since he'd met up with Martha Bentley, the big galoot had been mooning over her like some spotty adolescent with a crush. Now Martha was a pleasant girl all right, and what she planned to do with her old man's insurance money was like a gift from the gods as far as the business was concerned. *But a line had to be drawn.* Harry wanted his partner back.

Just then his attention was diverted by the sight of a two-man helicopter buzzing overhead on its way downriver. Such aircraft were not uncommon around Flamingo Creek – they were a quicker and safer alternative to using the roads, and one day Harry vowed he was going to have one himself instead of the twenty-year-old Land Rover that was his present mode of transport.

But as he watched, the chopper reared up in mid-air and hovered over the creek like a dragonfly considering its next move. Then, to his surprise, it suddenly banked sharply on itself and landed beside the workshop, casting out a stinging cloud of dust. The passenger door opened and two white men in dark suits climbed out. Covering their faces with their sleeves they ran across to where Harry was ducked down on the jetty.

'Are you Jake Moore?' one of the men shouted into Harry's ear over the waning din of the rotors. He was mid-fifties with buzz-cut greying hair and a full moustache. The accent was American.

Harry opened his mouth to speak, but it was instantly filled with dust. He shook his head instead.

'Is this where Jake Moore lives?'

Harry nodded.

'My name is FBI Special Agent Clarence Bryson,' the American bawled. He gestured to the other man, who was perhaps twenty years younger and with the physique of someone who worked out regularly. 'This is Special Agent McCrickerd. Let's go inside, shall we? We need to talk.'

8

Heading north on the Mombasa – Malindi highway, Jouma had also noticed the small helicopter as it swept low overhead. And, like Harry, he too had regarded it with a certain amount of envy as the engine of his ancient Fiat Panda clanked ominously, the way it always did when the speedometer went over forty mph.

'Did you know, Mwangi, that it takes less than twenty minutes to fly from Mombasa to Malindi in a helicopter? Think of the man hours that would save.'

Detective Constable David Mwangi was twenty-four years old and six foot three inches tall. In order to fit into the passenger seat of Jouma's Panda he'd almost had to fold himself in half.

'A helicopter would be most beneficial, sir,' he said with heartfelt sincerity.

Jouma smiled to himself. Mwangi had been his new junior officer for less than a week, but he liked him already. He was enthusiastic, sharp and respectful – everything, in other words, that his predecessor, Sergeant Nyami, was not. He was also

Oxford-educated and green as a palm leaf. But he clearly had promise, otherwise he would not have been among the dozen or so rising stars that Simba had brought with her from Nairobi.

They crossed the bridge over Flamingo Creek, then turned off the highway and followed the north bank of the broad river. This road was metalled and freshly asphalted, as befitted one of the coast's wealthiest enclaves. There were imposing granite walls to keep prying eyes from the homes beyond, and gates manned by uniformed *askari* from private security firms.

'I wonder how much it costs to live here?' Mwangi said, gazing out of the window.

'Start saving, Constable. On CID wages it will only take you three hundred years to afford a down-payment.'

After a mile or so the gated community abruptly ended and the smooth road disintegrated again into a rutted track leading through a dense forest of casuarina, flame and *mbambakofi* trees. From the smell of woodsmoke, they were approaching the village now. Jouma tentatively manoeuvred his car around stupid goats and excited children while villagers stood and stared with grim suspicion at the vehicle and its two occupants.

'What are they looking at?' asked Mwangi.

'Two Africans in suits, Constable. It is not a common sight in these parts.'

The road ended at an open patch of wasteground, where dogs picked at the rubbish heaps, women washed clothes in a brackish stream and the men, inevitably, just sat around smoking and playing cards.

Beyond was a ramshackle collection of wooden shacks leading down to the river, where a handful of wooden outriggers were lashed together at anchor. As the two detectives got out of the car they could hear the distant crump of the waves where the creek emptied into the ocean beyond the headland.

'Let's make this as quick and painless as possible, shall we?' Jouma said. 'And keep your cool, Mwangi. Brother Willem can be a tricky customer.'

The inspector led the way through the village to a whitewashed wooden church built on a spit of land overlooking a shallow cove. It was sturdily built in a four-square, European style. A cross had been fixed to its tar-paper roof and, above the door in foot-high painted letters, were the words: *Redeemed Apostolic Gospel Church.*

'I am not familiar with this particular order,' Mwangi said.

Jouma nodded. 'Until Sister Gudrun disappeared, neither was I.'

The door to the church opened and a thin, bearded man in his mid-thirties strode into the sunlight. He wore a long white and red robe with a thick rime of dust around its hem. He appeared startled by the appearance of the two detectives.

'Inspector Jouma.'

Jouma took his outstretched hand. 'Brother Willem.'

'I was not expecting you,' the priest said, his blue eyes darting behind steel-rimmed spectacles. 'Have you found her?'

Willem spoke with the nervous, distracted manner of a man who had other, more pressing concerns

41

than the welfare of a seventy-five-year-old nun. In fact, he looked like a man who was hiding something, Jouma thought, just as he had forty-eight hours earlier when he had first paid a visit to Jalawi village.

'I'm afraid not,' Jouma said smoothly. 'Brother Willem, this is Detective Constable Mwangi. He has recently joined my department from Nairobi CID.'

The priest nodded absently and shook hands with Mwangi out of politeness; but there was barely any eye contact and once the formalities were over he impatiently returned his attention to Jouma. 'If there is no news, then why are you here, Inspector?'

'Perhaps this is not the best place to talk,' Jouma said.

Inside the church two dozen metal and plastic chairs were arranged in rows on either side of the dirt floor. They faced a wooden altar table and pulpit. A particularly mournful-looking Christ hung from a cross on the wall behind, next to an amateurish, hand-painted mural depicting scenes from the Gospels.

Willem sat on the front row, agitatedly picking at the skin around his thumbnail, and Jouma drew breath, knowing that the purpose of the visit could no longer be put off.

'I am here to inform you that I have been assigned to a different case by my superior officer,' he said. 'Detective Constable Mwangi will be taking over the investigation from me.'

Usually, when people were told that their case was being fobbed off on to a junior officer, the reaction was one of furious indignation. But Willem merely blinked like some sort of reptile.

'What does that mean?' he said.

'In terms of the investigation, nothing,' Jouma insisted. 'I can categorically assure you that finding Sister Gudrun remains our highest priority.' Yet even as he launched into a vigorous defence of Mwangi's abilities, he found himself unnerved by the blank expression on the priest's face. 'Detective Constable Mwangi is an extremely capable officer and I have every confidence in his ability,' he concluded, his voice trailing off. 'The sooner you tell him every- thing you know about the missing lady—'

'*Again?*' Willem exclaimed. The outburst was sudden and unexpected, and Mwangi flinched.

'Yes,' Jouma said firmly. 'Again. And now, if you will kindly excuse me, I think I will go outside and stretch my legs. The potholes on the road are very bad for my joints. Mwangi – take over.'

As Jouma walked away, he noted with a certain amount of sadistic pleasure that Mwangi had the same beseeching expression as a dog whose owner has just left him in kennels for the first time.

9

American Airlines flight 368 from New York touched down at Moi International Airport three minutes ahead of schedule – but it would be at least another hour before the first of the passengers cleared immigration control and collected their luggage from the carousels. By then the occupant of seat 3B was already in the back of a taxi heading towards a five-star hotel north of Mombasa island. Such were the advantages of travelling first class and with hand luggage only, Martha Bentley's killer thought.

The name on the airline manifest was eastern European in origin. The face in the passport photograph was lean and unsmiling. The colour of the AmEx charge card was impressive enough to warrant the finest suite in the hotel and a personal welcome from the general manager.

'If there is *anything* we can do to make your stay more comfortable, please do not hesitate to ask,' he said.

'I appreciate your hospitality,' the killer said. 'I'm sure I'll have a wonderful stay.'

★

As the esteemed guest poured a large Scotch from the minibar and stepped into a hot bath, Harry listened with disbelief as FBI Special Agent Clarence Bryson described how, twenty-four hours earlier, Martha Bentley had been murdered in her apartment in New York's Upper East Side.

'It was a professional hit,' Bryson said. He described how the assassin had slipped a stiletto blade between the cervical vertebrae of Martha's spine and into her spinal cord, killing her instantly.

'But ... *why?*' Harry said. He was slumped in his chair in the office of Britannia Fishing Trips Ltd as if he'd just been felled. 'Why would anyone want to kill her?'

'Because of her boyfriend,' Agent McCrickerd said. 'Patrick Noonan.'

'Noonan?'

'Alias John Whitestone, Donald Ridgeway, Peter Miller, Salvatore Bruni, Karl Mayerling, Jean-Pierre Coutin – the list is as long as your arm, Mr Philliskirk. The only thing we know for certain about that bastard is that he's dead.'

Bryson, the senior man, leaned forward in his chair. 'We believe Noonan was a key player in an organisation responsible for the illegal trafficking of thousands of innocent kids across the world. The Bureau has been on the trail of this organisation for months, but without a sniff – until Noonan's east Africa operation was blown wide open.'

'We think they're running scared,' McCrickerd said. 'Tying up any loose ends they can.'

'Loose ends like Martha Bentley,' Harry said sombrely.

Bryson nodded. 'They couldn't take the chance that she might know something, that Noonan let something slip while they were together.'

Harry's eyes widened as a sudden, blood-chilling thought occurred to him. He jabbed his finger at them. 'You think the killer is coming for Jake and me now, right?'

Bryson smiled. 'Relax, Harry. No offence, but I think you and Jake are pretty low down on the list of priorities for these people.'

Harry did not seem convinced. 'So why are you here?'

'Because one of Noonan's key African operatives is still very much alive here in Mombasa – and we aim to keep him that way until we can get him Stateside.'

It took Harry a few moments to register just who the American agent was talking about.

'*Conrad Getty?*'

Getty was a coast hotel owner who also happened to be Noonan's logistics man and whose wealth and prestige had been built on procuring young girls from across east Africa for greedy European clients.

'Obviously Getty is our priority,' Bryson said, his easy smile masking the understatement. 'But we're keen to find out whatever we can. Anything you and Jake can tell us would be helpful.'

Harry reached in a desk drawer and produced a bottle of Pusser's rum. He took a long, throat-burning swill and thought about how he had been duped by Getty and his sidekick Tug Viljoen into becoming a courier in their vile human trade.

'Of course,' he said.

'When are you expecting him back?' McCrickerd asked.

'Any time now. I'll raise him on the ship-to-shore and find out where he is.'

The killer got out of the bath and dressed casually in jogging pants and T-shirt. Outside the room the temperature had cooled noticeably. Now, with the scent of tumbling frangipani rising up from the gardens below, it was positively pleasant – the perfect time for a stroll before supper.

Having grabbed a small shoulder bag containing a digital camera, a notebook and a six-inch stiletto knife in a leather sheath, the killer went down to the hotel lobby and sought out the concierge.

'I requested the hire of a motor scooter. I wondered if it was available?'

The concierge beamed. 'Of course! I will have it brought to the front door at once.'

'You are very kind.' The killer pressed a ten-dollar bill into his hand.

'You are going into Mombasa?'

'No. I thought I'd stay local.'

'Would you like a map showing locations of interest?'

A pleasant smile. 'No, thank you. There is only one place of interest I want to visit – and I know exactly where it is.'

10

Spurling Developments was the largest private construction company in east Africa, and its coastal depot was a vast, twenty-acre compound that had once been a quarry supplying the cement works in Mombasa. Inside, surrounded by three miles of ten-foot-high electrified fencing, were over a hundred construction vehicles, from forty-ton earthmovers to pile-driving machines that could hammer a steel pole thirty feet into bone-hard ground. There were office buildings, catering facilities, satellite dishes, cell-phone masts, electricity generators, oil and water tankers and, stacked up like shoeboxes, ten prefabricated cabins that housed the two hundred and fifty-strong army of men who were based there.

It was, to all intents and purposes, a fully functioning town, with better facilities than any of the roadside slums within a forty-mile radius.

The company's chief operations manager was a Scotsman called Frank Walker. He was forty-two, small and wiry, with close-cropped gingery hair so pale as to be almost translucent when he removed his protective hard-hat. At that moment, even though he was sitting in an air-conditioned cabin, Walker reflected that wearing it would be advisable, such was the deluge of shit that had been tipped on him from on high that morning.

'Where the fuck is Mathenge now, Tom?' he demanded.

'In the tool room, Boss.'

Sitting opposite him was a hulking, shaven-headed African called Tom Beye. The black polo shirt and steroid-boosted muscles immediately marked him out as a member of Spurling's internal Security Division – but right now the look on his face was that of a child who had just been told off for pulling the legs off spiders.

'I suppose I should be grateful he's still alive,' Walker said under his breath.

Beye stared at him with red-hazed eyeballs. His lids were hooded, his mouth slightly open. Walker shuddered. *Jesus, but he was a scary one.* He had seen some psycho nut jobs back in Glasgow, but nothing to match this bastard.

'He *is* alive, isn't he, Tom?'

Beye nodded slowly, and Walker sighed with relief. It was the first piece of good news he had heard since the depot manager had called him at six that morning to report an incident involving one of his digger drivers. The driver, a half-wit by the name of Baptiste Mathenge, had got drunk at a roadside hostelry the previous night and decided to drive his Cat D10 crawler six miles back to the depot along the Mombasa highway with his lights off. Mathenge was lucky that he had not been stopped by the police. The old man he had inadvertently driven over in the dark had not been so fortunate. He had been found snarled up in the caterpillar tracks and, judging by the expression on what was left of his face, had died an excruciating death under eighty tons of steel. 'I take it you've interviewed him about what happened?'

'He remembers nothing,' Beye growled.

'I bet he doesn't,' Walker said.

He was still annoyed that Beye had got to Mathenge first, and wondered just who had tipped off Security Division about the incident. Its members were not known for their interpersonal skills, nor did they pay much heed to disciplinary procedures. The speedo of Walker's company SUV had hovered at 100 mph all the way north from Mombasa that morning because he knew that every second the hapless Mathenge spent in the company of Tom Beye increased his chances of severe injury or even death.

'OK, I want you to get him cleaned up, given a month's pay and sent on his way. Understand?'

Beye frowned. 'But—'

'Just *do* it, Tom.'

'But what if he ... remembers?' Beye protested.

'Trust me, he won't.'

No – after a run-in with Security Division, Baptiste Mathenge would regard the termination of his job with a month's pay as akin to winning the lottery.

'We should shut his mouth for good.'

Walker put his head in his hands. 'Jesus Christ, Tom! Do you ever fucking listen to a word I say?'

Beye's face slackened again. No, Walker thought, he would never understand. Beye acted solely on instinct, and in all cases his instinct was to smash skulls and not even bother asking questions later. The fact that life was so cheap in Kenya had its advantages sometimes – but it didn't make it any more palatable. And there was still the problem of disposing of the old man's body. The last thing Walker needed was a police inquiry into a missing person.

Tom, of course, had his own solution. Even now he was convinced the remains should have been left on the highway for the early-morning pantechnicons to pulverise. He didn't seem to understand that even here in Kenya there were pathologists who could tell the difference between the damage caused by rubber tyres and those made by steel caterpillar tracks.

Instead, Walker ordered the remains taken to the plains far beyond the Vipingo Ridge, dowsed in kerosene and burned in a pit deep enough to prevent the charred bones being dug up by wild animals. It was the most effective, discreet and respectful solution – three words that did not appear in Tom Beye's or Security Division's vocabulary.

'Right,' Walker said with finality. 'We've wasted enough time. Let's do what has to be done and then we can get on with some real work.'

As he made his way across the dusty compound to his SUV, Walker removed his car keys and paused for a moment. Any big-game hunter would have immediately identified the two-inch-long brass cylinder attached to the key ring as a .300 Winchester Magnum cartridge. Walker kept it there for days like these – a reminder of those fleeting but idyllic times in his life when he could leave all his problems behind him; when he and Malachi, old man

Spurling's trusted game warden, would pack the Jeep with a few supplies and head off into the wilderness and not see another soul for days at a time.

He got into his car and pulled on to the highway. It would take him thirty minutes to reach Mombasa and his office on the eighteenth floor of Spurling Developments' headquarters on Nkrumah Road. From there he could see the Shimba Hills forty miles to the south. On a clear day he felt he could almost reach out and touch them. It was the one perk of a job he wished he'd never been given.

11

As he left the church and stepped outside into the heat of the day Jouma was lost in thought. Something stank to high heaven about the case of the missing nun, but he didn't know what. And, now that he had been taken off the case by Simba, he guessed that it would be up to Mwangi to find out. For now his priority was finding out why – and more to the point *how* – the late Lol Quarrie had fallen to his death.

Even after thirty years, he reflected, the life of a detective was anything but dull.

Just then he heard noise like the very gates of hell being opened, and he turned to see what appeared to be a garishly painted bus sputtering towards the village on grievously tortured axles. The inevitable crowd of children were joyously pursuing it until, a hundred yards from where Jouma had parked, the bus veered off into the trees and expired in a cloud of oily smoke. To his astonishment a steady stream of young people began climbing down from it, weighed down with rucksacks, pots and pans, musical instruments and other bags and accoutrements.

Very deliberately, and knowing that he was acting against his own professional curiosity, the inspector turned away and set off along a narrow track which led from the church in the direction of the creek. He had too much on his plate as it was and, as long as the people on the bus weren't here to rape and pillage the village of Jalawi, he was more than happy to mind his own business.

Away to the south, clouds were gathering and the air was thick with the smell of burning vegetation as the villagers along the coast readied the ground for the rainy season. It was a smell that always reminded Jouma of his own childhood on the fertile plains beneath Mount Kenya. There had been a church in his village too – nothing as grand as this one; in fact, it was little more than a hut where once a month a priest from the Christian mission in Meru would conduct a service. But Father Steele was a kindly man who preached that God loved all His children equally and without prejudice. By contrast Jouma had the distinct impression that, while Brother Willem read from the same Scripture, he did not practise what he preached.

A boy jumped out in front of him. He was wearing a pair of baggy shorts and a sky-blue football shirt with the word ROBINHO stencilled across the shoulders. He held up a green coconut in one thin hand. The other loosely gripped the handle of a machete.

'You want? Very pleasant. Very refreshing!'

Jouma smiled and nodded. '*Asante sana.*'

The boy grinned back and, with one deft movement, sliced off the top of the coconut. Jouma took the fruit to his lips and drained it of its warm, sweet milk. He handed it back and this time the boy used the blade of his knife to shave off a finger-sized chunk of the tough outer husk. With this he expertly scooped the moist flesh of the coconut into strips.

'*Asante*,' Jouma said, plucking a tender strip of white meat between his finger and thumb then dropping it into his mouth. It tasted delicious and indulgent, yet Jouma could remember a time when he had lived on little else. *Such carefree days, Daniel.*

A boat was turning into the creek from the ocean. It was travelling fast upriver and did not slow as a figure dived from the stern rail and began swimming towards the shore. Jouma watched the vessel pass just fifty yards from where he stood, and saw the name *Yellowfin* painted on its bow.

Jake?

He smiled with recognition and lifted his arm to attract his friend's attention – but up on the flying bridge the Englishman's eyes were fixed directly ahead, his face a mask of grim concern, and in a moment the boat was gone.

A boy emerged from the river, water sluicing from a body as lithe as a marlin's. There was something familiar about him, but it took a few moments before Jouma realised who it was. Of course! Jake's bait boy.

'*Sammy!*'

The boy looked up. There was a flicker of recognition, an unpleasant memory perhaps of smoky police interview rooms and a string of sympathetic doctors trying to ascertain the degree of psychological trauma he had suffered. Sammy's kid brother had been murdered by one of Patrick Noonan's men. Sammy himself had killed the man by firing a harpoon bolt through his head. What child should ever have to go through such an ordeal?

'Inspector—?'

'Jouma. Daniel Jouma. How are you?'

'I am well, sir,' Sammy said respectfully, but there was something in his eyes that suggested otherwise. 'But I must go now. My mother is waiting.'

Jouma put a hand on his shoulder. 'What is it, Sammy?'

The boy sighed. 'Mr Jake – he get some bad news on the boat radio. Very bad news indeed.'

'Then you must tell me what it is,' Jouma said, concerned.

When Sammy told him, the inspector reeled. Moments later he was hurrying past the church towards his car. As he drove as fast as he could along the dirt road, back towards the highway in order to get to the boatyard on the south side of the creek, he realised that Mwangi and Brother Willem would wonder where he had gone – but some things were more important than professional courtesy. His friend needed him. The priest and the rookie detective would just have to get along with each other a little longer.

12

The 10-seater Dauphin 365N, the fastest commercial helicopter in the world, lifted off from a private helipad at Mombasa Airport and immediately swung south in the direction of the Tanzanian border. Twenty minutes later it landed in the grounds of a sprawling ranch house in the shadow of the Shimba Hills, sixty miles from the city. There was only one passenger. He was in his early twenties with a flop of fair hair hanging over piggy features and a body that had yet to shed the puppy fat of adolescence. Bobby Spurling did not wait for the rotors to stop spinning before he dashed over to a waiting Jeep driven by a tall, white-haired Masai ranger wearing bush fatigues.

'Good afternoon, Mr Bobby. It is nice to see you again.'

'Cut the crap, Malachi, and take me to my father,' Bobby said.

The ranch was set in 33,000 acres of rolling grass-land adjacent to the Shimba Hills National Reserve; and on days like this, with the rains tamping down the dust clouds on the plains, it was possible to see nearly a hundred miles. But Bobby Spurling did not care about the spectacular panorama. He had seen it a million times, and each time he cared for it less. He preferred to live in the city – even if that city was currently Johannesburg – because he liked to go to restaurants and nightclubs, because he enjoyed access to women and drugs, and because he would rather fucking *die* than spend the rest of his life festering in the sticks like his father. In fact, the only good thing about the ranch was that he'd had it valued in excess of nineteen million dollars only last week – a windfall he now hoped would be coming his way sooner rather than later.

Money and land were not all Bobby stood to gain when Clay Spurling died. There was, of course, the small matter of Spurling Developments itself. And finally becoming the king, instead of the eternal heir to the fucking throne, was a prospect that sent a tingle down his spine.

The Jeep swept round to the front of the sprawling house, with its ornamental tea bushes and imported turf lawn, but instead of stopping outside the colonnaded portico the driver kept going.

'What the hell are you doing, Malachi?' Bobby demanded. 'I want to see my father.'

Malachi, his father's longest-serving employee and the man who had looked after the Spurling reserve for nearly forty years, looked straight ahead. 'Your father is waiting for you at the stables, Mr Bobby.'

Bobby felt like someone had driven a fist into his guts. The *stables*? His father was supposed to be on his fucking *deathbed*! Six months after his heart attack and God knew how many millions spent on life-saving treatments in clinics from Atlanta to Zurich, the old man had finally come home to die. Wasn't that the whole point of his being invited here? Wasn't this why he was being brought out of exile after eighteen long months?

Unless one of the treatments had actually worked!

No – the thought was just too appalling for words.

The stable block was situated two miles from the house, along an interminably winding track which passed through an area of arid wasteland occupied only by desert rose plants. With their grotesquely swollen stems and twisted branches it seemed almost perverse that these plants should produce such an abundance of glorious red and pink flowers, yet entirely appropriate that their sap, roots and seeds should contain a toxin strong enough to kill a small army. As a small boy Bobby had always been ordered to keep away from them – not that he needed any encouragement. He hated the obscenely ugly plants and soon, when the ranch was his, he would take great pleasure in burning the whole fucking lot of them to the ground.

The Jeep arrived at the stable block and Bobby climbed out. There were a dozen stables arranged in an L-shape around a dirt paddock. Beyond, on the slopes of the hill, his father had built gallops – almost three miles of loamy terrain in the middle of Africa that would not have looked out of place at Newmarket. There were those who had said it couldn't be done: but then you didn't build Kenya's pre-eminent civil engineering company from scratch without knowing how to create something out of nothing.

Clay Spurling, a short man with a shock of pearl-white hair, was standing at the far side of the paddock, deep in conversation with one of the stable lads. When he saw his father, Bobby was horrified. He had fully expected to confront a paper-skinned skeleton wheezing its final words from its deathbed. Instead, the old *cunt* was a picture of health! He had lost weight and in his polo shirt, jodhpurs and leather riding boots he looked as if he had just come in from playing a leisurely chukka. He was seventy-four years old, but to his son's disgust he looked ten years younger.

'Papa!'

The old man looked up and fixed his son with piercing blue eyes. In that instant Bobby felt the old familiar symptoms of panic and inadequacy – sweating hands, palpitations – he always experienced in his father's presence.

Clay strode across the paddock.

'Good trip?' he barked. 'How's Jo'burg?'

'Fine, fine. But, Papa, I thought—'

'Thought I was dead?'

'No—'

Clay Spurling laughed harshly. 'It's amazing what they can do nowadays, isn't it?'

Bobby looked at him blankly.

'*Nanotechnology*. Miniature robots. Barely the size of a molecule. Can you imagine – millions of these tiny little machines chomping away at the fatty deposits in your coronary arteries? Not a scar in sight. Of course, I'll be on pills for the rest of my life. But I'm not complaining. Are you, Bobby?'

It was a pointed question. 'I just can't believe it, Papa,' Bobby said.

It was a reply that was true whichever way you looked at it.

13

Since leaving CID training school in Nairobi nine months before, David Mwangi's career as a detective had consisted of sitting behind a desk with a calculator in one hand and a guide to fiscal law in the other. Exposing tax impropriety was not what he had expected when he had joined the plain-clothes division.

Which of course proved what a naïve fool he was.

When you were the son of a prominent government minister, educated at a leading public school in England and the recipient of a first-class degree in mathematics from Oxford University, you were too valuable to waste on such mundane tasks as murder investigations. No, your analytical brain was of far more use identifying and unpicking complex accountancy frauds – especially when the alleged fraudsters were political enemies of the government who, after all, paid your wages.

A lot of people in the tax fraud investigation department were annoyed when Superintendent Simba seconded him to Coast Province CID, because they had become used to Mwangi doing all the work. But for Mwangi, leaving Nairobi was like being reborn. At last he was free to work on cases that did not involve sifting through dizzying columns of figures. After being a detective in name only, here was his chance to prove himself – and, now that he had it, he was not about to squander the opportunity.

He sat with Brother Willem in the cool sanctuary of the church and removed his notebook from his jacket pocket.

'Tell me about Sister Gudrun,' he said pleasantly.

Willem's face twitched with irritation behind his spectacles and his long fingers drummed impatiently against the plastic chair in front.

'I have already told all this to Inspector Jouma,' he snapped.

'I am aware of that,' Mwangi said, taken aback by the priest's reaction but determined to maintain the upper hand. 'Now I would like you to tell me.'

Willem expelled a theatrical sigh and, in a sullen voice, explained that, like most of the elders of the Redeemed Apostolic Gospel Church, Sister Gudrun was of Dutch descent. She had been involved in missionary work in Africa for over forty years, and no – he didn't know exactly how many. It was not the sort of question one asked.

'And what about you, Brother Willem?'

'What about me?'

'What is your background?'

With a roll of the eyes, Willem explained that he was from Delft and had come to help with the Church's missionary work in east Africa three years ago – but was all this strictly relevant to the current investigation?

'Everything is relevant, Brother Willem,' Mwangi said. 'Do you know Sister Gudrun well?'

'What is that supposed to mean?'

'Is she popular?'

'She is *devout*, Detective Constable. If you were to ask her, she would say that popularity is unimportant when compared to fulfilling God's work.'

'Of course. So please – tell me about Sister Gudrun's trip to Mombasa.' Mwangi flashed the biggest, most endearing smile he could manage.

Slowly, grudgingly, the priest described how, three days earlier, Sister Gudrun had boarded an early morning *matatu* minibus and travelled thirty miles south to Mombasa. There she was due to meet with a number of prominent local businessmen to discuss funding for Church projects along the Kenya seaboard. It was a routine trip and she was expected back before nightfall.

'Before you ask, I supplied Inspector Jouma with a full list of her appointments,' Willem said.

Mwangi nodded. 'I am grateful. What time was her last scheduled meeting?'

'Four o'clock in the afternoon.'

'So she should have been back here at, say, seven in the evening?'

'If you say so.'

'Were you not worried when she had not returned by the following morning?'

'Sister Gudrun is an independent woman,' Willem said. 'She often changes her plans.'

'Changes her plans?'

'It's entirely possible that she decided to pay a visit to one of the other missions. She is one of the Church elders. She takes her responsibilities very seriously.' Willem gave him a withering look. 'I would remind you that it wasn't me who called the police, Detective Constable.'

No, Mwangi thought. The call had come from the last person on Sister Gudrun's list, a Chinese rice importer from the Old Town who became concerned when she didn't show for her four o'clock appointment. Sister Gudrun, it seemed, had a special place in his heart after converting him and his family to Christianity upon their arrival in Africa twenty years earlier.

Willem, by contrast, was so unconcerned he had gone off to Malindi on a fund-raising mission of his own the next morning. The first he knew about Sister Gudrun's disappearance was when he returned to Jalawi to find Jouma waiting for him.

'It's been three days, now, Brother Willem,' Mwangi pointed out. 'Aren't you even slightly worried?'

The priest sighed. 'If she was a teenage novitiate straight off the boat, then perhaps I would be. But Sister Gudrun knows Kenya better than most Kenyans, Detective Constable Mwangi. She'll turn up sooner or later. She always does.'

If Gudrun was indeed prone to going walkabout for days at a time then his irritation at the police investigation might have been understandable. But, as he diligently scribbled in his notebook, the young detective thought back to the briefing Jouma had given him in the car on the way here. Sister Gudrun might have been a responsible Church elder, the inspector said, but there were four Redeemed Apostolic Gospel Church missions within a hundred-mile radius of Mombasa, and none of them had seen her for months.

'So she has vanished off the face of the earth?' Mwangi asked him.

'In my experience, Mwangi, people do not simply vanish off the face of the earth,' Jouma had said. 'They are always *somewhere*, and someone always knows where. Which makes me think somebody is not being entirely truthful with us.'

'You think Willem is involved?'

'I think he knows more than he is letting on.'

Now, as he filled the pages with notes, Mwangi could not help but agree.

14

A table had been erected on a bluff overlooking the gallops and together Clay and Bobby Spurling shared a light, open-air luncheon of crawfish tails and chilled white wine. Below them a magnificent thoroughbred was being put through its paces and they said little, on the face of it content to watch the magnificent animal perform. But then the old man suggested they take a ride around the ranch and, as they mounted a pair of Arab stallions, Bobby knew that the purpose of this nightmarish father-and-son reunion was at hand.

The Spurling reserve was vast. It abutted the Shimba Hills reserve, and was almost the same size. Clay Spurling thought of himself as a conservationist – which Bobby always found hugely amusing considering the old bastard had made his millions from pouring concrete over Kenya – and as a result employed a large team of rangers to patrol against the ever-present threat of poachers. It was said locally that any elephant that valued its tusks would make a beeline for the Spurling reserve because it was the safest place in Africa.

But they did not ride far that day. Clay had summoned his only son from exile in Jo'burg for one reason, and he was not a man to waste time with preamble.

'I'm stepping down as company chairman, Bobby,' he said.

Bobby felt his heart begin to pound. *This is it.* 'It's the sensible thing to do for your health, Papa.'

'William Fearon will be taking over. And I'm making Frank Walker CEO.'

For a moment he found it hard to get his breath and he almost toppled backwards off his horse. '*What?*'

'With immediate effect once I've ratified the decision with the executive board.'

Bobby's mind raced. William Fearon, the long-serving company CEO, was always a certainty to be promoted to chairman. But—

'Frank *Walker*?'

'That's my decision.'

'Papa—'

'Frank has been a loyal servant to me and this company for over twenty years. He knows the business inside out. He deserves it.'

Bobby was too numb to feel his father's barbs. 'But what about *me*?'

'You're twenty-three years old, Bobby. You don't have the experience. Not yet. But your time will come, so don't worry – you'll be looked after.'

They had ridden a circuit that had taken them away from the stables, up around the bluff and back down past the house. Now, as the sun began to set, they were returning to the stables along the track where the desert roses thrust out of the arid soil like bloated hands. As a boy Bobby always felt an eerie sensation that the towering plants were *watching* him, and that their fat, underground roots contained the bodies of small boys dragged from their beds by the contorted branches.

But right now any irrational, childish fear was replaced by cold adult fury.

The selfish, senile old fucker! Handing over the reins of the company to someone else – and to Frank Walker of all people!

He brought his horse to a halt and dismounted.

'Don't sulk about it, Bobby!' his father snapped. 'And don't tell me you've ever had any interest in the business either.'

'But it's *our* business, Papa. The *family's*.'

'It's bigger than the family now.'

'*Papa!*' With a howl of anguish, Bobby took a hunting knife from his belt and jabbed it into the trunk of the nearest desert rose. A rivulet of oily sap oozed from the wound when he withdrew the blade and, fascinated, he touched it with the finger of his thick leather riding glove.

'Come on, Bobby,' Clay Spurling was saying, his tone placatory now. 'Running a business this size is just one big fucking headache. Believe me, I'm doing you a favour.'

'A favour?' Bobby stuck the knife into the plant again, but instead of removing it he began sawing absently at the flesh. 'You do know that by appointing Frank Walker you'll make me a laughing stock.'

'Don't be ridiculous—'

'"Look at Bobby Spurling. Passed over by his own

father for some truck driver from a fucking Glasgow housing estate!"'

'For Christ's sake, Bobby!' the old man exclaimed. 'Do you think you've given me a choice? You live like a playboy with your whores and your cocaine and your gambling! You seriously imagine I would let you anywhere near the company I built up from scratch? You'd bankrupt it in a month.'

'You always hated me,' Bobby spat.

'Oh, stop feeling sorry for yourself. It makes me sick.'

'And I could never understand why – because I worshipped you, Papa.'

'Bobby—'

Bobby moved quickly. Two, three rapid steps and suddenly he had reached up and dragged the old man from his saddle. Clay Spurling landed on the baked earth with a sickening thump and somewhere inside his weakened body a bone splintered loudly.

'You miserable old bastard,' Bobby said, grasping his father by the throat and speckling his purple face with white spittle. 'You think I'm going to let you fuck me over?'

Clay Spurling's blue eyes bulged in their sockets and, as his mouth opened in a silent bellow of rage and pain, Bobby pushed a freshly carved chunk of succulent desert-rose flesh into it with one gloved hand.

Had Clay Spurling been healthy to begin with, thirty seconds might have been an accurate estimate of his life expectancy. But against such a sudden and heavy concentration of fast-acting cardiotoxic glycosides, the old man's punished heart stood no chance.

He was dead before his son had finished screwing the last of the flesh into his mouth.

Breathing heavily and shaking with exertion and adrenaline, Bobby got to his feet, brushed the dust off his trousers, then bent down and, with difficulty, heaved the body over the saddle of his horse. In a few moments he would return, distraught, to the stables and inform the staff that his father had suffered one last, fatal heart attack while out riding. Yes – that was what he would do. But at least, he would tell them, Clay Spurling had died doing what he loved, and with the person he loved the most.

There would be the funeral to arrange, of course. He would bury his father beside his mother, at the foot of the ancient flame tree at the western perimeter of the reserve where they loved to watch the sun coming up over the Shimbas. It was only right that his parents should be united in death as they had been in life, in the corner of Africa they loved so much. And he hoped that, when he sold the estate for nineteen million dollars, the next owners would respect their graves.

But that was a long way in the future. For now Bobby Spurling was filled with a sudden urgency to get things done. There were phone calls to be made, meetings to arrange. There was no time to lose.

As he mounted the Arab and set off towards his destiny, his dead father's pearl-white head thumped against the muscular flanks of the other horse with the solemn beat of a funeral procession.

15

After half an hour in Brother Willem's company, even Mwangi's copious reserves of patience had been exhausted. With relief he terminated the interview and left the priest fussing over the altar ornaments in the gloom of the church. It was getting late. He was now anxious to get back to Mombasa, to begin retracing the last known movements of the missing nun. But when he stepped outside he discovered that not only was Jouma nowhere to be found, but his car had gone too.

What was it about Jalawi that made people disappear? he thought to himself.

After several minutes self-consciously hanging around outside the church, Mwangi concluded that the inspector was not coming back. Maybe, he thought, he was being subjected to some arcane initiation rite in which new recruits to Coast CID were abandoned in the middle of nowhere and expected to make their own way back to the city.

Or maybe Jouma was testing him in another way. The case was now his. Perhaps he was being encouraged to make the most of it without a senior officer peering over his shoulder.

Sister Gudrun's house was on the other side of the village. Like every other building in Jalawi it was constructed of wooden lattice, dried mud and coconut thatch. The only difference was its size. While the other houses were designed to accommodate as many as twenty people from the same family, the nun's was defiantly single-person occupancy. Peeking through the slatted door, Mwangi saw that apart from the cot the only other item of furniture was a crucifix on the wall. It was not so much a house as a cell.

Mwangi was debating whether to go inside when he heard the sound of approaching footsteps and girlish laughter. He turned to see two young nuns in red and white robes coming around the corner in the direction of the house. The older of the two was white-skinned with a pretty face framed by short dark hair cropped in a severe fringe. Mwangi guessed she was about four or five years older than the second girl, who was African and who could not have been more than sixteen years old. Both were carrying folded bedclothes in their arms and they stopped sharply in their tracks when they saw him. The younger girl seemed to shrink behind her companion like a small child with her mother.

'Forgive me, I did not mean to startle you,' Mwangi said. He introduced himself.

The older girl said something to the other, who handed over her blankets and then hurried back the way she had come, head bowed.

'I am Sister Constance,' she said, and he detected a

strong European accent. 'You will forgive Sister Florence but she is very shy of strangers. If you are looking for Sister Gudrun's house, you have found it.'

Mwangi shuffled awkwardly. 'I thought it might be helpful to my investigation to see where she lived.'

Constance moved past him and went into the house. 'There is not much to see.'

'So it would appear.'

Mwangi watched the young nun briskly strip the blankets from Gudrun's cot and replace them with fresh ones.

'Where is the other policeman?' she said. 'The old man who was here the other day?'

The old man? Jouma would love that. 'He is ... making enquiries elsewhere.'

'Gudrun is still missing?'

'I am afraid so.'

'Then we will continue to pray for her,' Constance said, gathering the old blankets. 'And to change her bedclothes.'

Together they walked back through the village in the direction of the church.

'Sister Gudrun's seems a very frugal existence,' Mwangi remarked for want of something better to say. 'I'm not sure I could ever do without my luxuries. I'm lost without my laptop.'

Constance laughed. 'I have 50 Cent's new album on my iPod, and my brother sends me DVDs. If I was to tell you that Sister Gudrun considers such things to be the Devil's work, perhaps you will get some idea of how single-minded she is in her devotion to the Lord.'

'I see. And what about you?'

'Ever since I was a young girl I always knew that God would be my vocation, Detective Mwangi. It was just a case of how best to serve Him.'

'How long have you been here in Jalawi?'

'I arrived here six weeks ago from the mission at Malindi. Sister Gudrun and Brother Willem were in the process of setting up the mission and wanted help with the children's education.'

Mwangi looked at the large cross on the church, visible above the thatched roofs of the villagers' huts. 'They built a church in six weeks?'

'Donations are the lifeblood of the Church. Money and labour get things built. When it comes to begging both Brother Willem and Sister Gudrun are in a league of their own.' Constance smiled coquettishly. 'Although I'm sure they would prefer it if you used the term "appealing to people's charitable nature".'

They were near the riverbank now. Less than a hundred yards away was the mouth of Flamingo Creek, and Mwangi could hear the sound of children shouting and screaming as they played.

'We hope one day to raise enough money to build a school,' Constance said. 'Florence and I try to help the kids with some rudimentary reading and writing. But, as you can hear, children aren't designed to sit still and learn. Not when the sun is shining outside. And of course the sun is always shining here.'

Mwangi grimaced. 'I was educated in England. There it was always raining.'

'The curse of northern Europe.' Constance laughed. 'I try to explain our climate to the children but they don't believe such a place exists. They think

74

we have white skin because we live in caves. Sometimes I think they are right.'

The detective stopped. 'I have to ask you, Sister – do you know of any reason why Sister Gudrun did not return from her trip to Mombasa? Any reason someone might have wished to cause her harm?'

She shook her head. 'No.'

'And you subscribe to Brother Willem's opinion that she is safe and well?'

'Brother Willem knows her better than most. If that is what he says then we must believe him.'

It struck Mwangi as a curiously offhand, noncommittal comment.

'And what about you? What do *you* think of Sister Gudrun?'

'As a woman who has given herself to God I have nothing but respect for her,' Constance said. 'But can you keep a secret, Detective Constable Mwangi?'

'Of course.'

'As a human being I despise her.'

16

On *Yellowfin*'s bridge Jake watched the sun going down over the distant mainland but saw only Martha Bentley lying dead in her kitchen. It was unbearable to imagine her final few seconds, yet he could not help himself: the shock and puzzlement as she was grabbed, pressure against the back of her head, a sudden cold wave of terror – then nothing at all.

It was the nothingness that Jake found hardest to bear.

The boat was drifting five miles off the coast, at the mercy of the current and the breeze. For the last hour Harry had been trying to raise him on the ship-to-shore, no doubt working himself into an even greater state of panic. The visitation from Special Agents Bryson and McCrickerd had spooked the life out of his partner, who was now convinced there was an assassin on his way to Mombasa to stick a knife in his spine.

But Jake had ignored the radio. So far that day it had brought nothing but bad news. He felt like throwing the fucking thing into the sea.

How was it possible that someone so full of life could now be dead? The question kept repeating itself over and over in his head; but still he was no nearer an answer.

Agents Bryson and McCrickerd had been waiting for him like a pair of undertakers when he'd got back to the yard that afternoon. As a young cop he'd broken bad news plenty of times but had only received it once; and his father's death from cirrhosis was not unexpected. This was totally different. To hear it first hand from someone who had actually watched Martha being zipped into a bodybag was like being punched in the stomach.

Then came the questions. Gentle and respectful at first. Bryson mainly. Did Martha ever mention the company Patrick Noonan worked for? Did she ever travel with him? Did Noonan say anything unusual in the minutes before he died?

Then McCrickerd, the pit bull: what was your relationship with her? Why was she going to give you her old man's insurance money? *Were you fucking her, Jake?*

And Jake, who knew the good cop/bad cop routine like the back of his hand, still couldn't help himself from lunging at the thick-set American with his fists whirling until Harry and Bryson dragged him away.

Sometime later, when the FBI agents had gone, Jouma had arrived at the boatyard; but Jake couldn't be sure when. He'd been at Jalawi, he said, something to do with the mission over there, and Sammy had told him about Martha. There were words of heart-felt consolation. If there was anything he could do –

But what *could* he do? What could anyone do that already wasn't too late?

Tomorrow he was supposed to be taking *Yellowfin* to Missy Meredith's repair yard. He had been looking forward to spending the morning sitting outside Missy's workshop with a mug of her industrial-strength Irish coffee, while her put-upon brother Walton got to work transforming *Yellowfin*.

But now the realities of the situation were beginning to hit him. *How the hell was he supposed to pay for the work?* The reason Martha had gone back to the States was to set the financial wheels in motion, to set New York's finest legal eagles to work unfreezing her father's insurance money. Now she was dead, who was looking after his assets? He could imagine the predators circling already. The chances of their allowing the money to go to a couple of English deadbeats in Africa were remote to nonexistent.

Yet the more he thought about it, the less he cared. It was the unedifying, immoral pursuit of money that had created monsters like Patrick Noonan. It was money that had taken Martha away from Africa, where at least Jake could have protected her.

In the supernatural glow of sunset, his eyes alighted on a coolbox stowed under the dashboard of the flying bridge. A dozen bottles of chilled Tusker winked up at him through the swirl of condensation. Martha never liked to travel without some cold ones to hand for just this time of the day.

Jake smiled sadly. That was how he would remember her: one hand clasped around a beer, the other expertly easing forward *Yellowfin*'s throttles, and the warm Indian Ocean breeze in her hair. He grabbed one of the frosted bottles and flipped its metal lid; then, lifting its neck to the darkening sky, he offered it in one last silent toast to his friend.

To you, Martha Bentley.

It was getting late.

It was time to go home.

Day Three

17

In a small village near Kisumu, in Nyanza Province on the shores of Lake Victoria, ten people suspected of witchcraft had been lynched by a vigilante group. The killings were in revenge for the abduction of a villager who had been made to dig up a dead body and then eat the decomposing flesh of the corpse. Meanwhile, in the Uasin Gishu district of the Rift Valley, north of Nairobi, one hundred and forty pigs had been hanged and then set alight by villagers who were under the impression they had been cursed by a witch doctor from a rival tribe.

Sometimes, when he read the overnight crime reports that came diligently chattering out of the ancient CID national network autoprinter, Jouma wondered if certain remote parts of Kenya would ever enter the fifteenth century, let alone the twenty-first.

But there were other times, like today, when he longed for the primitive simplicity of superstition and witchcraft.

He thought about Martha Bentley and how she

was a victim of a very modern conspiracy; one that was only possible because its perpetrators around the world could communicate with each other in the blink of an eye and could order another person's death without even having to say their name. It frightened him that he knew so little about the workings of the modern world, yet at the same time he was relieved that he was so ignorant.

He thought about Jake Moore. The Englishman was not one to openly show his emotions, but Jouma could tell the news of Martha's murder had hit him like a train. Yesterday at the boatyard it was as if all the life had been sucked out of him. And while the inspector had wanted nothing more than to console his friend he also knew there were times when there was simply no consolation that would suffice. At times like this, grief could only be reconciled in the privacy of one's own soul.

Jouma sighed. It was almost a relief to turn his attention to a mystery he at least felt comfortable with – even if he had yet to solve it conclusively. Two days had passed since Lol Quarrie had fallen from the walls of Fort Jesus, and Jouma was ninety-nine per cent sure that it was suicide. All the evidence pointed to the fact that a retired widower, in his twilight years and suffering from post-operative depression, had broken into Fort Jesus and flung himself from the ramparts in a fit of lonely desperation.

The alternative scenario – that the former police-man, all sixteen stone of him, had been abducted from a busy downtown street in broad daylight, smuggled into Fort Jesus through a locked gate, forced or manhandled on to the wall and thrown off it – was so unlikely it was, quite frankly, laughable.

Yet the fact nagged at Jouma's mind that ninety-nine per cent was not one hundred; and, however small, that one per cent of doubt could not be discounted.

He could not help recalling the words of Dutch Alice, the last person to see Quarrie alive: '*If you ask me he was drunk. Staggering about. Talking to himself – you know, like drunks do.*'

But Quarrie was not drunk. The analysis into his blood alcohol levels had come back negative, proving that on the day of his death he was resolutely teetotal and therefore in full command of his faculties. Christie, meanwhile, had concluded that Quarrie's heart – once clogged with a lifetime's worth of sludge – had been working as perfectly as a man half his age, which precluded any suggestion of a coronary.

Then there was the question of how he had got on to the walls of the fort in the first place. The gates were locked and showed no sign of being tampered with. According to the fort administrator there *was* no other way of getting into the compound, other than a hundred-foot ladder or a grappling hook.

And then there was the mystery of Quarrie's clothes.

That first morning, while the corpse was being prepared for Christie's tender mercies, Jouma had gone to see the fearsome Mrs Jubumbwe who ran the evidence locker at police headquarters.

'You do know that this is highly irregular, Detective Inspector?' she had barked at him. 'You are supposed to have the correct form filled out and signed.'

'I appreciate that, Mrs Jubumbwe. But if you could

overlook the formalities just this once I would be very grateful.'

Mrs Jubumbwe tutted through the metal grille separating her and over three thousand case files and evidence boxes from the grasping, disorganised hands of the outside world. She was a short, almost perfectly spherical woman whose encyclopaedic knowledge of her domain meant that, even though she was a civilian employee, she was probably Coast Province CID's most valuable asset.

'What was the name of the deceased?'

'Quarrie. Q-U-'

'I know how to spell, thank you very much.'

She turned, waddled off towards the groaning rows of shelves and returned less than a minute later with a reinforced cardboard box.

'As you don't have the correct form, you may not take the evidence out of this room,' Mrs Jubumbwe said. 'You may sit at that table where I can keep an eye on you.'

She lifted the grille and slid the box through the window.

Jouma carried it to a wooden table and lifted the lid. Inside, secured in plastic bags, were Lol Quarrie's clothes and possessions. He could feel Mrs Jubumbwe's laser eyes fixed on him as he carefully removed the dead man's blazer, shirt and flannels and laid them out on the table.

All three were covered in the same large brown bloodstain, and the shoulders and collars of the blazer were still speckled with brain matter and fragments of bone. But Jouma could see something else, something he was sure he had noticed the previous night but was now confirmed in the harsh strip light of the evidence locker.

Quarrie's clothes were filthy. The smart blazer and neatly pressed trousers were smeared with some sort of thick, greeny-brown sludge as if he had been crawling through mud. Except it was not mud. It smelled like – well, Jouma could not say for certain except that it caught in his throat and made him feel sick. There was dust, too. And soil. In fact, Lol Quarrie's clothes looked as if he had been sleeping rough in them for several days.

How he wished Coast CID had its own fully operational forensics laboratory, with white-coated experts who could analyse the substances on Quarrie's clothes and tell him precisely what they were and where they came from. But, as he sat in his office in Mombasa, he knew full well that the only available forensic department was in Nairobi and was so understaffed and ill-equipped it could take months to get any sort of result.

Jouma sighed. How uncomplicated life had been when his only concern was the whereabouts of a missing nun. How he envied Constable Mwangi for being able to pound the streets, reinterviewing shopkeepers, café owners, *matatu* drivers and stall proprietors in the vain hope that they had been suffering some form of temporary amnesia the last time they'd been asked if they had seen a seventy-five-year-old woman of God.

Even his colleagues in the sticks had pig killers and grave robbers to round up. Daniel Jouma, the man who cleaned up Mombasa, was just twiddling his thumbs in his office, waiting for something to happen.

18

Jake was up early that morning. There were no book-ings in the ledger, but instead of mooching around the yard he planned to park up in sight of the hotels at Watamu, north of Flamingo Creek, and go touting for trade among the Ernies poolside, just like he and Harry had done five years ago when the business was just starting out. The regular skippers up there wouldn't be too pleased – but fuck 'em. Business was business, and most of the Ernies would be financial-meltdown victims from the States and Europe looking for a cut-price afternoon's fishing.

First, though, he had to pick up Sammy from Jalawi. He anchored *Yellowfin* in the shallows oppo-site the village and waited for his bait boy to swim ashore. It wasn't down as a work day, but he knew as soon as Sammy saw him he would be over like a shot. The kid had been through hell in the last few weeks, with the murder of his younger brother by Patrick Noonan's goons, but the one thing he lived for was working on *Yellowfin*.

Jake had just lit a cigarette when he became aware

of a commotion on the north shore. Squinting across, he saw people waving at him.

Then he heard them shouting for help.

The hippie had fallen twenty feet from a fifty-foot palm tree and broken his leg in three places. Jake's first thought was that it served him right for being so stupid: the local kids who harvested coconuts by the water's edge made it look easy because they had been scampering up palm trees since the day they learned to walk.

'You need to get him to a hospital right away,' he said, peering at the kid's misshapen leg. 'The nearest is Mombasa General.'

'Can you help us get him there?'

The speaker had introduced herself as Evie Simenon. She was the oldest of a handful of the great unwashed who were gathered round their fallen comrade, and the only one who appeared to know what the hell to do next.

'We'd take him in our bus – but the rear suspension is shot,' she said glumly. 'We've got a motorbike, but a couple of our guys went to Kilifi this morning to see if they can get some spare parts.'

'Bus?' He looked at them. 'Who are you people? The *Scooby Doo* gang?'

Evie wore a wearied expression that suggested that in her time she had heard just about every smart-alec comment.

'Can you help us?' she said. 'If not, we'll try our luck with the Yacht Club down the road.'

'Trust me, lady, you don't get past the *askari* on the front gate unless you're worth at least a million.'

Jake looked at the injured hippie, who appeared to be in some sort of trance – although judging by the smell of marijuana drifting from the campsite it was hardly surprising. Then again it was most likely shock. Judging by the angle at which his right fibula had snapped he would be lucky to walk properly again.

'What's his name?'

'Michael. Michael Gulbis.'

'Have you given him painkillers?'

'A morphine shot,' Evie said.

That explained the stupor at least.

'Well, that won't last for ever. And when it wears off he's going to be in agony.' Jake shook his head. 'There's no way I can get him to hospital on the boat. But I can try to raise Harry on the ship-to-shore. He'll patch a call through to the paramedics at Kilifi. They'll have an ambulance here in half an hour – assuming there's not the usual carnage on the highway.'

Evie looked at him. 'Did you say *Harry*? You mean Harry from the boatyard on the other side of the river?'

'You know him?'

Evie told him about their meeting the previous day.

'He never mentioned it.' *But then neither man had been in the mood to swap stories yesterday.* 'Who are you people anyway? What are you doing here?'

When Evie told him about the proposed development at Jalawi village, Jake looked at her sceptically.

'A five-star hotel? Here?' He laughed. 'Well, it's the first I've heard of it, and my bait boy lives here.'

'Then you should ask your friend Harry,' Evie said. 'He seems to know a lot more about it than you do. Or maybe he never mentioned that either.'

19

The Colonial was a jaded, two-star hotel in downtown Mombasa. Room 507 had two single beds, a television set and a view over a timber yard. It stank of coffee and cigarettes. FBI Special Agent Clarence Bryson lay on one of the beds and felt the caffeine- and amphetamine-suppressed jet lag from a sleepless, fourteen-hour flight from Washington beginning to win the battle with his brain and body.

McCrickerd, by contrast, looked sickeningly robust. He had just returned from a two-hour jog around the island and was now sitting at a writing table in his sweats, fiddling with a laptop AppleMac.

'So how was he?' the younger man asked presently.

'The sonofabitch has lawyers costing three hundred dollars an hour,' Bryson said. 'He isn't saying anything.'

'He will, as soon as we get him back to the States.'

'Don't hold your breath on that one, John. The lawyers will contest every clause of the extradition papers. It could take months.'

And Conrad Getty knew it, Bryson thought

despondently. He'd just returned from a fruitless morning at a high-security prison north of Mombasa, where the last surviving member of Patrick Noonan's east African cell was currently incarcerated in solitary confinement. Getty, a cadaverous South African hotel owner with a comb-over, had simply sat there smirking, while his lawyers, who flanked him like a couple of linebackers in $3,000 suits, answered, 'No comment' to every question Bryson had asked.

'Can't we say that human trafficking is a threat to homeland security?' suggested McCrickerd. 'We'd have him on a fast plane to Algeria with a sack on his head by the end of the day.'

'Sadly not,' Bryson sighed. 'But if that arrogant bastard thinks he's going to have it easy he can think again. I'll be in his face every fucking day until we get the papers. Let's see how long he can afford 24/7 legal representation at three hundred dollars an hour.'

McCrickerd chuckled approvingly, then slapped the table. 'We're in business. The feed is in from Hoffman.'

Bryson levered himself slowly from the bed and went across to where his partner sat at the window. The two men stared at the laptop screen and waited patiently for a download to finish. After a few moments an image appeared on the screen and Bryson suddenly felt slightly queasy. He was not looking forward to this. Having your nose rubbed in it was not a pleasant experience.

A busy city thoroughfare with cars and pedestrians moving rapidly from side to side.

Footage from a security camera outside Martha

Bentley's apartment building on East 74th Street in New York on the day she was murdered. It had been beamed across the world from FBI headquarters in Washington. It was the first time either man had seen it. *The first time they had seen the killer everybody in the Bureau was calling the Ghost.*

'There he is,' Bryson murmured.

A figure walks towards the camera. He is slightly built, but wearing a bulky windcheater. His thin face is obscured by a baggy cap and a large pair of sunglasses. Is there a slightly Middle Eastern look about him – or is that just the received wisdom about every murdering bastard these days?

'Looks like Elton fucking John,' McCrickerd said. He froze the face and zoomed in – but other than a pair of narrow lips framed by a wispy goatee they were none the wiser. Martha Bentley's killer could be anyone.

But then, with a hired assassin, that was the point.

The playback shot forward by a further twenty-three minutes.

A yellow New York cab pulls up outside the apartment building and a blonde woman gets out of the back seat. The cabbie heaves Martha Bentley's suitcases on to the side-walk.

So glad to be home, Bryson thought. Yet with so little time left to live.

The cabbie thanks her profusely for what must have been a generous tip and follows her into her apartment building with her bags. The timer reads 11:04.

The download ended.

'Hoffman says his guys have been looking at the internal footage – lobby, elevators, hallway – but it looks like they were all fucked with,' McCrickerd reported. Dean Hoffman was from the Bureau's New York office and, in Bryson's absence, was in the capital heading up the Stateside investigation into Martha Bentley's murder. 'Some sort of electrical interference.'

'Convenient.'

'He says they'll keep trying to enhance what they've got, but so far it still looks like chicken noodle soup.'

'And Hoffman says there's no record of this guy leaving the building?'

'They say he must have walked through the walls.'

Bryson stared at the face on the computer screen. *The Ghost.* The sonofabitch would probably relish the soubriquet. Hired killers always did, because even though they claimed to be detached from society they were as vain as everybody else when it came down to it. Bryson had to admit that this guy was pretty damn good, though. He had rubbed out their number-one witness without a trace and made the FBI look like assholes in the process.

But that was where it ended.

Conrad Getty was going to tell them everything they wanted to know about the trafficking syndicate, whether he or his expensive lawyers liked it or not. Bryson's job was to ensure that, however long it took, the hotel owner would be extradited back to the States – and, Ghost or no Ghost, that was precisely what the veteran FBI man intended to do.

20

When Jake tried to hail him on the ship-to-shore, Harry wasn't in, or wasn't answering – which was probably just as well, because there were a few things he needed to sort out with his partner. Like why the hell he had kept the small matter of the Jalawi hotel development to himself, for example. Instead, he got through to Missy Meredith's yard and spoke to her brother. Walton was only too happy to help and said he would get on to the Kilifi paramedics right away: anything if it meant a break from crawling round in sump oil.

When he returned from *Yellowfin* Jake found Evie on the beach, in conversation with one of her tribe, a fresh-faced youngster with an unkempt thatch of matted black hair.

'The paramedics are on their way,' Jake said. 'As long as you keep Michael's leg stable he should be OK.'

'Thank you,' she said, and for the first time he saw her smile.

'Yeah – thanks, man,' the kid with the hair said in

what Jake identified as a rather incongruous Home Counties accent. 'Mikey is my bro', you know?'

Jake looked at him blankly.

Sheepishly, the kid offered his hand. 'Alex Hopper. Pleased to meet you.'

'Where you from, Alex?' Jake said.

'Ah – Berkshire, actually.'

'Does your mum know you're out?'

Now it was Alex's turn to look bemused.

'Alex is about to start his shift on the viewing platform,' Evie said.

'Viewing platform?'

'Why don't you come and see for yourself?'

'Yeah,' Jake said. 'Maybe I should.'

They set off along a dirt footpath through the trees, back towards the village and the hippie camp on the outskirts. Jake now saw the garishly painted thirty-seater school bus that was parked in a clearing just off the road. Nearby was a smouldering fire and a handful of pup tents where the hippies had pitched camp. Most were sitting in numb-looking clusters in the shade of the trees and reminded Jake of the feckless youths who hung around street corners and shopping malls back in England. The same dopey, bored-looking expressions on their faces.

Be nice, Jake. Be nice. They're just kids trying to save the world while smoking as much pot as humanly possible.

Beyond the bus was a huge baobab tree. There was a sharp whistle from above and Jake looked up to see one of the hippies peering down at him from a platform lashed to its boughs.

'I hope you have a head for heights,' Evie said with

another half-smile, and began shinning up the fat trunk on a knotted rope hanging from one of the branches. 'I'd hate for you to fall and break your leg.'

The gauntlet thrown, Jake grabbed the rope and attempted to climb the tree with the same athletic insouciance as Evie. But he was fourteen stone compared to her eight; it took him several minutes to heave his bulk to the platform, and when he finally clambered over the side he was gasping and sweating profusely.

'Bravo, *signore*,' said the hippie on the platform, clapping ironically. He was an Alex-lookalike, but with a swaggering Italian accent and a sleeveless T-shirt to enhance the appearance of his tattooed biceps. He introduced himself as Jacopo, then lit a cigarette, said, '*Ciao*,' and abseiled down the rope like he was Errol Flynn.

'You OK?' Evie said.

Jake got to his feet with as much dignity as he could muster. 'It's been a long time since I had a tree-house,' he said.

Alex guffawed as he climbed on to the platform behind them. 'Tree-house. Fucking radical.'

'Shut up, Alex, and give the man the binoculars,' Evie said.

Alex handed Jake a pair of ancient, leather-bound Zeiss binoculars that Jacopo had left hanging from a branch. With them he was able to gain a clear view of Jalawi village stretched out beyond the edge of the trees. Even magnified, he thought, the place seemed impossibly small, just a ramshackle collection of mud huts that looked like they'd been knocked up by a bunch of kids.

'Hardly worth the fuss, eh?' Evie said, as if reading his mind. 'Except if it's your home, of course.'

Much as he baulked at the bleeding-heart routine, Jake had to accept that she had a point. He thought about Sammy, and how the kid lived with his mother in one of the rudimentary houses down there. To them Jalawi was the very centre of the universe – but maybe that was because they knew no better. What annoyed Jake about people like Evie Simenon was that they assumed people were happy with their lot, when in fact their lot stank.

'So what happens to the villagers if Spurling Developments gets the go-ahead?' he challenged her. 'I presume they'll get compensation?'

'Yeah, I'm sure they will,' Evie said, her voice dripping with sarcasm. 'The last hotel they built, they offered the villagers half-price introductory membership of the leisure spa. A snip at 10,000 shillings. Another time they offered to relocate two hundred people from a fishing village near Lamu to another site – sixty miles inland. No one took up the kind offer, so they kicked them out anyway. When they tried to rebuild their village from scratch half a mile down the coast, Spurling's lawyers sued them for trespassing. Believe me, these guys are all heart, Mr Moore.'

'Don't they have to get approval for the development first?'

'That's right. You know how many building applications Spurling submitted to the district councils last year? Sixty-three. How many were approved? Sixty-three. They've got the planning committees so far in their pockets they usually start digging the foundations before the applications are submitted. But if they come we'll be ready for them.'

She went across to a small padded bag hanging from another of the branches. Inside was a compact digital movie camera.

'I'm impressed,' Jake said. 'I'd like to see you stop a bulldozer using that thing.'

21

When the call came it was not a voice that Jouma recognised. It was neither brutish nor ill-educated like most of his contacts – in fact, it was the very opposite, and for a moment he thought it might be a wrong number. But then the caller gave an address on Ndia Kuu Road in the heart of the Old Town and told the policeman to be there in thirty minutes.

The road was a claustrophobic thoroughfare connecting Fort Jesus to the dhow harbour. The address was a furniture workshop halfway along it. The caller was waiting for him in the shade of a canvas awning above the entrance. He was an Arab in his early forties, bearded and bespectacled and wearing a shirt and tie. He introduced himself as Salim Mukhtar, a teacher of chemistry at the Aga Khan High School on Vanga Road. He seemed agitated.

'My father does not trust the police, Inspector,' Mukhtar said. 'He believes any law other than Sharia is corrupt. It has taken a great deal of persuasion on my behalf for him to agree to talk to you.'

Mukhtar's father sat on the bare floorboards of an

upstairs room, sucking on a hookah pipe, surrounded by offcuts of wood and frames of intricate fretwork. He was an old man with a white beard, and he wore traditional Muslim attire. He studied Jouma with small rheumy eyes as the detective sat down opposite.

'Father, tell the inspector what you told me,' Mukhtar said in the kind of loud voice grown-up children reserved for their elderly, senile parents.

The old man put-putted serenely on his pipe for a while. When he did speak, it was in a strange, guttural tongue that Jouma did not understand.

'My father is a Berber,' the teacher explained. 'Although he has lived in Mombasa for fifty years, he refuses to speak anything else. He believes any other language to be inferior.'

Jouma sighed inwardly. With his superior attitude the stubborn old goat could make this little encounter last all day.

'What did he just say?'

'He said he saw the dead man. The man who fell from the ramparts.'

'Where did he see him?'

'My father has a small handcart he uses to transport wood from the timber yard at Chamgamwe. He says he was returning from making a collection when he saw the man on Mbaraki Road.'

Mbaraki Road was the very street Jouma and Jake had walked along the night Lol Quarrie died. It ran parallel to Ndia Kuu in the direction of the harbour. Jouma produced a blown-up copy of the dead man's passport photograph and held it up to the old man. 'Is this the man you saw?'

The furniture-maker shrugged.

'My father says he was too far away to see his face. But he saw what happened.' The old man spoke again, and made a curious gesture with his clenched fists. 'He says the man was fighting.'

'Fighting?'

Mukhtar frowned. 'Fighting ... *Struggling* perhaps would be more accurate.'

Jouma leaned forward. 'Can your father describe who with?'

There was a gabble of dialogue between father and son. Presently, Mukhtar turned to Jouma and smiled apologetically. 'My father's eyesight is not what it once was. Too many years peering at intricate carvings by candlelight, I'm afraid.'

'Anything he can remember would be a great help.'

'He says he thinks it was a child.'

'A *child*?'

'A boy.'

'Black, white? How old?'

'He was wearing a hood. My father thinks he was possibly thirteen or fourteen.'

'What time did this occur?'

'Three thirty. My father knows this because he plays kalooki every afternoon at four, and he was hurrying so as not to be late.'

'And did he see where the man and the boy went?'

'An alleyway connecting Ndia Kuu with Mbaraki Road,' Mukhtar said. Then he frowned. 'My father says that, when he looked, both of them had vanished.'

'Vanished?'

'From the alley. As if by magic.'

Jouma's heart sank. He was getting heartily sick of people who simply vanished into thin air. But then the old man said something.

'My father says there was a sound.'

'What sound?'

The old man drew himself up and raised his chin imperiously.

'*Clank!*' the furniture-maker exclaimed. '*Clank! Clank!*'

22

The paramedics eventually arrived in an ambulance that looked even older than the hippies' bus. They gave Michael Gulbis a whiff of laughing gas and then strapped him in the back for the long and bumpy ride to Mombasa General. When they had gone Jake and Evie walked through the village, pursued by children and chickens and stray dogs. The kids knew Jake, but the strange-looking woman clearly still fascinated them. They plucked inquisitively at her clothing and the great loops of cheap and colourful jewellery hanging from appendages. They seemed particularly enchanted by Evie's dreadlocks.

'They aren't used to seeing them on white women,' she explained. 'They think I've stolen them.'

Sammy lived with his mother and a handful of goats in a shack on the edge of the village. Gladys Eruwa was sitting in a straight-backed chair in the doorway, beneath an awning made of rice sacks and bamboo cane. When she saw Jake, the old woman clasped his hand in her own and kissed his knuckles with her dry lips. Then she shouted for Sammy, who dashed out with a large bowl of cassava chips and a set of wooden false teeth which his mother fitted into her mouth.

'God bless you, Mr Moore!' she wheezed. 'The boy told me about what happened to your friend Martha. My heart is broken. Sammy! Get Mr Moore and his friend something to sit on!'

Jake introduced Evie and they sat on a couple of upturned vegetable boxes in the shade of the sun.

'Evie's here about the hotel they're planning to build here,' he said.

'I know why she is here,' Gladys said sternly, her lips pursed disapprovingly. 'And I have to say I am not happy.'

'Why, Mrs Eruwa?' Evie said. 'We're here to help.'

'Only God can help us, young lady. And He does not approve of your lifestyle.'

'Mrs Eruwa—'

'It is true! Brother Willem has taught us that we must pray for salvation, not to rely on those who are without faith.'

Evie smiled bitterly to herself. 'And I suppose Brother Willem told you that it's God's will if your houses are destroyed.'

Gladys Eruwa placed her hands on her large bosom and snorted gently. As far as she was concerned, the matter was closed. She turned to Jake and smiled maternally. 'Do you need Sammy today?'

'I was planning to go to Watamu, yes, Mrs Eruwa.'

Sammy, who had been listening uncomfortably to the exchange between his mother and Evie Simenon grinned and darted back into the house. He returned a few moments later with his gutting knives and a packed lunch of dried fruit.

'OK, let's go,' Jake said, standing up, as eager as his bait boy to beat a hasty retreat from the confrontation.

They walked back through the village, but Evie did not say a word. As they passed the clapboard church, a priest in white and red robes was welcoming villagers through the door. Willem's eyes met Evie's and for a moment Jake felt an almost palpable animosity pass between them. Then the priest looked away.

'I take it you don't get on,' he said as they continued walking.

Evie grunted. 'You could say that.'

'I'm surprised. They've got God on their side – and you could use all the help you can get.'

'Those bastards aren't motivated by God,' Evie said. 'They've got a habit of turning up just before the bulldozers move in – and they always insist on cash up front rather than leisure-club membership.'

He looked at her, half-expecting some sort of smile to indicate she was joking. But Evie's face was set in a venomous scowl and Jake could not be sure just who she despised more: those who claimed to have God on their side or those who didn't.

23

'"*Clank! Clank!*"?' Superintendent Simba looked up from Jouma's report. 'What does that mean?'

'I think he was being descriptive, ma'am,' Jouma said, feeling his cheeks start to burn. Why was Simba concerned with sound effects when he had brought her information that could be of vital importance in the investigation into the death of Lol Quarrie? 'What interests me is what the old man saw. In his statement he says Mr Quarrie was *struggling* with someone. A boy.'

There was a snort of derision, and a thin-necked African in a European suit waved a copy of Jouma's handwritten report in the air. 'And so it takes the statement of a half-blind, half-mad Berber furniture-maker, who speaks no English and regards Kenyan law as an ass, to stir the great Inspector Jouma into action!'

The man's name was Frederick Obbo. He was twenty-six years old and from the mayor's office. And, although Jouma had no idea what he did there, or what he was now doing in Simba's office, he instinctively knew that the little *mavi* was bad news. All politicians were when they stuck their noses in police business – especially when they were part of a new administration. This one was barely a fortnight old. With the previous mayor currently on the run from a corruption investigation, the vacuum had been filled with indecent haste by the opposition leader, who could hardly believe his luck.

'I think any development is welcome in such an unusual case as this,' Simba said.

'*I* think, Superintendent Simba,' Obbo sneered, 'that no significant progress has been made in solving this crime whatsoever. It begs the question: what has Inspector Jouma been doing?'

As he looked at Obbo, with his air of arrogant superiority, Jouma yet again wondered if he had done the right thing by exposing the widespread civic corruption in Mombasa. It seemed that all he had done was enable a whole new breed of scavenger to gorge themselves on power.

'With respect, Mr Obbo,' Simba said, 'it is only two days since Mr Quarrie's death, and it is yet to be decided if it *was* a crime.'

'You do realise, Superintendent, that Mr Quarrie was a highly respected pillar of the Mombasa community? Not only was he a tireless fundraiser for local charities, but he was a pivotal member of the Rotary Club and the ex-pat liaison committee. A number of very prominent people in this city, *including the mayor*, are most anxious that the perpetrator of this heinous crime is apprehended.'

Simba cleared her throat. 'As I said, Mr Obbo, Inspector Jouma is our most experienced detective.

That is why I had no hesitation in assigning him the case. *If* there is a crime to be solved, I am confident—'

'I am well aware of Inspector Jouma's track record,' Obbo snapped. 'And I can't help thinking that, if he had treated the case seriously in the first place, then the killer might already have been apprehended.'

'Perhaps, ma'am, Mr Obbo would like me to arrest the furniture-maker,' Jouma said, his temper flaring. 'Or perhaps the whore and the Moroccan who found the body. I'm sure I could beat a confession from one of them before the day is over.'

'Don't be impertinent, Inspector!' Obbo said. 'Remember who you are talking to.'

'I don't believe we have ever met, Mr Obbo.'

'Daniel, I think that will be all,' Simba said smoothly.

But as Jouma left the room the instincts of thirty years as a detective told him this was only the beginning.

24

Woken from his mid-afternoon nap by the rasp of the launch's outboard motor, Harry emerged blinking and yawning into the light. He was barefoot and hollow-eyed, his lank greying hair sticking up at improbable angles beneath his baseball cap.

'What are you doing here?' he said. 'I thought you were supposed to be raking in the Ernies at Watamu.'

Jake hopped up on to the jetty. 'Change of plan. I need the keys to the Land Rover.'

'Why? Where are you going?'

'I'm going to see a man about a five-star hotel.'

Harry slid one hand into his camouflage pants and scratched thoughtfully. 'What are you on about?'

'You know exactly what I'm on about, Harry,' Jake said, eyes narrowing, and Harry's face fell as he told him about his encounter with Evie Simenon up at Jalawi that morning.

'I never took you for a bleeding-heart sandal-wearer, old boy.' Harry chuckled unconvincingly.

But Jake's expression was cold. 'Why didn't you tell me?'

'Must have slipped my mind. Anyway, what's the big deal?'

'The big deal? Why don't you ask Sammy that? You seem to forget the kid saved your life that day on *Yellowfin*. If he hadn't put a bolt through Tug Viljoen's head, there would have been a bullet through yours. Yet you're prepared to let Spurling Developments flatten his village and build a fucking hotel on it?'

Harry puffed out his chest defiantly. 'We're talking mud huts here, Jake. These people can build themselves a new village before breakfast. And don't tell me they won't be compensated. Sammy and his mother will be able to live in a palace.'

'You're fucking unbelievable, Harry.'

Harry raised his hands placatingly. 'Think about the extra trade that will be coming our way! A five-star hotel means five-star Ernies. And that means big bucks, Jakey-boy.'

Jake looked despairingly at his partner. 'It's all about the money, isn't it, Harry? You never learn.'

'All I'm saying is that we could use all the income we can get now that—'

Jake grabbed a handful of Harry's greasy vest. 'Now that *what*? Now that Martha is dead? Is that what you mean? Now that the money is gone?'

'You're upset, Jake! We're all upset about Martha. But we have to be realistic. We have to plan for the future. Remember the shit we were in with the Arab? I never want to be in that situation again. But what do you want me to do? Tie myself to a palm tree?'

'I wouldn't want you to do anything you don't want, Harry.'

Harry shook his head sadly. 'You have to understand, old son: Spurling *will* win. They *always* win. There is absolutely nothing you or Evie Simenon can do about it. It's the way the world works.'

Jake stared at his partner for a long time. 'Just give me the keys, Harry,' he said.

25

After leaving Simba's office and the police compound, Jouma followed Mama Ngina Drive around the headland and beyond the yellow, bone-dry fairways of the Mombasa Golf Club. He reached the Likoni ferry terminal just as the boat was disgorging its cargo on to the island, and he watched a thousand people swarming over the causeway like ants. After thirty minutes or so, when he had stopped shaking with fury, he turned and retraced his steps.

When he returned to his office the phone on his desk was ringing. As he expected, it was an internal call from Simba's secretary – and five minutes later he was back in the superintendent's office. Obbo, he noticed ominously, had gone, and from the solemn expression on Simba's face Jouma suspected that the man from the mayor's office had achieved whatever it was he had come for.

'I have been ordered to replace you as chief investigating officer on the Quarrie case,' she said briskly.

Despite the rage he felt in his veins, Jouma was determined to remain civil. '*Ordered*, ma'am?'

Simba spoke mechanically, as if reciting a rehearsed script. 'The mayor is extremely anxious that the case is solved as quickly as possible. He believes it will send a positive message to the people of Mombasa and the rest of the Province. He intends to bring in his own man to oversee the investigation.'

'And may I ask who that might be?'

Simba told him, and for a few seconds Jouma thought he had misheard. When it became clear that he hadn't, he was unable to stop himself exclaiming out loud.

'You are *serious*?'

Simba could not look at him. 'The mayor happens to regard him extremely highly,' she said. 'As does the lady mayoress, who also happens to be his sister.'

The pieces fell into place with a deafening clatter. Jouma had become so used to positions of authority in Kenya being filled either by bribery or tribal hierarchy, it was almost refreshing to be confronted by a case of good old nepotism.

'I see,' he said. 'And when does he start?'

'He will be here in the morning. You will work with him, but he will be primary investigating officer.' Only now did she turn her head to face him across the room. 'And I expect you to afford him every courtesy, Daniel.'

Jouma took a deep breath. 'With respect, ma'am, I must inform you that this man is a charlatan. Worse than that, he is a dangerous charlatan. He has spent his career catching goat thieves and speeding *matatu* drivers and bringing false evidence to ensure their convictions. Who knows what damage he could cause if he is let loose on a sensitive inquiry of this nature?'

'You will do as you are told, Detective Inspector!' Simba snapped. 'We will *all* do as we are told.'

'As you wish, ma'am.'

And with that Jouma turned for the door. His fingers were on the handle when she called his name, and he turned to see Simba with an expression of torment on her face.

'You know how things work more than most in this city, Daniel,' she said softy.

'Regretfully I do, ma'am.'

'Then please understand my position. I too have superior officers, and it seems the new mayor has friends in far higher places than this office.'

'Of course.'

She nodded, and suddenly the efficiency of old snapped back into action. 'The furniture-maker is a good lead,' she said, 'although I doubt whether the mayor will see it that way. I want you to follow it up, Daniel – but be discreet. I have no desire to join you in filling out parking tickets for the rest of my career.'

As he left her office Jouma felt for the first time that he and Simba were actually working for the same side. It was just a shame that it seemed to be the losing one.

26

An occluded front was sweeping in from the sea, bringing with it a mass of dark unsettled cloud, and away to the south it was raining hard over the Shimba Hills. When it rained after a long, dry spell, the smell of the earth was almost overpowering. As he stood at the window of his office on the eighteenth floor of the Spurling building, Frank Walker closed his eyes and breathed in, imagining himself on the vast open plains. But all he could smell was the sour stink of air conditioning and window polish. Even after eight years working a desk job it still stuck in his throat. Clay Spurling had told him it was a promotion, but to Walker it was a jail sentence.

The intercom on his desk buzzed.

'What is it, Janice?'

'Sorry to disturb you, Mr Walker, but there is a gentleman here who is very anxious to see you.'

'What does he want?'

The door to Walker's office burst open and Jake marched in, followed by a flustered-looking secretary. 'What I want, Mr Walker,' he said, 'is to know what you plan to do with the villagers at Jalawi if you get planning permission for your hotel?'

'I told him you were busy, Mr Walker,' the secretary said, close to tears. 'Shall I call security?'

Walker, momentarily taken aback, recovered his composure and waved her away. 'It's OK, Janice. Please take a seat, Mr—?'

'Moore. Jake Moore.'

'Can I get you a coffee?'

'I'm fine. I'm here to—'

'If I'm not mistaken, that's a Geordie accent I'm hearing,' Walker interrupted. 'Where are you from?'

Now it was Jake's turn to be off balance. 'North Shields,' he said, his momentum lost. 'Although now I—'

'I'll be damned!' Walker exclaimed, and his face split in an unexpectedly warm smile of recognition. 'You know, when I was driving trucks for a living I used to get the ferry from North Shields to Amsterdam every month. You're a long way from home, pilgrim.'

'You too, Mr Walker.'

'Aye, well. The game hunting here is better than in Paisley.'

Jake watched as Walker fidgeted with a high-velocity cartridge on his key ring.

'Do you hunt?'

'I run a fishing boat.'

'Fishing? Dah – that's not proper hunting, man!' the Scotsman exclaimed. 'Any time you fancy some real sport, just give me a shout. I'll take you to the plains, show you what it's all about. And by the way

– call me Frank, for Christ's sake. "Mr Walker" makes me sound important.'

'About Jalawi,' Jake said, determined to wrest back the initiative. But he knew he had blown his chance.

Walker knew it too. 'Aye – well, I don't know what to say about that, chum,' he said apologetically. 'I mean, as far as I know the application is still to go before the planning committee. My job is to make sure we get the damn thing built on time and on budget. You'd need to speak to someone else about the villagers.'

'The sign on the door says Chief Operations Manager, *Frank*,' Jake pointed out.

Walker shrugged and smiled sheepishly. 'I know – and one day someone will tell me what the hell it means. Listen, I'm just a small cog in a big wheel. I just do what I'm told, and most of the time the top brass tell me nothing. But do you want the truth?' Walker stared at him with piercing blue eyes. 'Companies like Spurling Developments only do what the politicians let them. And the only reason politicians do anything is if it's worth their while. It's them you should be protesting about – because *they're* the ones pouring concrete over Kenya, not us.'

'Bravo. I bet you give that speech to everyone.'

'Only because it's true.'

'I'll remember to tell the villagers when their houses are being bulldozed.'

As a pay-off line, Jake knew it stank. But he was already in headlong retreat. Walker had stood up from his desk, and now there was steel behind his smile.

'It's been nice meeting you, Mr Moore. And my offer stands about the hunting trip.'

★

Walker watched impassively from his office window as, two hundred and fifty feet below, Jake crossed the busy thoroughfare of Nkrumah Road to where his battered Land Rover was parked. As he drove away, Walker rested his forehead against the warm plate glass. Christ, he hated this job. The lying, the misery. When he thought about what he had become it made him sick.

He was no saint, of course. But then the path of righteousness was not always easy to follow for a young man growing up in Glasgow in the 1980s. The east end tenements were overflowing with hard cases, and even if you weren't a hard case you still had to pretend to be one. You wouldn't go far in schemes like Ruchazie and Easterhouse by writing poetry or painting in watercolour.

But he'd escaped all that – and on the plains of Kenya he'd found a place where, for the first time in his life, he could follow his own destiny rather than one scrawled on a concrete wall. The expensive suit and the flashy title were a mistake. He should never have accepted Clay Spurling's offer. He should have told the old man he was happy working on the reserve with Malachi.

It was too late now, though.

The terrible news had just reached him: Clay was dead – and Bobby was back. Frank could feel his malevolent presence in the very bricks and mortar that surrounded him.

Bobby was back, and soon he would be coming for him.

'Janice,' he said into the intercom. 'Get Gordon Wallis at the Consulate on the line.'

A few moments later the phone rang.

'Gordon,' Walker said to his contact, dispensing with formalities. 'What do you know about a Geordie fishing-boat captain from Flamingo Creek? Aye – name of Moore. Jake Moore.'

27

Agent Bryson ate alone in the dining room of the Colonial Hotel. His supper was an uninspiring grey steak served with limp French fries and washed down with a bottle of beer. His face was haggard with fatigue as he shovelled the food into his mouth.

He looked, the Ghost thought, with a modicum of sympathy, like a man in need of a damn good holiday.

The assassin was in the lounge bar, with the sales reps and the pimps who used the Colonial for business and pleasure. In one corner a group of British airline pilots and their cabin crew were getting steadily pissed playing a drinking game. In another a Eurasian whore was telling a fat German businessman that he was hot and that she wanted to go up to his room. Behind the bar a glum-faced African in a polyester bus-boy jacket rearranged the liquor bottles for the hundredth time.

Bryson looked up and their eyes met through the cigarette smoke. Then the American agent returned to his steak and his preoccupations, unaware that the person he was searching for was just fifty feet away through the sliding glass door. Again the Ghost almost felt sorry for him. But who exactly *was* Bryson looking for? Someone in a dark raincoat and fedora, holding a fizzing bomb in their hands?

In the dining room, Bryson had had enough of his meal. He wiped his mouth with a napkin, which he threw over his half-eaten steak. He rose stiffly from his table and wandered through to the bar. He ordered a large Scotch and lit a cigarette.

'How was the steak?' the Ghost asked him.

Bryson snapped out of his reverie and smiled weakly. 'I'm not convinced it was from a cow.'

'I think that's why most residents here eat elsewhere.'

'Does that include you?'

'Absolutely.'

Bryson extended his hand. 'Clarence.'

'Sasha.'

'What brings you to Mombasa, Sasha?'

'You don't find too many big fish in Belorussia.'

Bryson laughed. 'Then I guess you've come to the right place.'

'What about you?'

'Computer systems.'

'Must be interesting.'

'It is if you're interested in computer systems.'

The Ghost laughed. 'I don't know one end of a mouse from the other.'

'You want to know a secret, Sasha? Neither do I.'

Bryson's cell phone cheeped. It was his wife calling from Maryland. The FBI man downed his Scotch.

'It's been nice talking to you,' he said. 'But I've got to go.'

'Sure,' the Ghost said.

'Good luck with the fishing.'

And good luck with the computer systems, the Ghost thought as Bryson trudged wearily towards the elevators, his phone pressed to his ear.

As darkness fell the killer walked through Jamhuri Park and reflected on a career which had now resulted in the liquidation of more than fifty people across six continents.

In the early days, the Ghost had, like most professional assassins, used a silenced handgun. It was a vintage Spanish-made 9mm Astra 400 – which had also been the weapon of choice of Franco's *Guardia Civil* death squads during the Spanish Civil War and discerning members of Hitler's SS in World War II. But, although it was undoubtedly effective, the gun was essentially a youthful affectation. When it came to the true mark of a top-level assassin – the ability to kill silently, discreetly and without ambiguity – there was no question that the stiletto was an infinitely preferable choice and had been since before the time of Christ.

The Ghost's knife was a bespoke design, created to exacting specifications of weight and length by a Japanese armourer based in Osaka. Its six-inch-long, eight-millimetre-wide blade was fashioned from thirteen layers of woven steel and honed to razor sharpness along both edges. The same armourer had also manufactured its slim leather holster, which was worn around the chest at the level of the twelfth left rib for instant access with the right hand.

The Ghost never failed to marvel at its

craftsmanship. Yes, it was essential to know how to use the knife for ultimate effect – but, once it was unsheathed, it almost seemed to have a life of its own.

It knew how to kill.

Take this trinket salesman, for example. The man, toothless and reeking of *chang'aa* liquor, had appeared from nowhere as the Ghost strolled through the park. Now he was trying to persuade the killer to part with ten US dollars for a wooden charm he claimed was carved from a chair that had once belonged to President Barack Obama's Kenyan father. Having already instinctively computed the hawker's height, weight and skeletal structure, the Ghost knew precisely what manoeuvre would be required to get him into a position where the *coup de grâce* could be administered. But the killer also knew that once the knife was unsheathed it would *unerringly* direct itself to the exact point on the man's neck where the delicate vertebrae met the skull, and where the spinal cord was at its most vulnerable. A single smooth movement and death would be instantaneous.

'Each unique charm comes with a certificate of authenticity personally signed by President Barack Obama himself!' the hawker insisted chirpily.

'Let me see.'

The Ghost stared at a grubby sheet of cheaply Xeroxed A4 printer paper.

I Certifie this Good Luck Charm is Genuin, it said. It was signed by *Mr Barak Obbama (Pres. United States America).*

'There are only five hundred of these charms in existence,' the hawker said. 'Very popular! By tomorrow they will all have gone.'

The Ghost smiled. The man deserved full marks for audacity if nothing else. He certainly did not deserve to die – although that would have been of absolutely zero consideration had the Ghost been contracted to kill him. Once an assassin started questioning what they did, then it was the end.

'I'll take one.'

The hawker masked his surprise as the Ghost gave him ten bucks, and handed over the chunk of wood and its accompanying certificate before scuttling away into the shadows.

The Ghost looked at the trinket. It was worthless, of course, but it would be a nice souvenir of this trip to Mombasa. One to keep with the others picked up on various contracts around the world. Everyone needed to store memories and keepsakes while they could, because before you knew it, when your body and mind had turned to mush, that's all you had left.

And the Ghost had no intention of spending decrepit old age with the faces of the dead for company.

Day Four

28

The boardroom of Spurling Developments' head-quarters towered twenty storeys above Mombasa. It was a huge, high-ceilinged room with a twenty-five-foot polished rosewood table around which the fifteen executive board members sat in impotent fury.

At the head of the table sat Bobby Spurling. He was wearing a $3,000 Brooks Bros suit bought in Jo'burg for this very occasion. In fact, he had been looking forward to this moment for so long it almost seemed like a dream that it was actually happening.

He stared at each aghast face with contempt. 'So there we have it, gentlemen,' he told them. 'In accordance with the wishes of my late father, as of today I shall be taking over as chairman *and* chief executive officer of Spurling Developments. Over the course of the next few weeks I shall be undertaking a thorough audit of the management structure, but for now I should like to thank you all for your loyalty to my father and to the company. I have taken the liberty of drawing up an official document ratifying my appointment, which you have in front of you. I would be grateful if you could please sign where indicated. Yes, Mr Fearon? There's something you wish to say?'

Oh, yes, Mr Fearon, I bet you've got something to say, all right. That's why everybody around the table is holding their breath. Urging you on with willing little eyes. How will the incumbent CEO react to having his job stolen from him and his big promotion to chairman ripped from his grasp?

William Fearon was a fat man with small features set dead centre of his doughy face. 'May I first reiterate my great sorrow for the death of your father,' he said in a firm voice. 'He was a great man.'

Oh, yes, he was a great man, all right. But get to the point, Mr Fearon. Say what it is that you want to say.

'But, while I would most certainly respect Mr Spurling's last wishes, I am nevertheless uncomfortable with the manner in which they have been executed.'

'Really, Mr Fearon? In what way?'

Yes, come on, you fat fuck. Spit it out.

'To be blunt, we have only your word for it, Bobby.'

Bobby remained calm. 'Whose word do you require, Mr Fearon?'

Fearon raised his palms quizzically. 'This document you wish us to sign – what is it? It appears to have no legal authority.'

'But I am Clay Spurling's son and I am carrying out his wishes,' Bobby said. 'I fail to see what other legal authority you need.'

'With the greatest respect, Bobby, I am afraid the

executive board – any executive board – would require substantially more than an unqualified verbal agreement before it handed over control of the company to you, or anybody else.'

'Then you refuse to sign the document?'

'Under the circumstances, I feel there is no way that I can. And I would advise my fellow board members to do the same.'

Oh, you self-righteous prick.

Bobby sighed and turned to the thin, white-haired man sitting beside him at the boardroom table. His name was Cyril Craven and he was the company lawyer. 'Mr Craven, will you please put Mr Fearon's mind at ease?'

'Of course,' Craven said briskly. He opened a leatherbound folder on the table in front of him and withdrew a thin pile of documents which he began to distribute to the board members. 'These are copies of Clay Spurling's last will and testament. You will see I have highlighted the relevant clauses in relation to Spurling Developments, and more specifically the succession of his son as chairman and CEO.'

Bobby watched William Fearon's piggy eyes darting from side to side as he digested the document. When he had finished, he crumpled it into a ball and threw it the length of the boardroom table.

'Congratulations, Cyril,' he said. 'Clay's still warm but you've already altered his will.'

Craven's eyes bulged. 'I absolutely resent that implication, William.'

Fearon laughed. 'I had lunch at the ranch three days ago. He told me in confidence that he was making me chairman and Frank Walker CEO.'

'And you expect us to believe that?' Bobby blurted, his face flushed with anger. 'You think either you or Frank Walker was more important to him than his own son?'

'With the greatest respect, Bobby,' Fearon said matter-of-factly, 'he also told me that he wouldn't put you in charge of a fairground ride. I think the word he used was *liability*.'

'Sign the fucking document, you fat bastard,' Bobby hissed, his lips flecked with saliva.

Fearon stood up and brushed particles of lint from the lapels of his jacket. 'I'm afraid I can't do that.' With that he left the table and headed purposefully for the exit. As he reached Spurling, he paused and looked him in the eye. 'You're playing with the big boys now, Bobby,' he said. Then he left the board-room without another word.

As the double doors swung shut behind him, every pair of eyes swivelled to the end of the table where Bobby Spurling sat, his knuckles white.

'Is there anyone else who would like to leave?' he said.

A full minute passed. The fourteen remaining board members glanced nervously at each other across the table. None of them moved.

29

Ndia Kuu is a famous Old Town street, and at its southern end is a door with a curtain of dried grass hanging from the frame and a large sign nailed above it on which the word PAHRMACIE is misspelled in hand-painted letters.

David Mwangi went inside, grateful to be out of the heat and for the thin blast of cool air coming from an electric fan positioned on the trestle counter facing the door.

'Good afternoon, sir!' exclaimed a cheery-looking man, springing from a chair behind the counter and disposing of his newspaper in one movement. 'How can I help you this fine day? Stomach pain? Fever of the innards? I have medication for all manner of illness.'

He gestured grandly at a paltry selection of indigestion potions, cough-medicine bottles and liver-salts tins displayed on a shelf behind him – but what Mwangi really needed was a headache pill. Forty-eight hours into the missing-nun investigation and he had lost count of the number of leads that had turned out to be dead ends, witnesses who turned out to be liars, doors that remained closed to his pummelling. He had attempted to interview the businessmen Gudrun had met in Mombasa on the day she disappeared – including the proprietors of the Shalimar Casino, the Foxy Dance-Now Disco Bar and the Hujambo Massage Centre – but most had found some excuse to be conveniently otherwise engaged. Those he had managed to speak to had simply looked at him blankly while shrugging their shoulders. Yes, they had seen her. No, they did not know where she was. And if that was all, Detective . . .

A day of footslogging around Mombasa in Sister Gudrun's tracks had established just one irrefutable fact about the missing nun: she was quite prepared to turn a blind eye to mortal sin if it meant a hand-out for the Church.

'Your name is Justice N'Pomba?' Mwangi said.

The pharmacist's smile froze. 'Yes, sir?'

Mwangi held up his badge and warrant card. 'I understand you had a meeting five days ago with Sister Gudrun of the Redeemed Apostolic Gospel Church.'

Still the smile did not flinch. 'That is correct, sir.'

'What was the nature of your business?'

'The lady was enquiring about donations to her Church fund, sir.'

'Mr N'Pomba, might I suggest you stop smiling now?' Mwangi said. 'Not only is it extremely off-putting, but I fear you may give yourself a painful cramp.'

N'Pomba did as he was requested. By contrast his face now looked suspicious and surly.

'Have you donated to the Church fund before?'

The pharmacist nodded, and when he spoke Mwangi could detect a hint of resentment in his voice. 'Six months ago. I gave ten thousand Kenyan shillings.'

Mwangi did a quick calculation in his head. The donation was the equivalent of about eighty pounds – not much by UK standards, but a substantial amount to a Mombasa shopkeeper.

'That was very generous of you.'

'My parents were killed by the Mau Mau at Lari. I was brought up in a Church orphanage. I believe I owe the missionaries a great deal.'

Lari, Mwangi knew from his history lessons, was the site of a brutal massacre in 1953. Rebels fighting for independence from the British attacked a village of loyalist Kikuyu, setting fire to their houses and then chopping them to bits with axes and machetes as they fled the blaze. More than three hundred were killed, including women and children. All that was found of the village chieftain the next day were his feet.

Mwangi now noticed the pharmacist's right hand had been neatly amputated at the wrist. N'Pomba was probably in his mid-fifties, which would have made him just a child when the Mau Mau came sweeping into his village. The thought made the young detective shudder.

'Yet six months after you gave her this money, Sister Gudrun returned for more?' he said.

'Yes. She said it was for a school at Flamingo Creek. But I told her I did not have any to give.'

'What did she say?'

'She said that I would fry in the fires of hell,' N'Pomba said bleakly.

Mwangi was not surprised by this. All the businessmen he had interviewed that day had told him a similar story: on the day she disappeared Gudrun had harangued them for money for her Church – and when they either said no, or offered her less than she was looking for, they had been subjected to a torrent of abuse and threats of eternal damnation.

'She is a bitch,' the owner of the Hujambo Massage Centre on Digo Road had told him. He had given her fifteen thousand Kenyan shillings just a month before and was of the opinion that this was more than enough to salve his guilty conscience. 'I am pleased she has disappeared,' he added for good measure. 'I hope she is dead.'

Justice N'Pomba was rather more circumspect in his opinion of Sister Gudrun – and with good reason. He was the last person to see her. After leaving his shop she'd had an appointment with a wealthy rice importer at the dhow harbour but never turned up. Somewhere between Ndia Kuu and the harbour, a distance of no more than a quarter of a mile, she had vanished off the face of the earth – and now, despite Jouma's cynicism, Mwangi was beginning to think such a thing might be possible after all.

30

Through the buzzing haze of cocaine, Bobby Spurling was only dimly aware of the two African hookers slavering at his groin like soft-mouthed Labradors worrying at a bone. They were not the best he'd ever had, and certainly not a patch on the roster of girls he had on call in Jo'burg. But it was eighteen months since he'd been banished from Mombasa. It would take time to re-establish his lines of supply. For the moment these two would have to do. Even so, for reasons not entirely connected to the drugs and the whores, his mind was elsewhere.

Why couldn't that fat fuck William Fearon have simply signed the document? It wasn't his company. Fearon's father hadn't built it up from nothing into one of the biggest in Africa.

He sat up in his office chair and, almost absentmindedly, pushed the whores away from him. It had been a pleasant interlude, but now he had things to do. Preoccupied, he stalked into the executive bathroom adjoining his office. By the time he had peed and splashed his face with water, the women had gone.

'Tell Cyril Craven to come and see me,' he ordered his secretary.

He went across to a vast plasma map of Kenya on the wall. On it each Spurling building project was highlighted in pulsing red. There were hundreds of them, stretching from Lake Turkana in the north to the Tanzanian border seven hundred miles to the south; so many that Kenya itself seemed to be a vast throbbing heart.

By rights they belonged to him now – yet it seemed to Bobby that they were mocking him.

'You wanted to see me, Bobby?'

Craven had appeared in the doorway. Never was a man better named, Bobby thought, looking with disdain at the hunched lawyer.

'What are we going to do about Fearon?' he said, waving the old man into a chair opposite his desk.

'We must be patient, Bobby,' he said. 'Negotiate with him.'

'*Never!* This was my father's company and now it is mine.'

'Offer him some money to go away. He's not getting any younger, he'll take it.'

'How much?'

'Three million dollars should do it.'

'Three million? You must be joking!'

'Believe me, Bobby, three million is nothing compared with the legal costs to resolve this matter in court.'

Bobby thought for a moment. 'You sure he'll take it?'

'I'd stake my house on it.'

'You'll be losing more than your house if this

doesn't work,' Bobby warned him.

'And it will, Bobby,' Craven said smoothly. 'You just have to be patient.'

'Patience is not one of my strong points,' Bobby said.

Craven felt cold sweat prickling at his brow. It was not the altering of the will that bothered him – Lord knows he had doctored hundreds of documents on Clay Spurling's behalf over the years. That was all part of selling one's soul to the Devil. What filled the lawyer with trepidation was that, unlike his father, Bobby was a loose cannon liable to bring the whole house of cards crashing down around their ears.

'What about Frank Walker?' Craven said, keen to turn the conversation away from the fat CEO.

'Don't you worry about Frank Walker,' Bobby said. 'I do not intend to give the eulogy at my father's funeral knowing that the company he started from scratch has been hijacked by a jumped-up truck driver from a Glasgow tenement.'

Craven didn't like the sound of that either, but he kept his mouth shut. In the short term Frank Walker was not a concern, and as long as he kept Bobby occupied then the lawyer could sleep easier.

After Craven had been dismissed, Bobby spun round in his high-backed leather chair so that he could look out through plate-glass windows at Mombasa island spread before him. Slowly, he swept his hand from one side of the horizon to the other, levelling the buildings at a stroke, turning the jagged panorama into a flat wasteland upon which he alone could impose his will.

31

Leaving the pharmacist, Mwangi turned left along
Ndia Kuu Road and, after just a few paces, emerged
into a bright, tree-lined square dominated on one
side by the imposing stone walls of Fort Jesus. He
crossed the square to another street branching off it.
This was Mbaraki Road, which led to Government
Square and the dhow harbour.

This is the way she would have come for her last
appointment, he thought. It was unnerving to follow
in her footsteps.

The street was groaning with shops and apart-
ments housed in tall, faded colonial buildings. There
must be thousands of people who lived and worked
here, and even more tourists – yet not one of them
had seen Sister Gudrun. Or if they had they had not
come forward. Mwangi stood at the entrance to the
street and stared at the bobbing sea of people flowing
along its length and concluded that it would be all
too easy to be swallowed up in this relentless human
tide.

He walked on for a few yards then paused. To his

left was an alleyway between two buildings, barely five feet wide and cloaked in shadow. It stretched for about fifty yards, and through the narrow aperture at the far end Mwangi could see more buildings and shopfronts. He realised that he was looking at Ndia Kuu Road once again.

There was someone in the alley. He could see a small, lean silhouette moving towards him, or was it away from him? It was difficult to tell. Then the figure stopped.

A voice said, 'Is that you, Mwangi?'

'Inspector?'

'I don't suppose you have a torch?' Jouma said. 'Foolishly I neglected to bring one.'

Mwangi entered the alley and immediately felt the onset of claustrophobia. He was a big man, and with every step the sheer walls seemed to be closing in on him. There was an acrid stink of piss and shit, both human and animal, mingled with that of rotting food and flesh. When he finally reached Jouma, it took him several minutes to regain his composure and slow his racing heart.

'What are you doing here, sir?' he asked, turning on a small pencil torch and shining it in the inspector's face.

'My job,' Jouma said peevishly, as if offended that Mwangi should think he was doing anything else. 'According to a furniture-maker on Ndia Kuu, the last sighting of Lol Quarrie was in this alleyway.'

'I heard you had been taken off the Quarrie case, sir,' Mwangi said, and immediately regretted his impertinence.

Jouma's furious stare cut through the gloom like

laser beams. 'I have *not* been taken off the Quarrie case, Detective Constable Mwangi, and I would strongly advise you *not* to believe the tittle-tattle of Mama Ngina Drive. I have merely been placed into a *coordinating* role, overseeing the investigations of Detective Inspector Oliver Mugo of Nyanza Province CID.'

'Who is Detective Inspector Oliver Mugo?'

'He is a charlatan,' Jouma said. 'Furthermore, Mwangi, he is a cockroach who somehow survives every catastrophe he creates.'

Mwangi was pleased the inspector could not see his astonished expression. He had never heard Jouma be openly critical of anyone – and certainly not of a fellow detective. But the venom in his voice left the young officer in no doubt that the bitterness between the two men ran deep, and he could not wait to find out why.

To his disappointment, however, Jouma was not about to elaborate.

'Now – I take it you have been making enquiries into the case of the missing nun, Mwangi?'

It was not pleasant to be reminded. 'Yes, sir. I was on my way to interview her last appointment. The Chinese rice importer in Government Square.'

'Well, while you are here you can help me,' Jouma said. He gestured at a heap of unspecified detritus piled against one wall of the alley. 'Take your torch and look over there.'

The torch was a free gift from a petrol station in Nairobi that, in his innocence, Mwangi had thought would come in handy in his new job as a CID detective. He might as well have brought a pair of plastic toy handcuffs. The beam was watery weak and extended barely twenty feet.

Mwangi gingerly shone it towards the pile. 'What am I looking for, sir?'

'I have no idea,' Jouma said.

The beam had picked out a stack of discarded fish boxes draped in some sort of oily rags. The stench was appalling and Mwangi was forced to jam a handkerchief to his nose. He flinched as something moved in the darkness. The beam fixed on a pair of gleaming rat eyeballs. The rodent, a foot long from nose to tail, stared back for several seconds before skittering away down the alleyway. Something else now glittered in the dirt where the creature had been sitting. Mwangi reached down with one arm, gagging at the smell, feeling unspeakable slime sliding into the cuff of his shirt. His fingers closed around the object and he gratefully dragged it back.

'What is it, Mwangi?'

It was made of enamel and perhaps an inch long, with a pin running along the back. Mwangi cleaned it with his handkerchief to reveal a spectrum of vertical stripes navy blue through pea green to black. He handed it to Jouma.

'It would appear to be a tie-pin, sir.'

Jouma clucked quizzically. 'I see. Thank you, Mwangi.' He put the item in his jacket pocket.

'I can take the item back to headquarters if you like, sir,' Mwangi said.

'I am perfectly capable of doing that myself, Constable.'

'Of course, sir.'

'And you'd better be on your way. The last time I

143

looked, Sister Gudrun was still missing.'

In the shadows Mwangi could not see Jouma's expression, but he had the distinct impression that the inspector was smiling.

32

Bobby Spurling was twenty-three years old. By pleasing coincidence, so was Alexander the Great when he acceded to the throne of Macedonia, and within ten years he had conquered the known world.

Right now, though, Bobby could not help wondering how the great conqueror had dealt with the flipside of ruling the world – namely the fucking paperwork.

He glanced surreptitiously at his Rolex. In a few hours at least he would be sipping the first of several pre-prandial Tanquerays at the Cashew Country Club. After that – well, who knew what the night held? It had been a while since he'd been out and about in Mombasa. There was a lot of catching up to do.

First, though, there was the onerous task of getting rid of the rather unpleasant-looking man currently occupying the chair on the other side of his desk.

'Sorry – which department did you say you were from, Mr—?'

'My name is Roarke, sir,' the man said in a rough

Kenyan accent. 'Douglas Roarke. I am the head of Security Division.'

That made sense. With his shaven head and flattened nose Roarke looked like he'd broken up one nightclub brawl too many. He was also wearing the sort of outmoded, double-breasted suit favoured by street thugs who had reached their late forties and were trying to look respectable.

'Really. Well, it's been nice to meet you, Mr Roarke, but I really must be—'

Bobby held out his hand, but Roarke had not finished.

'My condolences on your loss, sir,' he said.

'Thank you.'

'And also many congratulations.'

Bobby's eyes widened. 'What do you mean?'

'Your use of the desert-rose sap to cause fatal cardiac arrest. A master stroke considering your father's heart condition and the fact he was already using small doses of digitalis toxin as medication'

There was a pause while Bobby, white faced, assimilated this information. He had no idea what digitalis toxin was, never mind how he had apparently used it to kill his father. He thought he had simply choked the old bastard to death.

'You were seen, sir,' Roarke explained, his tone light. 'At the ranch.'

'You *saw* me?'

'Yes, sir. A major part of Security Division's duties involve the safeguarding of company executives. Mr Spurling Senior was under observation at all times. One of my team in position on the bluff to the north of the stables when you had your little

... tête-à-tête in the desert-rose plantation.'

Bobby got up and went to the window in an effort to clear his head. 'What do you want, Mr Roarke?' he said presently. There seemed no point in denying anything. 'Are you intending to blackmail me?'

Roarke looked affronted at the suggestion. 'Certainly not, sir! In many ways I applaud your actions.'

'You do?' Bobby was feeling totally creeped out now. Roarke *wanted* his father dead? It made no sense.

'And don't worry about the post-mortem examination,' the security chief continued. 'I've seen to it that Mr Spurling's body will be sent to a very amenable pathologist. One we have used on previous occasions.'

Bobby felt sick. He hadn't considered the possibility that his father's death would be investigated. He'd simply assumed the old bastard's corpse would be taken straight from the mortuary to the funeral parlour.

'Not that there would have been any controversy,' Roarke was saying. 'In such high doses digitalis mimics the symptoms of cardiac arrest almost perfectly.' He fixed Bobby with an expectant gaze. 'But of course you knew that anyway, didn't you, sir?'

'Of course, of course,' Bobby said hurriedly. 'But I still don't understand what you want, Mr Roarke.'

Roarke sat back in his chair. 'I have always firmly believed that, ultimately, the role of the Security Division is to protect the interests of the company. Unfortunately, over recent months I concluded that your late father was acting contrary to those interests.'

'How?'

'In the event of his death he planned to pass on control of the company to Mr Walker and Mr Fearon.'

'I know that. He told me.'

'Did he also tell you that those two gentlemen were to be issued with instructions to liquidate the company and use the money to create a charitable foundation dedicated to wildlife conservation in the national parks?'

Bobby gawped.

'Now that's all very well,' Roarke continued. 'Towards the end of his life Mr Spurling Senior was a keen conservationist, as you know. But I believe he failed to consider the implications of his plan on thousands of hard-working employees of this company. Not to mention the loss of many profitable development opportunities in the future.'

Now Bobby understood. 'You want the company for yourself, Roarke!'

The security chief shook his gleaming, shaven-headed dome. 'Not me, sir. I am here to serve the best interests of the company. And I have for some time now believed that you would be the ideal successor to your father. I am certain you share many of my own concerns about the future of the company should Mr Walker and Mr Fearon be allowed to take control.'

'I have already seen to it that my father's will was altered.'

'Yes, sir. But if you will forgive me for being so blunt – that will isn't worth the paper it's written on. In litigation I believe Mr Fearon will have a very good chance of overturning it.'

'But Cyril Craven—'

'—is a very capable lawyer. But there are no certainties in the law, and I prefer to deal in certainties.'

Bobby stared out towards the minarets of the Old Town. 'What do you propose?'

'First things first,' Roarke said. He had materialised from nowhere and now stood beside Bobby at the window. 'I hear you are having one or two problems with a planning application at Flamingo Creek.'

'I am?'

'Yes, sir. Some rather recalcitrant councillors and a group of environmentalists seem to be holding up the development of a very profitable five-star hotel.'

'I didn't know.'

Roarke smiled. 'Why don't you let me deal with that for you, sir? In fact, I will be going up there myself as soon as our meeting here is concluded. Once that's sorted, I'm sure we can deal with any other outstanding matters.'

Bobby looked at Roarke's teeth. They were small and sharp and seemed to slope inwards. When he smiled it was a terrible thing and it sent shivers up Bobby's spine. He knew that what the security chief was proposing would not be pleasant and to give him the consent he desired would be to enter a very dark and sinister place indeed. Yet Bobby knew that he had no choice. He was already well on his way there already.

33

The last time Jouma had seen Chief Inspector Oliver Mugo's idiotic gap-toothed grin it was beaming out at him from the front page of the *Coastal Weekly News*. The story beneath the colour photograph described how 'Malindi's leading investigator' had solved the mysterious death in an explosion of Flamingo Creek game-boat skipper Dennis Bentley in less than two days.

'*A careful and thorough examination of the evidence led me to the conclusion that Mr Bentley and his crew were the most unfortunate victims of a most dreadful accident,*' Mugo told reporters. '*The people of Coast Province can sleep soundly tonight, safe in the knowledge that foul play has been ruled out.*'

Five days later the same newspaper reported that Bentley and his crew had in fact been brutally murdered and his boat deliberately blown up. But on that occasion Malindi's leading investigator was strangely unavailable for comment.

When he heard that Mugo had escaped demotion as a result of the fiasco by being transferred five hundred miles away to a desk job with the plain-clothes division in Nyanza Province, Jouma assumed he had friends in high places. Now that Mugo was replacing him as lead detective on the Quarrie investigation he knew it was true.

It would be easy to blame Simba for caving in to the powers at City Hall. But, Jouma reasoned, it would also be unfair. The new mayor clearly had friends in high places, too. Which was why there was no point in getting annoyed or doing something dramatic like handing in his resignation – which he had to confess had, in a fit of unforgivable self-pity, crossed his mind momentarily.

In any case, the great Inspector Mugo was not here yet – and, until he was, the Quarrie case was still his.

The white-jacketed steward at the entrance to the Constabulary Club fixed him with a hard stare.

'Can I help you, sir?'

'I am here to see Assistant Commissioner Jardine.'

The steward's eyebrows shot up. '*Assistant Commissioner Jardine*, sir? Is he *expecting* you?'

'Yes he is, Long,' boomed a voice from somewhere in the cool shadows of the lobby. Confident footsteps rapped out on the marble floor and the dapper, balding figure of Assistant Commissioner Edward Jardine, late of Scotland Yard, appeared in the doorway. 'Good to see you again, Detective Inspector.'

They had met two days earlier in the course of Jouma's inquiry into the last hours of Lol Quarrie's life. Jardine, as well as being the highest ranked of the retired club members, was also its president. He had been all too pleased to help. Indeed, Jouma got the feeling after meeting him that the former assistant commissioner would have jumped at the chance of being invited to join the investigation.

He led Jouma into the heart of the club, past large oil portraits of equally fierce-looking men in uniform, glass display cabinets full of medals, hand-cuffs, whistles and hand-carved wooden truncheons, and rows of stuffed animal heads.

'Thank you for agreeing to see me at such short notice, sir,' Jouma said.

Jardine shook his head. 'Not at all. Could use a little excitement round here. Any joy with Sergeant Quarrie?'

'Not yet, sir.'

'They say he jumped.'

'That is one possibility we are looking into.'

'It wouldn't be the first time, I suppose. Some chaps find it hard to cope without the buzz, and I can't imagine a backwater like this was any substitute for the mean streets of Belfast as far as Quarrie was concerned. How old are you, Jouma? You must be nearing the dreaded day yourself.'

'Fifty-one, sir.'

'Then enjoy every last second of it, if you want my advice.'

They were now descending a short flight of steps which led in turn to a book-lined room dominated by a snooker table.

'This is the reading room,' Jardine said. 'It's where old duffers like me come when they want to relive their glory days. In here you'll find newspaper clip-pings of every successful police investigation in the last hundred years. But I won't bore you with old war stories. You say you've some sort of memorabilia you're interested in?'

Jouma placed a folded handkerchief on the baize surface and unwrapped the enamel tie-pin Mwangi had found in the alleyway.

Jardine snapped a pair of half-moon spectacles on to the bulbous tip of his nose and examined it. Then he went across to one of the bookcases and pulled a thick leatherbound tome. He opened it and flipped through the pages, comparing the tie-pin with photographs and drawings. After several minutes he emitted a satisfied harrumph.

'I can tell you exactly what it is, Jouma,' he said. 'It's a Royal Ulster Constabulary Long Service ribbon.'

Jouma blinked. 'Are they rare?'

'I should say so. You only get one of these if you've served twenty-two years in the RUC. Where did you find this, then?'

When Jouma told him, Jardine stared at the tie-clip again.

'Well, I can't explain what it was doing in some Old Town alleyway – but I can tell you one thing for sure: we've got refugees from pretty much every constabulary in the colonies, but Sergeant Quarrie was the only member of the Ulster mob. And unless there's another Paddy copper in town then I'd say this tie-pin belonged to him.' The former police-man's eyes glittered with an old fire. 'The sniff of a clue, eh, Jouma?'

'Possibly, sir,' Jouma said. 'But for now it tells me that an old furniture-maker may have been telling the truth.'

34

Jake's mood had been black ever since he'd left Frank Walker's office the previous day. He'd gone there to get answers but come away with snake oil instead and had been brooding on it all night. What annoyed him was how easily he'd been sidestepped. Walker was the consummate smooth operator, the kind Jake had seen hundreds of times in police interview rooms – yet he'd allowed the Scotsman to play him like a fiddle. All that flannel about North Shields, the man-to-man chat about big-game hunting, the knowing shrug of the shoulders – it was beautiful, and Jake had lapped it up.

I'm just a small cog in a big wheel, Walker had said. Sure – but if anyone knew what was planned for Jalawi it was the manager of Spurling Developments' entire coastal operation.

But then maybe it took a fraud to spot a fraud.

The welfare of the Jalawi villagers? Who was he trying to kid? Harry was right – this was all about Martha Bentley, and his pitiful attempts to prove he was worthy of her. In reality he was like a sixty-a-day smoker giving money to a cancer charity. His only motivation was guilt.

Twenty-four hours had done little to improve his mood. And neither had Harry. Jake looked across the workshop at his partner, who was in the office, studiously clipping invoices and receipts into a ring binder. The two men had spoken little since their blow-out yesterday, choosing instead to circle each other like wary scorpions until it was time to visit Suki Lo's bar and, once there, seek out alternative company. It had made for a tedious night, though; crotchety old skippers and morose, spare-part-obsessed mechanics did not make for great conversation. At least on nights like these Suki Lo, the Malaysian bar owner, could usually be relied upon to lighten the mood with her relentless and foul-mouthed banter. But even she was not her usual self. Her rotten teeth were giving her grief, and according to her horoscope she was about to develop cancer.

It was almost a relief to get home and go to bed.

'You won't forget about those Ernies from the Shellfish Marina,' Harry was calling from his desk. 'One o'clock kick-off.'

'I'll be there.'

'And we need to get some supplies in. Thought we could nip to the trader at Kilifi first thing in the morning.'

'All right.'

Jake fixed his attention on the lures he was working on. Harry went back to his paperwork.

'Jake?'

'Harry.'

'Are we friends?'

Jake looked across at his business partner. 'You're a thoughtless prick, Harry.'

'I am aware of that.'

'Of course we're friends.'

The Shellfish Marina was just a couple of miles north of the creek, so Jake was in no tearing hurry. Shortly after noon that day he raised *Yellowfin*'s anchor and set off downriver at a pedestrian ten knots, enjoying the opportunity to watch the kingfishers, heron and spoonbills feeding at the water's edge and the yellow baboons watching gimlet-eyed from the uppermost branches of the mangroves.

It was a peaceful scene – but one which was abruptly shattered by the roar of high-powered engines from the north shore. The birds and the monkeys scattered as a convoy of three high-powered SUVs in identical black livery came speeding along the Jalawi road, dust spewing out from their fat tyres. In just a few seconds the powerful vehicles were level with *Yellowfin*, and Jake could see each contained burly-looking men. One of them, a bullet-headed black man behind the wheel of the lead vehicle, looked across and flashed a broad smile. Then they were gone.

Evie Simenon gazed at the village from her vantage point on the viewing platform and wondered out loud whether she was deluding herself. Could a group of enthusiastic amateurs *really* take on and beat the corporate might of an organisation like Spurling Developments? More to the point, did she have the stomach for the fight any more? She was twenty-nine years old, and this had been her life for more than a decade. In all that time she had never questioned her own belief. But ten years of constant attrition was beginning to wear her down. How long could *she* continue?

She looked away towards the ocean and breathed in the warm, salt-laden breeze. How much easier it would be not to care, to look after Number One for a change rather than carry everyone else's problems on her shoulders. Could she live with herself if she did, though? The more she thought about it lately, the more she thought that maybe she could.

'What's that?'

Evie realised she must have been talking to herself, and flushed as she remembered she was not alone on the platform. Alex Hopper was sitting cross-legged against the trunk of the baobab, sucking contentedly on a king-sized joint.

But Alex was standing now, peering beyond the furthest houses at the large cloud of reddish dust that appeared on the river road. 'We've got company.'

Evie took the binoculars and her stomach lurched at what she saw.

'Go back to the camp and get the others,' she said urgently, grabbing the camera bag and slinging it over her shoulder.

Sister Constance was by the riverbank, teaching a handful of children the rudiments of soccer's offside rule, when she heard the commotion. Lifting her heavy robes to her knees she ran back through the scrub to the village.

At the church she nearly collided with Sister Florence, who was running in the opposite direction, her young face drawn with fear.

'What's happening?' Constance demanded.

'Men are here,' Florence said, gesturing frantically towards the other side of the village. 'Men in big cars.'

'What do they want?'

'I don't know. *I don't know!*'

Constance grabbed her by the shoulders and shook her firmly. 'Calm down. Where is Brother Willem?'

At that moment Willem emerged from the church. 'What is going on?' he said, his face twitching.

'Men are here,' Florence repeated.

'What men?'

'They could be from the construction company,' Constance said. 'The woman protester said they would come when we least expected it.'

Was it her imagination, or had the colour drained from Willem's face?

'Into the church with you,' he said.

'But what about the children?' Constance protested.

'This is none of our concern,' the priest snapped. 'Now into the church. Both of you. *Now!*'

There were six men. Four black, two white. Each with the physique of a weightlifter. They stood in a line in front of the parked SUVs, arms folded, staring menacingly at the huddle of villagers who had gathered to see what the commotion was about. One of them was Tom Beye, chief enforcer of Spurling Developments' Security Division. As if to accentuate his position in the pecking order, he was the only one carrying a metal baseball bat.

The tableau set, Douglas Roarke climbed meaningfully from one of the cars and stepped forward in front of his men. The security chief had changed out of his suit and was now wearing army-style combat fatigues which seemed far more in keeping with his shaven head and battered face

His pale eyes swept the crowd. 'Where is Chief Akimbala?' he said.

Presently an old man stepped forward. Chief Akimbala, the most senior of a dwindling number of village elders, walked with the aid of a forked stick and wore a look of weary resignation on his weathered features.

'Good afternoon,' Roarke said, but the greeting was perfunctory. The old man hung his head as Roarke turned him round to face the other villagers like a teacher making an example of a naughty pupil. 'My name is Roarke,' he told them. 'I represent a company called Spurling Developments. Several weeks ago, one of my colleagues met with Chief Akimbala to discuss a proposal which would transform all of your lives beyond your wildest dreams. I am disappointed to learn that Chief Akimbala has seen fit not to pass on the details of this proposal to you, the people of Jalawi. I have come here today to ensure that the message *is* passed on.'

He stooped to the old man's ear and, in a low voice, said, '*Tell them what I said, and make it sound good, or I'll rip your head off your spindly fucking shoulders and feed it to the pigs.*'

★

Jake dropped anchor in the shallows and waited for Sammy. After a while he began to wonder where his bait boy was. Then it struck him as unusual that there appeared to be no life at all on the shore. Usually there were at least a few waving kids, or an old woman washing her clothes in the water.

Then he thought about the knuckleheads in the SUVs heading for Jalawi.

And he remembered what Evie Simenon had said about Spurling Developments moving in first and waiting for planning consent second.

Chief Akimbala's eyes were fixed on the ground. In muttered Swahili he explained how, in return for their land, Spurling Developments was prepared to relocate the villagers of Jalawi to a new purpose-built settlement a few miles along the coast. The crowd listened with bemused expressions to promises of new houses, a dock, road access and jobs at the magnificent new hotel that would stand where their village had once stood: the gleaming five-star Jalawi Hotel and Marina Complex, named in their honour. When he had finished they looked at each other and wondered what it all meant.

'This land has been farmed by the people of Jalawi for centuries, Mr Roarke.'

Roarke looked up and smiled with the recognition of an old and expected adversary as Evie Simenon pushed her way through the crowd.

'It contains their burial ground and most of the villagers regard the soil as sacred,' she continued. 'And you want to move them to a concrete concentration camp? Why do you think Chief Akimbala didn't tell his people about your kind offer?'

'Miss Simenon. I heard you were here.' The security chief hawked lazily and spat at her feet. 'Where is the rest of your tribe of misfits?'

'On their way.'

'Well, you must forgive me if I don't quake in my boots.'

'You've made your point, Roarke,' Evie said. 'Now why don't you and your men just leave?'

'Leave? But we've only just arrived.' He moved back towards the SUVs.

Just then a firm, clear voice rang out. 'You heard the lady.'

Roarke's eyes narrowed. *Who was this?* A tall, thickset man with the build of a rugby player had appeared at the edge of the crowd and was now moving towards him. *Hired muscle?* Behind Roarke his own hired muscle tensed.

'And you are?'

'You could say I'm a concerned neighbour,' Jake said.

Roarke shrugged. 'Well, thank you for your concern – but this really is none of your business.'

'Like Evie said: you've made your point, now fuck off.'

'I don't think I like your tone,' Roarke said, and as he did so Tom Beye moved forward ominously, the tip of the baseball bat nestled in the palm of his other hand.

Jake prepared himself for an onslaught, but instead Roarke turned to the villagers, who flinched like a flock of timid sheep as he approached with his arms outstretched.

'You should all be careful,' he told them. 'There are people here who claim to have your best interests at heart – but they are not to be trusted. My colleagues and I only came here today to pay our respects to Chief Akimbala and to the people of Jalawi, to tell you all about the better life we can provide for you – but look what they did to one of our vehicles.'

He gave a signal to Beye, who immediately hoisted the baseball bat above his head and brought it down with a deafening crash on to the hood of one of the SUVs. His next blow shattered the windscreen.

'Unprovoked vandalism,' Roarke said, as Beye swung his bat three more times against the gleaming exterior of the vehicle. 'These people are out of control.'

Evie scrabbled to open the camera bag slung on her shoulder, but one of Roarke's thugs stepped forward and ripped it from her grasp. Next he removed the camera and smashed it on the ground. Jake tried to intervene but his path was blocked by a second man. As he tried to push his way through, a fist smashed into his solar plexus and he dropped to the dirt.

'Stop it!' Evie cried as a wail of panic rose from the assembled villagers. 'Stop it now!'

But Roarke was already sauntering back to where his men were standing like a Praetorian guard. 'Then they set upon my men,' he said, still addressing the horrified crowd. 'A mob of so-called environmental protesters. We told them that we were unarmed, that we came in peace – but it made no difference.'

Beye swung the bat again, this time straight into the face of one of his own henchmen.

'You should see the state of poor Toby,' Roarke said as the man slumped to the ground with blood pumping from his ruined mouth. 'They say he may never recover.' The bat came down twice more on Toby's head until he lay still. 'To think only last weekend he was celebrating the birth of his first child.'

Roarke nodded to his men, and two of them dragged their stricken comrade into the back of one of the undamaged SUVs.

'We begged them to stop,' he said. 'But they were like a pack of wild animals.'

As he was speaking one of his men had been stuffing a petrol-soaked rag into the gas tank of the smashed-up SUV. On Roarke's signal he lit the rag and scrambled back into one of the other vehicles.

'I suggest you remember what happened here today,' Roarke told the villagers. 'Because one day they might just burn down your village – and I would hate that to happen.'

Roarke got into one of the vehicles and the convoy swept out of the village, just as the tank of the battered SUV erupted with a deafening explosion, sending a ball of oily yellow flame high into the cloudless sky above Jalawi.

35

Unlike Evie and the rest of the hippies, Alex Hopper did not see the confrontation with Roarke's men. In fact, as the SUV's petrol tank exploded the public schoolboy from England was already half a mile west of the encampment. As far as he was concerned the arrival of Spurling Developments' heavy mob and the subsequent panic in the village could not have come at a more opportune moment.

It was strange to think that at Wellington College Alex had been a model pupil. Yet three months travelling with Evie Simenon and her motley brigade of footloose activists had swiftly unravelled eighteen years of premium-grade education. His hair had grown long and unkempt, his limbs were covered in henna tattoos courtesy of an Australian girl called Raeleen with whom he had been intermittently sleeping; and, thanks to his new best buddy Mikey Gulbis from California, he had developed a voracious appetite for marijuana.

Mikey was a walking cannabis encyclopaedia. There was not a strain of sativa that he did not know about or had not smoked. Indeed, the American's quest for the finest hash Africa had to offer was the reason Alex was now making his way along a narrow hunter's track that hugged the north bank of Flamingo Creek.

'I got a tip from one of the nightshift cleaners, man,' Mikey had whispered into his cell phone that morning. He was speaking from Mombasa Hospital where he was recuperating from an operation on the leg he'd shattered when he'd fallen out of the palm tree. 'There's a dealer, name of Gangra – he's got his hands on a shipment of Algerian Spitbush that he's selling at rock-bottom prices.'

Alex, who had taken the call while doing yet another mind-numbing shift on the observation platform, had no idea what made Algerian Spitbush so special. But he didn't want to lose face with Mikey.

According to Mikey's directions Gangra lived in a tin shack a mile west of the village. The further he walked, the spinier and more impenetrable the undergrowth became. Alex was wearing a T-shirt and shorts that soon became ripped by thorns and speck-led by his own blood. Secured in a waterproof bag down the back of his underpants was a hundred US dollars belonging to Mikey. His buddy, Alex had learned, was a hippie with a keen sense of commerce; he believed in buying in bulk and selling at a profit. And that was fucking cool.

It took him nearly an hour to get there. The shack was decrepit. The corrugated metal sheets were rusted and flaking. Grass and weeds had been allowed to grow unchecked outside and, were it not for a weak column of woodsmoke coming from a hole in the roof and the flickering glow of an oil lamp hanging from the door, anybody would have assumed it was derelict. Alex felt a *frisson* of unease as he approached the plywood door and knocked twice.

'Mr Gangra?'

There was no reply. Alex pushed the door and it swung inwards.

The interior of the shack was illuminated only by a pile of smouldering embers in the centre of the room. Alex could make out a bed made of sacking against one wall and, beside it, a portable gas stove with a small saucepan on top.

'Hello? Mr Gangra?'

Gangra was facing the door in a sitting position, his back resting against a wooden pole supporting the roof, his chin on his chest. He was an elderly man, with patches of white hair on his flaking scalp. He appeared to be asleep.

'Mr Gangra?'

Alex reached down to shake the old man's shoulder. Gangra slumped to one side and now, in the glow of the fire, Alex could see that the back of his skull had been beaten to a pulp by countless blows of a blunt instrument.

Alex Hopper cried out and ran from the shack – and it was this sudden exit that undoubtedly saved his life. The two uniformed *askari* waiting outside were taken momentarily by surprise by the sudden blur of movement. The moment of hesitation before they levelled their AK-47 assault rifles at him and opened fire was just enough for Alex to bolt left

166

towards a goat corral, and hurdle the low wooden palisade as shots rang out and bullets whanged into the metal walls of the shack.

He kept running, oblivious to the urgent shouts from behind him. There was another crack, and this time a palm trunk splintered barely a foot from his head.

Jesus, they really were going to kill him.

As he ran for his life through the clinging undergrowth and down among the fetid mangroves, with no idea of where he was going or why anyone would want him dead, Alex Hopper wept tears of terror and wished his mother was here to make everything better. But Alex was just a public schoolboy on his own in a big bad country – and his mummy wasn't coming to save him.

Day Five

36

Shimo la Tewa maximum security prison, five miles north of Mombasa, has a well-earned reputation as one of the toughest in Kenya. Behind its grey concrete walls and rolls of razor wire, it is said that, if the guards or your fellow inmates don't kill you, then diarrhoea, typhus, tuberculosis or the Aids virus almost certainly will. Overcrowding is chronic, torture systematic, rape endemic. Water is stagnant, food contaminated. Inmates exist five to a cell in a state of almost continuous malnutrition. Many are vicious murderers who will never see freedom again. Many more are simply there on remand for offences they almost certainly did not commit, their only crime to be dirt poor and utterly worthless in the eyes of the state. At Shimo la Tewa, they say the only fate worse than death is surviving.

There was a time, very recently, when Conrad Getty kept a loaded pistol in the drawer of his office at the Marlin Bay Hotel, just in case the police arrived to arrest him. Firing a bullet into his own brain was unquestionably preferable to incarceration

171

in a hole like Shimo la Tewa. The very thought of being caged like an animal filled him with terror.

But how marvellously contrary life was! Barely a fortnight after being locked up on remand, pending a trial in which he was charged with over three hundred counts of child abuse, trafficking, conspiracy and murder, Getty had never been happier. Certainly, his cell was poky and infested with cockroaches – but it had a bed and a small writing table and chair, and at least he was in solitary confinement, away from the seething, sodomising masses elsewhere in the jail. And the fact that he was clearly regarded as a valuable commodity by the FBI meant that he was treated with a pleasing reverence. *Which made their frustration even sweeter to behold*. Getty could not help a self-satisfied smile when he thought about Special Agent Bryson's barely contained *fury* at having his every move baulked by the prisoner's legal team. Yes, the lawyers were expensive – but as far as Conrad Getty was concerned they were worth every penny if they succeeded in scuppering the FBI's attempts to extradite him to the USA. He knew all too well that the legal process would be a lot harder to pervert in the States than it would here in Kenya.

The lawyers were convinced that the Bureau didn't have a cat in hell's chance of securing the necessary paperwork without a long and costly court battle. And, privately, they had told him that – with the right sort of inducement – he could expect a sentence of no more than five years from a Kenyan judge. After good behaviour and plea bargaining had been taken into account, he would be a free man in less than three. And with the Marlin Bay worth at least five or six million on the open market he could very easily enjoy the rest of his life in the manner to which he was accustomed.

Despite the inconvenience of being incarcerated, Getty now had no doubt that he could survive the ordeal – especially if his lawyers ensured the sort of preferential treatment that allowed him a supply of fresh water, access to bathing facilities, regular exercise, and, most importantly, kept him far away from the other prisoners. Wary of their star prisoner being gang-raped or stabbed to death with a home-made shiv, the FBI had insisted that he avoid all contact with other inmates.

How strange it was that here, in Mombasa's most notorious jail, Getty should feel *relaxed* for the first time in years. He might have been unable to get out, but nobody could get in. And after living with the murderous spectre of Patrick Noonan – the man he had known only as Whitestone – the hair-trigger violence of his partner-in-crime Tug Viljoen, and the constant torture of his own assorted demons, his stay in the secure wing of Shimo la Tewa had, so far, been the equivalent of a break at a health farm. He was off the booze, eating sensibly and even getting regular exercise in the prison yard. As a result his stomach ulcer had disappeared and he felt ten years younger.

That morning his routine had been as normal. At six am he was woken by the polite tapping of one of the guards on his solid steel cell door. The same guard had then escorted him to the shower block where, in glorious solitude, he had performed his ablutions. Back in his cell, dressed in prison-issue overalls, Getty ate his breakfast. If he had one complaint it was the rather unimaginative nature of the prison cuisine – breakfast, lunch and dinner was unfailingly a bowl of maize porridge and a banana – but then again there had been a time, very recently, when everything he ate came back up again. Right now he was, to all intents and purposes, weaning himself back on to solid food.

Afterwards, having enjoyed a brisk stroll around the prison yard, listening to the birds and enjoying the early warmth of the sun, Getty returned to his cell and emptied his bowels into a stainless-steel lavatory attached to the wall. This arrangement was perhaps the least attractive aspect of his incarceration. But again he could hardly complain, when the majority of inmates at Shimo la Tewa were forced to shit *en masse* into a hole in the ground.

Shortly after nine am he was sitting at his desk, attempting to complete the crossword in the previous day's *Daily Nation* when there was the clank of keys in the lock and the cell door opened.

'You have a visitor, Mr Getty,' the guard said.

Getty swung himself round in his chair and peered towards the door. In the gloom his visitor appeared slightly built with a thin face and hair shaved down to dark stubble on the skull. Around the neck was an ecclesiastical collar, worn with jeans and a casual jacket.

'Good morning? Can I help you?'

'I am from the Society of Prison Chaplains,' the visitor said.

As far as Getty could make out in the pitiful light of the caged 40-watt bulb that lit his cell, he was a smooth-skinned young man of around twenty-five, with a straggly attempt at a goatee beard framing a thin-lipped mouth. His voice was so quiet Getty had to lean forward to hear what he was saying.

'Where is Father Kabuga?'

'Unfortunately Father Kabuga is ill.'

What the visitor did not say was that in fact Father Kabuga was dead, and his weighted-down body was currently at the bottom of a small man-made lagoon no more than a mile from the prison compound.

'Oh. How unfortunate.' Getty nodded at the guard, who went out and closed the cell door behind him.

'He asked me to give you this.' The Ghost held up a folded copy of that morning's *Daily Nation*. 'Father Kabuga tells me you and he enjoy doing the crossword together.'

Getty smiled ruefully. 'No offence, but I was rather hoping he would be here today. Yesterday's 23 across has got me absolutely stumped.'

'Then maybe I can help.'

The Ghost crossed the cell and peered over Getty's shoulder.

'It's an anagram,' the hotel owner said, tapping the grid with his finger. '"*Vanished, like the Red Sea*", six letters.'

'"*Erased*",' said the killer, sliding the stiletto knife from its holster and easing it beneath Conrad Getty's occipital bone and through the second and third cervical vertebrae into his spinal column with a single movement. As his chin lifted involuntarily the expression on Getty's face was one of beatific puzzlement, but it was merely a spasm and he had already been dead for at least two seconds. The Ghost gently withdrew the blade and eased him over to the bunk, closing his eyes and covering the body with a thin blanket.

It would be lunchtime before the guard realised that the prisoner in the solitary cell was not sleeping. By then the Ghost would be enjoying a light meal of sailfish on the hotel veranda and debating how to spend the rest of the day. In the feature pages of that morning's *Coastal Weekly News* there had been an article about an exhibition of the craftwork of the *mijikenda*, the nine ethnic tribes of the Kenyan coastal region, which was being held at the Haller Nature Reserve just outside Mombasa. According to the writer it provided a fascinating insight into what was rapidly becoming a dying tradition and should not be missed.

The job of a professional assassin entailed a great deal of travel to unusual parts of the world, yet there were some who preferred to spend their time closeted in hotel rooms waiting for the phone to ring. The Ghost always made a point of absorbing the local culture, however.

To do otherwise just seemed like a wasted opportunity.

37

Detective Inspector Oliver Mugo, late of Malindi Constabulary and now, scandalously, of Nyanza Province CID, had arrived on an early-morning shuttle flight from Kisumu. He now sat in Jouma's office, his burnished Loake boots propped on Jouma's desk.

'Good morning, Daniel!' He beamed from over the top of a newspaper as Jouma entered the room. 'I was beginning to think you weren't coming!'

Jouma regarded him as one might regard a burglar sitting in one's favourite armchair in the living room of one's house. 'They have not given you an office?' he said. 'I understood all great detectives at least had their own office.'

Mugo smiled. 'I understand one is being prepared as we speak. Superintendent Simba said I should use yours until then.'

Jouma glared at him through narrowed eyes. 'Then get your boots off my desk.'

Like a rowing couple forced to put on a show of

unity for a dinner party, the two detectives set about retracing the last-known movements of Lol Quarrie.

'I know this must be difficult for you, Daniel,' Mugo said, putting one bear-like paw on Jouma's shoulder. The fingernails were perfectly clipped and buffed to a gleaming finish. 'But, if it is any consolation, your name is spoken with reverence by everyone in Nyanza Province.'

He hadn't changed at all, Jouma thought. The bristling moustache, the shaven head perched comically on its fat neck, the demeanour of an overstuffed bantam cock. He peeled the plump fingers from his suit.

'Please do not patronise me, Mugo,' he hissed. 'Everyone knows full well that if it wasn't for your sister, and the fact her husband is the mayor, you would be issuing parking tickets instead of playing detective.'

Mugo drew himself up so that the padded shoulders of his double-breasted Hugo Boss suit almost blotted out the sun, and for a moment Jouma hoped the charlatan would hit him because that would bring this whole sordid episode to a swift conclusion.

But Mugo had not survived this long without a finely honed instinct for self-preservation. He flashed his gap-toothed smile and chuckled indulgently.

'I appreciate you are a busy man, Daniel,' he said. 'And I appreciate your assistance in this case. I have read your report into this unfortunate incident and I must commend you on your professionalism.'

'I am honoured.'

'But, if you don't mind me saying, professionalism can often leave a lot to be desired.'

'Really? In what way?'

'The people you interviewed – I get no sense of who they *are*. They exist only as words on a page.'

'I see.'

'And the scene where the victim was found – it is just an arrow on a map. There is no *description*. No sense of *place*.'

'Perhaps I should have set my report to music,' Jouma said.

Mugo grinned. 'I am pleased to see you have not lost your sense of humour, Daniel. I was concerned in case you took my observations as criticism. Now – I take it we are nearly there?'

They were standing in the inner compound of Fort Jesus, having threaded their way across the Old Town from Jamhuri Park. On the way they had paid a cursory visit to the alleyway connecting Ndia Kuu and Mbaraki Road. Mugo, reluctant to get his boots dirty, had merely peered into it. Jouma did not bother to tell him about the tie-pin – it seemed a shame to waste such a valuable clue on such a bone-headed idiot.

They walked across the compound, past the rows of Portuguese cannon and the old soldiers' barracks towards the crumbling tower in the north-west corner. This was known as the San Filipe bastion and had once housed the prison warden's house. Now it consisted of a couple of empty rooms connected by a worn stone staircase which led eventually on to a flat roof surrounded by a low, crenellated wall. Police tape was still strung across the bottom of the steps. Jouma and Mugo ducked under it and presently emerged on the roof of the bastion.

'So this is where he fell,' Mugo said, peering down a sheer hundred-foot drop to the ground below.

'According to the whore, Mr Quarrie appeared to be unsteady on his feet in the moments before he fell. I believe that to be of some significance.'

'I have read the report, Daniel,' Mugo said cheerfully. He looked out at the rooftops and minarets of the Old Town. 'He would have had a fine view of the city.'

Jouma did not bother to tell Mugo that any possible forensic evidence, such as footprints, had been obliterated by the first uniformed officers on the scene. Such clod-hoppering ineptitude was par for the course. Indeed, Mugo had made a career of it.

Mugo stalked around the roof for a few minutes, stroking his chin thoughtfully to give the impression he had the first idea of what he was looking for.

'Are you getting a sense of place, Mugo?' Jouma asked him.

Mugo was not listening. 'This whore. I am interested in her.'

'Her name is Dutch Alice. She is well known around this area.'

'And where was she on the night in question?'

Jouma pointed back across the compound to the loading-ramp entrance in the far wall, which was blocked off at the top end by a wire-mesh fence.

'The ramp leads down to a disused wharf which can be accessed by a path leading round from the square outside,' he explained. 'The whore used the wharf as a meeting place for her clients, and then took them to the top of the ramp to ...'

'I see. And who was the man she was with that night?'

'His name is Abdelbassir Hossain,' said Jouma. 'He is a dockhand at the harbour.'

'You have interviewed both suspects?'

'You read the report.'

'Yes. And according to the file the dockhand ran away.'

'He confirmed the whore's story when we brought him in for questioning.'

Mugo's eyes narrowed. 'But did he explain why he ran away? Or indeed why he did not hand himself in of his own accord?'

Jouma forced himself to remain calm. 'Listen, Mugo, forget about the dockhand. I have checked the fence and it is secure. There was no way he could have gained access to the fort, even if he'd wanted to. He is not even of any use as a witness because at the time of Mr Quarrie's death his back was up against the fence. He was facing the other way. The only solid lead you have is the statement from the furniture-maker. He saw Quarrie struggling with someone near the alley-way.'

'Yes, yes,' Mugo said, but it was obvious to Jouma that he wasn't listening. 'Where is Hossain now?'

'*What?*'

'The dockhand. Where is he?'

'For goodness sake, Mugo! You need to find more witnesses. Somebody else *must* have seen Quarrie.'

'Well, why don't I leave the door-to-door questioning to *you*, Daniel? Meanwhile, I want the dockhand brought in for further questioning.'

'*Why?*'

Mugo looked at Jouma and shook his head. 'Because he is a *suspect!*'

181

38

The blue Suzuki 125cc scooter had been on their tail for more than five miles, heading north on the Mombasa highway towards the Flamingo Creek junction. The rider was wearing a nondescript jerkin and a full-face helmet with a silvered visor.

From his days in the Flying Squad Jake knew that scooters were the transport of choice for contract killers. They weren't powerful, but they were nippy and manoeuvrable and easily disposed of. And there was a bag slung over the rider's back that was the perfect size to conceal a handgun.

Was this how it was going to end? he thought. Gunned down on the fucking supermarket run with eighteen cases of Tusker, sixteen bottles of Jack Daniel's and enough cartons of Marlboro to sink a battleship in the back of the Land Rover? How humiliating.

But how utterly in keeping with everything that had happened in the last twenty-four hours. Given the runaround by Frank Walker, his big chance to redeem himself had ended with him retching his guts up in the dirt, courtesy of a fist in the belly from one of Spurling's hatchet men. *Nice one, Jake. The villagers of Jalawi must think you're a real hero.*

'What's wrong?' Harry said anxiously from the passenger seat.

'Nothing.'

'Then why do you keep looking in the mirror?'

'I don't.'

'Yes you do. What is it?'

'You're being paranoid,' Jake told him.

But the scooter was still on their tail.

Maybe *he* was the one being paranoid. Maybe he had actually let all this talk of assassins spook him, too.

He had reached the Flamingo Creek junction now. He indicated and slowed as a six-axle oil tanker came steaming towards him on the other side of the road. The scooter slowed behind him. At the last second Jake yanked the steering wheel to the right and swerved across the tanker's path. The blare of its air horn was still sounding as the Land Rover careered along a dirt road heading east towards the boatyard.

Harry squawked as he was thrown around in his seat.

'Put your belt on,' Jake ordered, but his partner was already scrabbling with the buckle.

The Land Rover was kicking up a cloud of dust, making it difficult to see anything, and for one happy moment Jake thought that he must have imagined the whole thing, and that right now the scooter rider was still heading north on the highway, wondering why the madman up ahead had almost killed himself.

But then – *shit!* There he was in his wing mirrors, a hundred yards back, weaving around the divots and scars in the road. Jake gripped the wheel as the vehicle hit a huge pothole and skittered towards the trees. Bringing it back on to the road, he frantically checked his mirrors again. The scooter was still there, but the distance between them had closed to less than a hundred yards.

The boatyard was still more than a mile along the track, but the scooter was getting closer and now it seemed to Jake that the rider's right hand was lifting from the handlebars and reaching for the bag.

Fuck this.

He dragged the steering wheel hard right, at the same time as he yanked on the handbrake, so that the Land Rover entered a dizzying spin and blocked the road. The scooter, following in thick dust just fifty yards behind, had nowhere to go except into the bushes at the side of the road. Its front wheel went into a ditch and the rider went cartwheeling into the undergrowth.

For a long time the only sound was the ticking of the Land Rover's cooling engine. Then came bird-song and the frantic shrieking of monkeys. Jake slowly unclipped his seatbelt and extricated himself from his seat, feeling the tortured muscles in his neck and back screaming with indignation.

'You all right, Harry?'

Harry looked at him with wide, startled eyes. 'Did you get him?'

'I don't know.'

'Where are you going?'

'Get behind the wheel. If anything happens, put

your foot down and head straight for Mombasa police station. Ask for Jouma.'

Jake grabbed the nearest weapon, which happened to be a bottle of bourbon, and gingerly stepped down from the Land Rover.

39

Cyril Craven had worked as Spurling Developments' in-house lawyer for twenty years. Long enough to know the way the wind had blown the instant he walked into Bobby Spurling's office and saw Roarke standing at his left shoulder like one of the hounds of hell.

It was what he had feared might happen the moment he'd heard Clay Spurling was dead.

Clay had always regarded the Security Division as a necessary evil, an instrument to call upon when all other options had been exhausted. Wherever possible he preferred to use Craven's legal department to overcome problems in a manner that was as above board as possible. And, while Roarke had always deferred to the boss's wishes, Craven knew that, beneath his obsequiousness, the rabid security chief was just waiting for his chance to turn the tables.

Now it seemed his opportunity had arrived.

'You wanted to see me, Bobby?'

Bobby came straight to the point. 'What is the hold up with the Flamingo Creek hotel?'

Flamingo Creek? How on God's earth did he know about Flamingo Creek? But of course the answer was staring straight at him with evil eyes.

Craven cleared his throat and tried not to look at Roarke. 'There has been a widespread corruption investigation in Coast Province,' he explained. 'Many of the councillors and planning officials who were, shall we say, *on our side*, have been replaced or are facing charges. Those that are left are inclined to be more circumspect about what they will or will not approve.'

'This is a sixty-million-dollar development, Cyril,' Bobby said. 'What do you propose to do about it?'

Craven sighed. 'We have been in negotiations with Dr Kosgei, the Chairman of the District Planning Committee at Flamingo Creek. But so far he has made it perfectly clear that he is not open to the normal channels of persuasion.'

'You mean he won't be paid off?'

Craven nodded – and as he did so an alarming image appeared in his mind of Dr Kosgei, an unassuming family man, watching as his wife and children were tortured by Roarke's henchmen.

'Then you will go and see him again,' Bobby said. 'You will tell him the situation has changed.'

'Changed?'

'Yes. Changed.'

Craven sat and listened in growing disquiet as Bobby Spurling told him about the Security Division's visit to Jalawi village the previous day. He glanced at Roarke and saw the merest hint of triumph in the security chief's otherwise impassive features.

'And you will tell that parasite priest that if he

wants his money then he had better earn it,' Bobby said by means of a final flourish. His plump white cheeks were rosy with the exertion.

'As you wish, Bobby,' the lawyer said. 'I will arrange a meeting immediately. But are the police involved in this ... unfortunate incident?'

'The police are *far* too busy for that,' Bobby said. 'It seems there was also a murder at Flamingo Creek yesterday.'

Craven went cold. 'A murder?'

'Some old man. A sisal cropper, I believe. Beaten to death in his shack less than a mile from the village.'

'My God.'

'Yes,' Bobby nodded. 'The prime suspect is one of the hippie protesters. He was seen running from the scene. Perhaps you will see fit to mention this to Dr Kosgei when you see him. Just so that he is fully aware of who these unsavoury people really are.'

'Of course,' Craven spluttered. 'But I did not read about any murder in the newspapers.'

'Give them a chance, Cyril.' Bobby smiled. 'We've only just told them.'

As he left the office, it struck Cyril Craven that Roarke had not said a word during the entire meeting. Then why should he bother, Craven reflected, when he had the chairman and chief executive officer of the company to speak for him? He was merely the silent executioner – and it seemed that blood had already been spilled.

40

The scooter lay in the bushes by the roadside. It seemed remarkably undamaged. Of the rider there was no sign. Then, from further in the undergrowth, Jake heard a loud groaning and he moved forward slowly, the bourbon bottle clutched like a cudgel.

The rider had landed in a ditch running parallel to the road. The ditch was overgrown with thorn bushes, which had torn strips from his jerkin but also cushioned him from the impact and most probably saved his life. As Jake approached, the rider weakly moved his limbs in an attempt to free them.

'Don't move, or by Christ I swear I'll smash your face in.'

He knelt and tentatively lifted the silvered visor of the helmet. The face framed in the protective foam pads was not what Jake had been expecting. In his imagination hired killers had brutal, Slavic features with cold, pitiless eyes. This one was just an African kid with a half-hearted moustache, and he was terrified.

'Please do not kill me, sir,' he pleaded.

'Who the fuck are you?' Jake demanded.

'My name is Enock Mambili. I am a reporter.'

'A *reporter*?' Jake raised the bottle higher.

Enock raised his hands defensively and put one in his pocket. He handed Jake a business card. 'I work for the *Coastal Weekly News* newspaper.'

Jake scrutinised the card. 'You're lucky you're not dead.'

Grabbing Jake's outstretched arm, Enock Mambili sat up, checked to see he was still in one piece, and nodded enthusiastically. 'Extremely.' He removed his helmet.

'Why were you following me?'

'I was not following you.'

'Then what are you doing here?'

'I am en route to Jalawi village.'

'Why?'

Enock cleared his throat and thrust out his chest. 'I have been assigned by my newspaper to investigate reports of violent aggression by members of an ecological protest group. It seems that yesterday employees from Spurling Developments were set upon. One of them was so badly injured he is in hospital.'

'Who told you this?'

The reporter shrank slightly at Jake's accusatory tone. 'I am not at liberty to reveal my sources.'

Jake nodded grimly. Enock Mambili didn't have to reveal his sources. He would be prepared to wager an afternoon's fishing money that the call had come from Spurling Developments. Most probably Frank Walker, the operations chief. Hell, Spurling himself was probably on the board of the *Coastal Weekly News*.

'Well, I've got bad news for you, Enock,' Jake said. 'For a start you're on the wrong side of the river.'

'Ah.'

'And what's more, your story is bullshit. That thug's wounds were self-inflicted.'

Enock flinched. 'My sources are highly reliable.'

'So are mine,' Jake told him. 'I was there.'

'You live in Jalawi?'

'I have a boatyard half a mile down this track.'

'Really?' the reporter said, and his eyes widened. 'Then perhaps you can tell me about the murder?'

Now it was Jake's turn to be taken by surprise, especially when Enock Mambili revealed how the brutal clubbing of Isaac Gangra had taken place no more than a mile from the yard on the other side of the river.

'The police believe it was one of the protesters,' Enock said. 'They are hunting him down at this very moment, and expect to have him in custody soon.'

'Is that so?'

'You should be careful, sir! Nobody is safe from these people!'

'Thanks for the warning,' Jake said.

He lifted the young reporter to his feet, dusted him down, and put him back on his bike. He even wished him well and told him he would most certainly buy a copy of the newspaper. But as Enock Mambili set off back towards the highway in search of his scoop, Jake couldn't help wondering why his editor had bothered sending him all this way to cover the story when, clearly, it had already been written.

41

Bryson stared at the body lying face down on the narrow prison bunk and a great wave of fatigue washed over him. He drew his hand down his face and noticed that he appeared to have no feeling in his forehead and cheeks. For one unnerving moment it was like touching the face of a corpse.

'A maximum-security prison,' he said. 'How?'

'He posed as a pastoral priest from the Society of Prison Chaplains,' McCrickerd said. 'Killed the real priest and took his ID card and dog collar.'

'Don't they have guards here?'

'None with any brains.'

'What about CCTV?'

'You must be joking.'

Bryson reached down and with one finger carefully moved a lock of suspiciously artificial-looking hair that had fallen from the dome of Conrad Getty's skull across the nape of his neck.

'I want this place locked down,' he said. 'I don't even want the Kenyan cops to know this has happened. This is a national security issue now.'

Just below the jutting nodule of the occipital bone at the back of Getty's head was a small blood-crusted incision.

'Jesus,' Bryson muttered. 'So the sonofabitch is here.'

In fact, at that moment the Ghost was drinking hot sweet tea at a souk in the inland town of Gongoni, killing time before sundown when a Cessna light aircraft bound for Somalia was due to take off from a nearby jungle airstrip normally used by dope smugglers. Once inside the unpatrolled borders of that lawless and chaotic country, leaving Africa would be a simple matter. It was, admittedly, a some-what circuitous and time-consuming exit – but by now the FBI would presumably have the airports, ports and border crossings under surveillance and there seemed little point in jeopardising the assign-ment for the want of a little comfort.

And it was not as if the financial rewards didn't make up for it. The Ghost had been paid sixty million euros to execute Martha Bentley and Conrad Getty, a fee far in excess of any other working contract killer.

Sitting amid the pleasing hubbub of the souk, reflecting on a job well done, it was impossible not to feel a twinge of regret that things would never again be this good. It was an unavoidable truth that when one was at the very top of one's game the only way was down.

Maybe it was time to quit. The life expectancy of an assassin was short enough without tempting fate. With every job the odds of failure increased astronomically.

It didn't matter how good you were, if you hung around too long in this profession it would kill you.

There were still several hours before the rendezvous with the Cessna pilot, and one minor administrative task left to perform. The Ghost removed a MacBook Air from a leather shoulder bag and booted up the flimsy machine. Using an encrypted messaging account the killer sent a brief, coded message confirming that the contract had been completed.

Almost immediately a reply landed in the inbox. This was highly irregular and for a split-second the Ghost was wary of opening it. It could be a trap. Agencies like the FBI sometimes fretted that they were losing the technological war against their enemies, but the truth was that their resources were far superior. They would always have the edge. A major strategy of winning for these people was to convince their enemy that it was more powerful than it actually was. To lead them into fatal over-confidence.

The Ghost opened the message. It consisted of the name of a target, a location and the number of a bank account into which a further twenty million euros would be deposited upon his elimination. The killer considered this new development carefully. The job would involve research. Careful planning. More importantly it would be dangerous, because Kenya was red hot right now.

But there was also a point to be proved. The Ghost needed to know whether the summit of a glorious career had indeed been reached, or whether there was one more pinnacle to be climbed.

Using a recognised confirmation code, the killer sent a reply accepting the new contract. The plane to Somalia would have to wait. And so would any premature thoughts of retirement.

At GCHQ, the British Intelligence listening post in Cheltenham, a team of technicians had been experimenting with newly developed decryption software which used probabilistic algorithms to identify, isolate and unravel highly complex but seemingly random bursts of electronic data. After three months of fruitlessly monitoring static, most of the team had reached the conclusion that the new software was a piece of shit. Indeed, the only reason it had not already been ripped out and consigned to the junk pile was that the technicians were retained on handsome contracts which did not expire until the end of the following month. As a result, they were anxious to try every possible permutation to ensure their contracts were not terminated prematurely.

Two of the team were dutifully monitoring the ether when the new software suddenly latched on to a burst of random traffic. A moment later it registered a second intercept. Fifty seconds later, a third. This in itself was not unusual. But what surprised – and delighted – the technicians was that this time the software was actually able to decrypt the intercepts. Or at least that was how it appeared: the decrypts made no sense to either man. But then it was not their job to interpret their significance.

The intercepts were sent upstairs to GCHQ's analysts. As had become customary, the information was also passed on to their counterparts on the other side of the Atlantic – which was how a computer at the CIA headquarters in Langley, Virginia, was able to identify an inter-agency flagged word combination contained within the three intercepted transmissions.

Less than an hour after the Ghost had sent the last message from a souk in Gongoni, a transcript of the decrypted exchange landed on the desk of FBI Special Agent Dean Hoffman in the Bureau's headquarters on Pennsylvania Avenue, Washington DC.

'Holy shit,' Hoffman said, picking up the phone.

Eight thousand miles away, as the Ghost left Gongoni and headed south towards Mombasa, Special Agent Clarence Bryson's cell phone began to ring.

42

Abdelbassir Hossain sat in the interview room of Mombasa central police station and described once again how, five days earlier, he had gone to Fort Jesus and paid the whore known as Dutch Alice four hundred shillings to suck his cock.

'And that is when you saw the victim fall to his death?' Inspector Mugo asked amiably, standing behind the Moroccan dockhand and gently massaging his bony shoulders.

'I told you – I didn't see anybody fall,' Hossain protested. 'I was facing in the other direction. The whore saw everything when she was—'

'When she was what, Abdelbassir?'

'When she was, you know ... *down there.*'

Through a grimy metal grille set in the door of the interview room, Jouma watched the dialogue with increasing frustration. Hossain had answered these same questions five days earlier when he had been brought in. It was all available in a carefully compiled transcript. The purpose of this charade was simply for Mugo to justify his existence. As to furthering the investigation into Lol Quarrie's death, it was a waste of time.

'One thing puzzles me, Abdelbassir,' Mugo was saying. 'You say you had nothing to do with the murder—'

'Murder?'

'Oh yes, my friend. This is a murder inquiry now. You see, the victim was seen fighting with someone before he died. And I wonder, Abdelbassir, if it was you?'

Abdelbassir's dumbstruck expression was matched only by that of Jouma on the other side of the door. *A murder investigation?* What the devil was Mugo playing at? There was not one single piece of evidence to suggest Lol Quarrie had been pushed from the San Filipe bastion. And as for him struggling with someone – hadn't Mugo read the report? The furniture-maker had quite clearly said it was a boy. Abdelbassir was at least forty years old. He had a *beard* for goodness sake!

'Why would I want to kill him?' Abdelbassir was saying. 'I never saw this man in my life.'

'You like Dutch Alice, don't you?' Mugo suggested.

'I—'

'She says you are her best customer.'

'I—'

'Maybe this man was trying to steal her from you. Maybe this was something that upset you very much. Maybe you were jealous.'

'She is a *whore*,' the dockhand said. 'She fucks men for a living. At least twenty a day. Why would I be jealous?'

Mugo looked up at the ceiling, his hands together as if in prayer. 'Jealousy is a strange thing. It affects men in many different ways. Even men who think they are immune to it can suddenly find themselves gripped and no longer in control of themselves.'

'I never saw this man before in my life. I swear.'

'And you did not push him off the wall?'

'No!'

Mugo smashed his fist theatrically on the table. '*Then why did you run away?*'

Jouma decided he had had enough. Three hours in Mugo's company was more than enough for any man.

'*Why*, Abdelbassir?' Mugo's voice echoed down the corridor. '*Why?*'

Because, you idiot, Abdelbassir Hossain is a married man with five children, Jouma thought as he strode towards the exit. *And the very last thing he wants is his wife to know that he spends his evenings in sordid clinches with whores down at Fort Jesus.*

Not that Mugo gave a damn about anything like the truth. Which was why Jouma had no intention of wasting any more time chaperoning him. There was a case to be solved, and now at last he had a clue. This afternoon, with the oafish Mugo tilting at windmills, he fully intended to knuckle down to some proper detective work.

But first things first.

'If anybody wants me,' he said to the corporal behind the front desk, 'tell them I have gone for my lunch.'

43

Back at the boatyard Jake and Harry unloaded the booze and cracked open a couple of beers.

'You think the kid will write what really happened at Jalawi yesterday?' Harry asked, lowering himself into his director's chair on the jetty.

Jake shrugged. 'Even if he's not toeing the editorial line he can only write what people tell him. And if the villagers or the missionaries won't talk then it's Spurling's word against a bunch of spaced-out hippies. In any case, who's going to believe that a hit squad from Spurling Developments smashed up one of their own cars and put one of their own men on life support?'

He knew fine well that the villagers would not speak out. They were all scared stiff of what would happen to them if Roarke and his platoon of meatheads paid them a return visit.

'What about this murder?' Harry said.

'I saw those kids, Harry. They wouldn't know how to pull the legs off a fly let alone batter some poor old bastard to death. It's all part of the same dirty tricks campaign to discredit Evie Simenon.' Jake glanced at his partner. 'Maybe you could raise the matter at the next shareholders' meeting.'

Harry grunted noncommittally. 'There is, of course, another option. Why not tell the newspapers how you and I are living under the shadow of imminent assassination? Now *there's* a good story. Far more newsworthy than some squabble over a village.'

Jake laughed. 'I told you: nobody wants us dead except spurned women and jealous husbands.'

'Is that why you nearly killed us both back there?'

'I overreacted. Don't worry about it.'

'But I *do* worry about it, Jakey-boy! What if we come back from Suki's one night and he's waiting for us at the yard?'

'Then we'll offer him a nightcap and tell him he's wasting his time. We don't know anything.' Jake finished his beer and looked over at the full boxes of Tusker on the jetty. 'In the meantime, I don't suppose you fancy giving me a hand to load the beer on to the launch?'

Harry winced. 'Still suffering from a spot of whiplash after our little adventure back there,' he said. 'Best I didn't aggravate it.'

By the time Jake had loaded the last box aboard *Yellowfin*, Harry was already dozing in his chair. *Silly old bastard*, he thought affectionately. Sometimes it was easy to forget what he had been through. Jake may have lost Martha Bentley, but Harry had lost his entire family, wiped out in a split-second in a car accident in England. His partner had his own eccentric outlook on life – but Jake doubted anyone could ever bounce back from that with their sanity completely intact.

He pulled another Tusker from the coolbox and savoured it with a cigarette. It was good to take stock, because events were beginning to spiral out of control. First Martha, now this business up at Jalawi – it was time to take a step backwards and let things simmer down a little. Christ only knew what might be lurking around the next bend.

Just then he heard something. It wasn't much, just a tiny scuffling sound from the cabin. It could have been anything – the gentle swell dislodging a cushion from one of the banquettes, or a door that hadn't been closed properly.

But then he heard it again, and now there could be no doubt.

Someone was on his boat.

Jake silently opened one of the cockpit tackle boxes and removed a metal boathook. Clutching it so that its evil-looking claw was above his head he edged towards the cabin. This was getting to be a habit, he thought. A shadow moved on the grimy window pane and he took a deep intake of breath before shouldering the flimsy door with all his might. The edge caught the intruder a glancing blow, and a body clattered backwards against the fold-down table between the banquettes. Jake was on him in a split-second, and the metal claw would have undoubtedly come down on his defenceless skull had he not emitted a pitiful wail of surrender.

The red mist cleared and Jake found himself staring down at a familiar face.

'What the fuck are you doing on my boat?' he demanded.

'You got to help me, man,' pleaded Alex Hopper. His face was pale and his clothes were torn and bloodied. He was also soaking wet. 'I'm in serious shit.'

44

Sunday, 5 February 1987. That was the day it all changed for Frank Walker. An unspeakably dreary winter's evening in the front parlour of a guest-house in North Shields. Just him and a Belgian trucker called Henning huddled around the single-bar fire, watching the telly. The usual Sunday-night shite: *Songs of Praise*, *Antiques Roadshow*, *Last of the Summer Wine*. Then Henning reached across and turned it over to BBC2, and Frank was about to have a word when suddenly he saw the rest of his life up there on the screen: a documentary about big-game hunters in the Masai Mara. Burly bastards in bush hats and fatigues, hanging out of speeding Land Rovers, armed to the teeth with high-velocity rifles.

And maybe Frank said something out loud, because Henning turned to him and said, 'You like this kind of thing?'

Turned out Henning had a cousin who worked as a ranger on some private estate in Kenya, and he was pretty sure they were always on the look-out for guys who weren't afraid of a bit of hard work to help out in the field.

Frank didn't even know where Kenya was – but the next day he made a few long-distance calls and quit his job. He didn't have much money but there was enough stashed away for a National Express coach trip down to Heathrow and a one-way economy class ticket to Mombasa on Kenya Airways. He was twenty years old.

He had been expecting the summons ever since he'd heard Clay Spurling was dead.

'Bobby would like to see you in his office, Mr Walker,' Janice, his secretary, said. Her voice was tremulous with tension. She could tell that this was the call he had been waiting for. 'Mr Walker—'

'It's all right, Janice. Tell him I'll be up right away.'

In the elevator to the top floor, the only thing that surprised Frank was that the call hadn't come sooner. What was Bobby waiting for? His dish of revenge to turn cold?

He felt the smooth copper casing of the Winchester Magnum cartridge in his pocket and reflected how uncomplicated life had been when he was twenty before Clay Spurling had taken him under his wing and treated him like a son.

If only Clay's own son had been worthy of the Spurling name.

'Hello, Frank,' Bobby said, leaning back in his chair. Even this early in the day his eyes had that tell-tale narcotic sparkle to them. Walker could recognise the signs. 'It's been a long time. How've you been?'

'As well as can be expected, Bobby. How was Jo'burg?'

Bobby shrugged. 'I have to say I was not best pleased to be shipped there. It really fucked up my social life, I'll tell you. But you know something? Compared to this dead-end town, it's like New York City.'

'I'm pleased to hear it.'

'Are you, Frank? Are you pleased to see me back again so soon?'

'My condolences on your loss,' Walker said noncommittally.

'People keep saying that,' Bobby said. 'I suppose we should be thankful that the old boy managed to hang around for so long. But we mustn't dwell on the past, must we?'

'No, Bobby. We mustn't.'

Bobby stood up and went to a drinks cabinet in one corner of the office. 'Whisky, Frank? I remember you were always partial to a drop of the hard stuff back in the day.'

Walker stood stiffly, arms folded behind his back, and watched Bobby select a fifteen-year-old malt with shaking hands. It was hard to believe the kid was still only twenty-three years old. In the two years he had been in exile his hedonistic lifestyle had given his boyish face the haggard look of a man in his forties.

'No, thank you. It's a bit early for me.'

Bobby raised an eyebrow as he poured himself a large slug. 'Early? You've changed your tune.'

'It's what comes of old age,' Walker said. 'You can't take your drink the way you used to when you were younger.'

'How depressing. In that case, here's to never getting old.' Bobby drained the glass in one and poured himself another. He moved back to his desk and sat down. 'So here we are. The dynamic duo, back together again. Who would have thought it, eh, Frank? By God, we had some rare old times together, didn't we?'

'If you say so, Bobby.'

Bobby smiled glacially. 'You know I used to look up to you, Frank. I really did. When I was a kid I thought of you like – I don't know, an uncle or something. And when my old man took you into the business, promoted you up through the ranks, I was really happy for you. It couldn't have happened to a nicer guy. Real rags to riches stuff. But you let me down, Frank. I thought we had something special between us – but you *betrayed* me.'

Walker sighed. 'For Christ's sake, Bobby – we both know why I'm here. If you're going to get rid of me, why don't you stop fucking around for once in your miserable life and get on with it?'

Bobby regarded him with hooded eyes. 'You never were one to stand on ceremony.' He buzzed his secretary. 'Tell Mr Roarke to come in, will you?'

Walker heard the door opening and felt the floor shudder. He turned to see Douglas Roarke, accompanied by the unmistakable figure of his personal pit bull Tom Beye. They stood behind him, Roarke calm as a vicar, Beye bristling with aggression like the wild animal he was. So this was how it was going to end, he thought. Thrown out on the street by security. He almost laughed out loud.

'You thought a lot of my father, didn't you, Frank?' Bobby was saying.

'A lot more than you ever did.'

'That's unfair. I loved him like any son loves his father. But he never loved me back.'

'I think he tried his best, Bobby,' Frank said. 'But it's hard to love a fucking sociopath.'

'*Sociopath?* That's an impressive word coming from a truck driver from Glasgow. Well, let me tell you something you *don't* know. People think my father died of a heart attack. That his poor old fuzzed-up ticker just gave up the ghost. Well, it did – but not from natural causes.'

Walker felt the blood draining from his face. 'What are you talking about, Bobby?'

'Let's just say I helped him on his way.'

'You – *killed him?*'

Bobby grinned as he described Clay Spurling's final moments. 'The toxin in the desert-rose sap is similar to digitalis extract, isn't it, Mr Roarke?' He looked at Roarke with the expectant expression of a child seeking approval from an adult.

'That's right, sir,' Roarke said. 'In small doses it can actually treat congestive heart disease.'

'Ironic, eh, considering his condition?' Bobby cackled. 'But only *very, very small doses.* Tell Frank what happens with larger doses.'

'Larger doses cause systolic heart failure and death,' Roarke intoned.

'And it did,' Bobby bragged. He had by now convinced himself that the murder of his father was an act of calculated genius on his behalf, rather than an extremely fortunate confluence of circumstances and plant toxins. 'And the clever thing about it is that no autopsy will ever be able to tell.'

'You *bastard*,' Walker said, lunging towards the desk. But Tom Beye was faster. The big security man's arms looped round him, and Walker gasped as the air was squeezed from his lungs. At that moment he realised Bobby had a far more sinister fate in store for him than simply stripping him of his job.

'He was going to make you CEO,' Bobby said. 'And that's just not on. You see, I'm his son. The company belongs to me.'

'You're a fucking maniac, Bobby!' Walker whispered.

Bobby stood up and put his face just a few inches from Walker's. 'No. I'm not. And to be honest, I'm getting a bit sick of people saying that I am. I demand *respect*.'

Walker spat in his face. The thick gobbet ran down the younger man's flabby cheek until he swiped it away with a handkerchief.

'You do understand that I'm going to have you killed,' Bobby said, confirming Walker's suspicions.

'Well, I didn't think *you* would do it,' Walker said. 'You haven't got the balls for that.'

Bobby slapped him hard across the face. 'To think we used to be friends, Frank,' he said.

Walker's gaze was poisonous. 'I was never your friend, Bobby. And as far as I'm concerned you can go to hell.'

Bobby shrugged. 'Get him out of here, Mr Roarke. And bury him deep, where the animals won't dig him up.'

45

'What is the matter, Daniel?' Winifred Jouma said. 'Are you sickening for something?'

Jouma looked at his bowl and saw that, despite ladling lamb stew with his spoon for the last five minutes, he had yet to take a mouthful.

'It's nothing, my dear,' he told his wife. 'I was just thinking.'

'Well, eat your lunch before it gets cold,' Winifred said. She did not ask what he was thinking about because she knew that it was bound to be police work. In more than thirty years of marriage she had never asked him about his job, and for that Jouma was grateful.

She was right, of course. He had come home in order to escape the madness of police work for a while – and yet he was *still* thinking about it.

The tiny apartment shook as a lorry thundered over the Makupa Causeway on its way to Nairobi. Winifred removed his bowl and took it into the kitchen.

'That was delicious,' he said.

'As if you would know,' his wife replied. 'I am going to do the ironing.'

Jouma leaned back in his chair and stared at the four walls. Then, from his jacket pocket, he removed the multi-coloured tie-pin that Mwangi had found in the alley. He placed it on the table in front of him. It had been presented to Sergeant Lol Quarrie for long service in the Royal Ulster Constabulary. Why was it on the ground in the alleyway? Had it been ripped off in the struggle? And if so, what else might be lying there amid the detritus? *And who was this boy the old furniture-maker had seen?*

It was no good. The bit was between his teeth now, and much as he loved his wife and her cooking, the mystery of Lol Quarrie was an itch that simply had to be scratched. He stood and put on his jacket. Mugo could bring the whole of Mombasa in for questioning – as far as Jouma was concerned there was only one place he was going this afternoon.

'I have to go,' he called to his wife. But in the bedroom Winifred was singing to herself and did not hear him. How he loved his wife. How he wished he could share her total disinterest in matters that did not concern her.

He opened the door and jumped as a figure emerged from the shadows of the stairwell.

It was Jake. He was not alone.

Alex Hopper sat at the kitchen table and shovelled Winifred Jouma's stew into his mouth. The boy looked dreadful, Jouma thought. His face was deathly pale and there were dark rings beneath his eyes. From the tiny bathroom came the sound of water spitting uncertainly into an enamel bathtub, and Winifred came in with a freshly laundered towel over her arm.

'I regret that the bath will take quite some time to fill,' she said. 'I will leave the towel on the bed when you are ready.'

'Thank you very much, Mrs Jouma,' Jake said. 'You're very kind.'

She looked at Alex with unmistakable concern, then turned and went back into the bedroom.

When the door had closed, Jouma cleared his throat and said, 'This is what the desk sergeant at Kilindini station told me on the phone just now. Yesterday a plantation worker called Isaac Gangra was found beaten to death in his house on the north shore of Flamingo Creek.'

'Plantation worker?' Alex blurted. 'He was a fucking drug dealer.'

'Watch your mouth, son,' Jake snapped.

'It is being treated as murder,' Jouma continued. 'A team of detectives has been assigned to the case. The suspect is described as a white male in his late teens.'

'Alex says there were guys there with guns taking pot shots at him.'

'They were *askari* from a private security firm employed by the Flamingo Creek Residents Association. They were investigating reports of illegal activity in the area.'

'What sort of illegal activity?'

'Drug transactions.'

'Convenient.'

'They were patrolling near Mr Gangra's house when they saw Mr Hopper. They claim he was armed, which is why they opened fire in self-defence.'

212

'They were trying to fucking *kill* me,' Alex insisted, his voice close to breaking.

'I won't tell you again,' Jake growled. 'Watch your language.'

Jouma sighed and turned to the boy. 'What were you doing there?'

'Mikey said he had some weed,' Alex said. 'He said the guy in the shack was a dealer. I swear he was dead when I found him, man. His head was all—'

Jouma rubbed his face wearily and turned to Jake. 'May I speak with you outside?'

They went out to the stairwell and looked out over the Makupa Causeway. Jake lit a cigarette. In the distance a huge freighter laden with containers was inching its way out of Kilindini harbour in search of the open sea.

'You should not have got involved in this,' Jouma said angrily. 'What were you thinking? There are officers swarming all over Flamingo Creek looking for him.'

'I didn't have much choice in the matter,' Jake explained. 'The kid was on the boat this morning, hiding in the cabin. He was terrified. I thought he was ... I nearly brained the little bastard with a boathook.'

'He is in serious trouble, Jake. By all accounts this was a brutal killing. By rights I should arrest him.'

'I know. But this whole thing stinks. An armed security detail stumbling on old man Gangra's shack, just as Alex is stumbling out of it? Come on. Those guys wouldn't even piss on a plantation worker if he was on fire. They're paid to look after the toffs from the Yacht Club.'

Jouma groaned. Right now – *at this precise moment* – this was the very last thing he needed in his life. 'This fellow Mikey. Who is he?'

'Michael Gulbis. One of the hippies up at Jalawi. He broke his leg falling out of a tree the other day. He's on a ward at Mombasa Hospital. It seems he got a tip from a hospital cleaner that Gangra had some high-quality cannabis he was looking to sell.'

'Who is this hospital cleaner?'

'I don't know. Yet.'

Jouma looked at him sternly. 'You must not take matters into your own hands, Jake.'

'What else can I do? You know how the system works, Inspector. If they catch the kid they'll lock him up and throw away the key. The only way I can help him is by finding the real killer. Or at least find out who's setting him up.'

'How can you be so sure he is telling the truth?'

'Because I saw his face. He was frightened out of his wits. He hid in the swamp all night then swam across the creek because he thought *Yellowfin* was the only place he would be safe. He really thinks those guys were out to kill him.'

Jouma sighed and shook his head in resignation. Jake Moore, he knew, was a man who did not change his mind when it was made up. All he could do was hope that the former Flying Squad detective would exercise both caution and restraint – because the only other option open to him was to throw the pair of them behind bars.

'The boy can stay here,' he said presently. 'But only until tomorrow. I cannot get involved in this.'

'I appreciate that, Inspector. And thank you.'

'What will you do?'

Jake rubbed the bristle on his chin. 'I thought I might take a bunch of grapes to his old friend Michael Gulbis,' he said.

46

In his well-appointed office north of Flamingo Creek, Dr Benson Kosgei, the Chairman of the District Council Planning Committee, peered over the top of thick-rimmed spectacles at the man sitting on the other side of his desk.

'What can I do for you, Mr Craven?'

'I would like to discuss the growing problem of Jalawi village,' said the head of Spurling Developments legal department.

'What of it?'

'Specifically, how many more lives will be lost before your planning committee make a decision on our application?'

Kosgei seemed surprised. 'Lives?'

'At this moment the police are investigating a brutal murder. An itinerant plantation worker beaten to death not half a mile from Jalawi yesterday. Their prime suspect is one of the environmental protesters camped near the village. This, I must point out, comes hard on the heels of an unprovoked attack on our men by those same protesters yesterday. Not only did they smash up a vehicle, but they put one man in hospital — and the doctors aren't sure he'll ever recover the sight in his right eye.'

As he recited the script Bobby Spurling and Douglas Roarke had given him that morning, Craven somehow managed to remain impassive — even though the very act of saying the words made him feel sick to the stomach.

'These people are dangerously out of control,' he continued ominously. 'Something must be done before there is more bloodshed. Before more innocent people lose their lives.'

Kosgei considered this. Then he said, 'Have the police arrested anyone in connection with these incidents?'

'No, but—'

'Not even for an assault which put a man in hospital?'

This was not the response Roarke or Bobby Spurling would have expected — but then they did not know Dr Kosgei like Craven did. Kosgei was not like other planning committee chairmen. He had none of the vanity and greed. He did not expect an envelope stuffed with hundred-dollar bills to be included with the planning application, nor did he want a new car, a holiday to Europe or even free hotel leisure-club membership for his family.

But Craven's pitch was not yet complete.

'You may think Spurling Developments have got a vested interest in this matter, Dr Kosgei,' he said. 'And you would be right. But don't just take my word for it.'

Craven sat back, his job done for the moment.

Now it was the turn of the man sitting beside him to lean forward in his chair. And, of the two of them, Craven knew that Brother Willem of the Redeemed Apostolic Gospel Church had the most to lose if this damnable hotel development went to the wall.

'Everybody is extremely worried, Dr Kosgei,' Willem said earnestly. 'I have villagers — even those who are not members of the church congregation — coming up to me to ask when the hotel will be built and when this nightmare will be at an end.'

'You mean the villagers are in *favour* of this development?' Kosgei asked suspiciously.

Willem nodded. 'Jalawi is a small fishing village — and it is dying. Young people today aren't interested in following the footsteps of their fathers or grandfathers. They know that beyond their village is a modern world full of opportunity. Ten years ago there were more than a thousand people in Jalawi. Now there are less than two hundred. Whether you grant this planning application or not, Dr Kosgei, the truth is that this village will soon be dead anyway. This development at least gives the people a chance to make new lives for themselves.'

Kosgei looked at the priest. His face was like stone. 'Is that so?' he said.

'I thought that went well,' Willem said optimistically, as he and Craven were driven away from Kosgei's office in the back of a Spurling Developments executive limousine.

'Did you?' Craven said. 'Then you must have been in a different meeting to me.'

'After everything that's happened I don't see how

Kosgei can possibly recommend anything *other* than granting your application.'

'Tell me, Brother Willem – would you be so in favour of the application if Spurling Developments *wasn't* prepared to pay you one million dollars to move out of Jalawi?'

Willem looked affronted. 'You are not paying *me*, Mr Craven! You are paying the Redeemed Apostolic Gospel Church. And your most generous *donation* will ensure that its vital missionary work in Kenya will continue for many years to come.'

'Although not in Jalawi,' Craven pointed out.

'Such is the way of the world,' the priest said. 'The Lord giveth and the Lord taketh away.'

'The Lord always was convenient in that way,' Craven said icily.

47

Frank Walker had always thought that, when he died, he would like to be buried somewhere on the Spurling reserve. Nothing special, just a discreet grave somewhere with maybe a whitewashed rock as a headstone.

Now it seemed he was about to get his wish. Except Tom Beye would not be supplying the memorial.

They had driven south for two hours and then inland for another hour, skirting the southern perimeter of the Shimba Hills National Reserve. Walker was hogtied in the boot of the SUV with a sack over his head for good measure. But when they finally stopped and Beye removed the sack, he knew precisely where they were. The rich, earthy smell was enough. Just beyond the low escarpment on which the SUV was parked was a vast expanse of rolling grassland and down there, at the heart of it, was Clay Spurling's ranch house.

'Get on your knees,' Beye said.

'You know that Roarke will run out of uses for

you eventually, Tom. Then it will be you on your knees waiting for a bullet.'

'Shut up.'

Beye smashed the butt of his .45 automatic between Walker's shoulder blades and he pitched forward on to the dirt. The big African reached down and effortlessly dragged him to his knees by the scruff of his neck.

Walker could smell the rank odour of his breath, and reflected that there was a certain poetry to his impending death. He was a boy from the tenements of Glasgow where life expectancy was dismally short, the living years hard, and death usually caused by a shiv knife or a broken bottle across the throat in some dismal drinking hole or piss-sodden stairwell. At least he would not die like that. His bones would be bleached under the African sun rather than incinerated at Bishopbriggs crematorium.

Behind him he heard the snap of the safety catch on Beye's pistol and he closed his eyes.

But the bullet did not come.

Instead, a familiar, rumbling voice said, 'Put the gun down, *bwana*.'

Malachi! Christ – those five short words were probably the most he'd ever heard the taciturn old Masai ever say in one go, but Frank Walker had never heard a sweeter sound.

He turned his head. Beye was directly behind him, the pistol aimed at his head. Behind Beye, wearing his usual attire of dusty canvas bush clothing, was Malachi, Clay Spurling's trusted game warden. His scored face was as usual impassive beneath the brim of his hat. In his hands was a Winchester hunting rifle, its barrel pressed hard against the back of Beye's head.

Walker wondered how long he had been watching them. The old Masai had an almost supernatural ability to blend into the terrain, to creep up on his prey without being seen or heard. Clay Spurling used to call him Whispering Death – and was only half-joking about it.

'Put the gun down, Tom,' he said. 'Or Malachi *will* blow your head off.'

There was fury in Beye's red eyes, but he knew when he was beaten. He lowered the pistol and tossed it on to the ground.

Walker got to his feet and used Malachi's bush knife to cut the rope that bound his wrists. 'And your telephone if you please.'

Beye did as he was told. With the rifle still pointed at him, he had little choice but to obey.

'Now turn around and walk to your vehicle.'

As soon as Beye was behind the wheel of the SUV, Walker picked up his gun and shot out the front tyres.

'I will kill you for this,' Beye rumbled. 'Be assured I will kill you both.'

'I've got to go now, Tom,' Walker told him. 'But if you start walking now you'll reach the highway by sundown – assuming the lions don't get you first. Alternatively you can try your luck at the ranch house. It's about three miles that way. I heard Bobby was planning to sell it, but maybe he hasn't had the phones disconnected yet.'

48

It had been a devil of a day, one which had frustrated him at every turn. First Mugo and Abdelbassir, then Jake and Alex Hopper – Jouma wondered who else could possibly get between him and his potentially vital police work.

Now, armed with a powerful torch requisitioned from Desk Sergeant Wa'ango at central police station, the inspector at last threw back his shoulders and strode into the alleyway connecting Ndia Kuu with Mbaraki Road. It didn't matter that it was oppressive and smelled like the very bowels of Satan himself; this, Jouma was convinced, was where the key to the mystery of Lol Quarrie's death lay. Call it gut instinct, call it experience – somewhere amid the squalor he knew he would find the answer.

His first discovery was where the many malevolent rats that seemed to appear and disappear from the alleyway were coming from. Under the detritus where Mwangi had discovered the tie-pin was a displaced manhole cover which presumably accessed the sewer system beneath Mombasa's streets. *Well, at least he could get one over on the vermin population.* He slid the heavy metal cover across the hole with his foot, where it settled back into place with a satisfying clang.

The noise reminded him of something. Something which he had been all too prepared to dismiss as the ramblings of a senile old man.

Clank! Clank! Clank!

That was what the furniture-maker had said. It was the noise he had heard from the alleyway on the day Lol Quarrie disappeared.

He thought about the strange, foul-smelling slime he had found on the dead man's clothes. *Was it possible that . . .?* His heart pounding, Jouma hunkered down and attempted to slide his fingers around the edge of the manhole cover. But it was made of inch-thick steel and was far too heavy for the little detective to prise open. What was needed, he concluded, was either a special key or else someone with a bit of muscle.

Cursing, Jouma hurried to the central police station and slammed the torch down in front of Desk Sergeant Wa'ango. 'I need one of your men,' he said. 'Preferably one who is very strong.'

But for some reason Wa'ango merely smiled in a curious manner and tapped his nose conspiratorially. 'Congratulations, Inspector Jouma.'

'What are you talking about, Wa'ango?'

'The news is all around the station.'

'*What* news?'

'About how you and Detective Inspector Mugo have arrested the killer of the policeman at Fort Jesus!'

224

Jouma stared at him with incredulity. 'Mugo and I have done no such thing, Wa'ango.' But even as he spoke, a clammy feeling of dread was beginning to spread through him.

'You should not be so modest, sir.' The desk sergeant grinned. 'The dockhand has confessed all. He was taken in handcuffs to Kingorani jail not an hour ago and Inspector Mugo has summoned the press to the station to receive the news.'

49

Michael Gulbis's shattered left leg was encased in plaster and raised on a traction device to an angle of thirty degrees. But this was the only source of discomfort for the kid from the San Fernando Valley. He was clean and well fed, there was a vase of flowers and a well-stocked fruit bowl by his hospital bed, he had access to books and magazines, and when he was not listening to his iPod he could always watch DVDs on his portable player.

'Looking good, Michael,' Jake said, drawing the privacy screens around the bed. 'How's it going?'

Michael, who had been enjoying a light nap after his lunch, jerked awake. It took him a moment to register his visitor, but then he smiled sleepily.

'Hey – what's up, man?'

Jake sat on the bed and tapped Michael's plaster with his knuckle. 'Just thought I'd drop by. See how you were.'

'I'm good, I'm good,' Michael said. 'Where's Evie?'

'Oh, Evie's out saving the world. But your friend Alex sends his regards.'

Uncertainty registered on Michael's face. 'Great. How is he?'

'Not too good, I'm afraid.'

'Really?'

'Yeah, really. You see, being on the run for murder is a real pain in the ass.'

Now the healthy glow drained from Michael's face.

'That little errand you sent him on yesterday. Turns out you were misinformed. The guy at Flamingo Creek wasn't a dealer after all. He was an old man with a couple of goats. Except when Alex got there, someone had smashed his head in.'

'Whoa!' The hippie raised his hands defensively. 'Back up, man. You want to tell me what the fuck you're talking about?'

'Who was it, Michael? Who told you about Isaac Gangra?'

'Wait a minute – why are you asking me all these questions? You're not the police.'

'You'd prefer it if the police were here?' Jake said. 'Because believe me that can be arranged.'

Michael flopped back against his pillow and stared at the ceiling. 'He's just a cleaner. Chinese guy. Nightshift. I don't know his name.'

'What did he tell you?'

'He said he knew a dealer at Flamingo Creek who was looking to offload some Spitbush.'

'Why you, Michael? Why did he tell *you*?'

'How the hell should I know?'

Jake reached for the pulley holding Michael's plaster cast in the air and gave it a yank. The American squawked as his leg was lifted almost vertical to his body.

'Come on, son – we don't have time for this. If you want to help your pal, stop fucking around.'

'OK. OK – listen, maybe he helped me out with some supplies.'

'You mean drugs?'

'A little weed, maybe. Look, man, the docs say I'm going to be in here for at least two weeks. I'm going fucking crazy in here as it is.'

'So this cleaner is supplying your weed but you don't know his name?'

'I don't want to get the guy in trouble. He could lose his job and that's serious shit—'

Jake's hand moved over the pulley again. 'Alex is about to go down for murder, Michael. Now give me a name.'

'OK, OK,' Michael said. 'It's Jimmy.'

'Jimmy what?'

'I don't know his second name. I swear it! Please – put my leg down.'

Jake released Michael's cast. There was a sigh of relief.

'What's going to happen to Alex?' Michael said quietly.

'Why would you care?'

'Listen, man – I didn't mean for any of this shit to happen.'

Michael's eyes began to fill up, but Jake had already gone.

50

The official line was that Abdelbassir Hossein had received a black eye and two broken ribs while attempting escape from the prison van taking him to Kingorani jail on the other side of Mombasa island. The Moroccan dockhand was too frightened of another beating at the hands of Mugo's thugs to deny the claim. Having resigned himself to the fact he was going to prison for the murder of Lol Quarrie, he saw no reason to aggravate his dismal circumstances any further.

'Mugo said you confessed,' Jouma said. They were sitting in Hossain's tiny cell. A mean-eyed guard stared at them through the steel bars.

'Then I most surely did,' Hossain said dully.

'You either did or you didn't, Abdelbassir!'

The Moroccan looked at him dolefully with his one functioning eye. 'Does it matter?'

'Do you want to spend the rest of your life in prison? What about your wife? Your children?'

'What does she care? Mugo told her all about the whores. Now she thinks I am filth, and she has turned my children against me.'

'But you are the person who puts bread on the table for your family. How will they cope without you?'

He laughed harshly. 'My wife will cope. But it's not her I feel sorry for. It's the next man. Husbands don't visit whores unless they are driven to it, Inspector.'

Jouma looked at Abdelbassir Hossain and saw a man who had been crushed flat by life.

'You must remain strong, Abdelbassir,' he said, gripping the other man's hand. 'Everything will be resolved.'

The dockhand did not look up. Instead, he hawked once and spat a gobbet of bloodied saliva on to the dirt floor of his prison cell.

Upstairs in central police station, in a commandeered office belonging to the uniformed inspector, Oliver Mugo and the mayor's fixer Frederick Obbo were putting the final touches to a statement the detective planned to give to the press later that afternoon.

'Instead of "*Hossain is under arrest*", Inspector, might I suggest "*an evil killer is behind bars and the people of Mombasa can rest easy in their beds*"?'

Mugo fixed Obbo with a hard, uncomprehending stare. Then he burst out laughing and wrapped one bear-like arm around the skinny shoulders of the man from the mayor's office.

'"*Evil killer*"!' he exclaimed, bending over the desk and scribbling the amendment on to a sheet of type-written paper. 'I like it, Mr Obbo! I like it!'

'Except he's not a murderer, you stupid fool,'

Jouma snarled. He had been watching them from the doorway, waiting for his anger to subside before trusting himself to speak. He was breathing heavily after a furious march across town from Kingorani.

Even Mugo seemed taken aback by the interruption and by Jouma's expression, although this was only a momentary lapse before the self-assured smile returned to his face.

'Daniel! I heard you had gone home for your lunch. What did you have?'

Jouma's eyes blazed. 'What the devil do you think you are doing, Mugo? Hossain is no more a murderer than I am, and you know it!'

'I believe Detective Inspector Mugo has performed a great service for the people of Mombasa this day,' Obbo announced.

'I repeat,' Jouma said coldly, ignoring the fixer, 'what possible grounds do you have to charge Abdelbassir Hossain?'

'He confessed,' Mugo said matter-of-factly.

'You mean you *beat* a confession out of him.'

'Inspector Jouma!' Obbo exclaimed. 'You will withdraw that outrageous slur immediately.'

Mugo placed a restraining hand on Obbo's arm. 'It is all right, Frederick. I'm afraid that, since his great triumph in uncovering corruption in Mombasa, Inspector Jouma thinks the achievements of others are not worth considering.' He looked at Jouma with a barely disguised glint of victory in his eye. 'Now if you will excuse us, Daniel – we have much to do.'

Jouma ignored him. 'Does Simba know about this?'

'Superintendent Simba appreciates the seriousness

with which the mayor regards the solving of this case,' Obbo said.

There were certain Swahili words that were so offensive Jouma had never in his life said them. Now, unable to control himself any longer, he used three of the choicest to describe the man from City Hall, and Obbo's eyes almost popped out of their sockets.

This time, Mugo did not smile. 'I never took you for a jealous man, Jouma,' he said, his voice sorrowful. 'But it seems I was wrong.'

51

Jimmy Chen lived in a municipal hostel near the docks at Kilindini. He was twenty-six years old and had graduated from the University of Nairobi with a first-class degree in geospatial engineering four years ago, around the same time he developed a ruinous addiction to heroin. These days he worked as a cleaner at Mombasa Hospital because the pay was so derisory nobody cared if he was a smackhead or not as long as he turned up occasionally. The arrangement also suited Jimmy because it allowed him free access to the hospital pharmacy. By stealing and selling prescription drugs he was able to maintain his own expensive habit to a satisfactory level.

Jimmy worked nights. His shift usually finished around seven am, by which time he would be starting to twitch. His own dealer was the owner of a Cantonese restaurant on Biashara Street, just a few minutes' walk from the hospital. After shooting up, the two men would play mah-jong until Jimmy felt able to walk home. On a normal day, he would expect to be in his bed by eleven am. He would not expect to stir again until the irresistible nag for another fix woke him six hours later.

It was understandable, therefore, that, when he was dragged from the black pit of sleep by a hammering at the door shortly before two in the afternoon, Jimmy was not best pleased.

'Who the fuck is it?'

'Rent,' said a voice from the other side of the door.

'I paid,' Jimmy said.

'There's a problem. Open the door.'

'What sort of problem?

'Do you really want me to discuss it in the hallway, Mr Chen?'

Cursing and wearing only a pair of flimsy under-pants, Jimmy opened the door. A white man in shorts and T-shirt was standing in the corridor.

'I told you – I paid my rent,' Jimmy said grumpily. 'You've got the wrong address.'

The man smiled. 'I lied, Jimmy. I'm not here about the rent. I'm here about Mr Gangra.'

Jimmy froze and for a moment Jake thought he was going to make a bolt for it.

'You police?'

'You could say I'm an interested third party.'

Jimmy smiled. 'OK. Let me put some pants on, yeah?' he said.

Jake looked at his watch. 'You've got thirty seconds.'

Jimmy nodded gratefully and went back inside, leaving the door slightly ajar. Forty seconds later, when he had not reappeared, Jake burst into the apartment to find the window wide open and Jimmy Chen, now wearing jogging pants, bounding down the fire escape towards the alley two storeys below.

Cursing, Jake hooked his leg over the window frame and squeezed out on to the narrow iron landing. By the time he reached the alleyway Jimmy was sprinting towards the looming cranes and container stacks and refinery chimneys of the port. Jake, already puffing and blowing as he set off in pursuit, knew that if he made it to the maze of warehouses at the quayside then he would be gone for good.

'Jimmy!' he shouted, even though he knew his voice would be lost in the noise of traffic and industry coming from the port.

Jimmy was young and lithe, but he was also a junkie. By the time he reached the port gates he was already slowing up. He stopped and gripped his knees as he gasped for breath. Then he stood up straight and looked back along the street at his pursuer. For a split-second their eyes met, and in that instant Jimmy seemed to understand that if Jake had wanted him dead he would be dead already.

'I just want to know who—'

Neither of them saw the container lorry that swung out of the gate at a reckless speed until it was too late. The driver of the lorry, iPod 'phones jammed in his ears and amphetamines roaring in his veins, certainly never saw Jimmy Chen. One moment Jimmy was there, the next he was under the wheels. The speed of it was shocking.

Jake reached him before the screaming started.

'Who put you up to it, Jimmy?' he said, cradling the young man's head as he lay on the ground with his brains spilling out of a fist-sized hole in his skull. 'Who told you about Gangra?'

Jimmy stared up at him with his mouth working, but the only thing that came out was blood and in a very few moments his dark eyes clouded over. A small crowd of observers crossed themselves or muttered an incantation or did whatever their religion or their tribal belief dictated, then hurriedly went about their business.

The world turned again while Jake sat in the gutter with Jimmy Chen's blood all over his hands.

52

With a theatrical flourish Inspector Oliver Mugo burst through the doors of Mombasa central police station and strode down the steps towards a thicket of photographers, cameramen and reporters. He was wearing his best Hugo Boss suit and a gleaming yellow tie.

Hovering a discreet distance behind the detective's broad shoulders Frederick Obbo surveyed the lenses and microphones with barely concealed delight – for this was all his doing. His own career as a reporter with the *Daily Nation* may have lasted less than a year before he was seduced by the substantially larger salary offered by a leading Nairobi public relations company, but he still knew what excited the pack. And nothing got their juices flowing more than a high-profile murder, a larger-than-life detective and – most importantly – a fast result.

The mayor would be thrilled. This was precisely the kind of publicity coup Obbo had been employed to engineer. A new administration needed positive headlines in its difficult early days, especially when it had come to power promising to erase the memories of the corrupt regime that preceded it. And it had not been easy. Even the mayor had had reservations about bringing in Oliver Mugo, despite the fact the detective was his brother-in-law.

'But Oliver is an idiot,' he had confided in Obbo, out of earshot of his wife. 'Are you sure this is wise?'

Of course it was wise, Obbo thought, because Mugo was perfect. The detective's service record was an exemplary catalogue of miscarriages of justice obscured by rampant self-publicity. Time and again Mugo had proved that, as long as there was even the most tenuous shred of evidence to connect suspect with crime, he had absolutely no interest in whether the right man was behind bars. All that mattered was that the newspapers knew Mugo was the man who put him there.

As he studied the list of convicted felons from Mugo's days as a uniformed chief inspector in Malindi, Obbo saw how almost all of them were dirt-poor nonentities or educationally subnormal dupes without access to lawyers. His entire career was, in fact, a scandal. And, had Obbo an ounce of scruples himself, this would have been the story he would have fed to the press.

But corruption was old hat. People were sick of the same old story. What they wanted, after everything that had happened, was some *good* news for a change.

So now they had it. The resistance of Elizabeth Simba and the holier-than-thou Inspector Jouma had been dealt with. Mugo had been parachuted into the investigation, and *that very same day* an evil killer was behind bars.

What could be better than that?

And Mugo, Obbo had to admit, was good. There on the steps of the crumbling old police station, reading out the statement they had prepared together, he had the assembled media eating from the palm of his almost comically large hands.

Obbo felt like rubbing his own hands with glee — but he knew how unseemly such an expression of delight would seem coming from a representative of the mayor's office. At that moment his cell phone began to vibrate in the inside pocket of his suit. He removed it surreptitiously and glanced at the number on the display. It was the mayor, as he suspected it would be.

As he moved away to answer the call, this time Frederick Obbo allowed himself just a small expression of pleasure — a discreet fist pump inside the lining of his jacket that no one but the most eagle-eyed of photographers would ever have spotted.

'Good morning, sir,' he said. 'Yes — it *is* marvellous, isn't it?'

Jouma did not watch Mugo's televised triumph. His intention on leaving central police station had been to go straight to Mama Ngina Drive, to confront Simba, to let the superintendent know in no uncertain terms what he thought of her and her craven capitulation to the mayor's office. But as soon as he stepped out on to the street it was as if all his anger and frustration had leached the very marrow from his bones. He simply couldn't be bothered. Why bother to fight when Simba had proved herself powerless?

Instead, he found himself wandering in the direction of the Old Town, and for a while considered returning to the alleyway. But it was getting dark now, and not even detective inspectors in Mombasa CID ventured into such places at night. The manhole cover would have to wait until morning.

After an hour or so of aimless walking, Jouma found himself back at central police station, like a moth unable to resist the lure of a white hot flame. The last of the TV camera crews had packed away their equipment from in front of the building and the steps where Mugo had given his address were empty. With a sigh, he turned away and walked to where his car was parked on the street outside. Twenty minutes later, having missed the worst of the evening rush-hour traffic, he wearily climbed the stairs to his apartment overlooking the Makupa Causeway. He was now thinking about the boy, Alex Hopper, and how, to compound everything else that had happened, he was also guilty of harbouring a wanted felon.

Oh, this day was just getting better and better by the minute.

Turning the key in the lock he entered the apartment, and was cheered at least by the smell of his wife's cooking. It seemed a long time ago since he had left this place filled with such energy and hopefulness.

Jake was sitting at the kitchen table, his shirt covered in blood.

Jouma blinked. 'Where is Winifred?'

'She's out. Alex let me in. He's sleeping now. When he wakes up I'll take him back to the boatyard. He can hide out there tonight. In the morning I'll figure something out.'

'What *happened* to you?'

Jake told him about Jimmy Chen. His voice was empty.

Jouma sat down beside him. For a while neither man spoke. The only sound was the strangely comforting drone of traffic sweeping north out of the city.

'Were you questioned by the police?'

Jake shook his head. 'I left before they showed up. Thought it would be advisable.'

'Then you should go home.'

'And the boy?'

'Leave him. He will be safe here.'

'I don't want you to get involved—'

'I am already involved, Jake,' Jouma sighed. 'Leave the boy. Go home and get some rest. We will see what tomorrow brings.'

Day Six

53

Dawn had been and gone but it was still gloomy in the canyons of downtown Mombasa. Bobby Spurling emerged from the Anaconda Club on Digo Road with a giggling Lebanese dancer on his arm and stumbled into the back of the company limousine. As the girl frantically attempted to loosen his belt, Bobby leaned back his head and listened to the blood sloshing in his brain. It had been a good night after a long and tiresome day. And, for all Kenya's second city lacked the metropolitan cool of Jo'burg, he had to admit it was good to be back on his old stamping ground.

The evening had begun twelve hours earlier with a toot or two of high-grade coke at his apartment in the Old Town and half a dozen sharpeners at the yacht club. And, as the limo sped him across town to a succession of his favourite drinking holes, there had even been a flutter of excitement in his stomach that had nothing to do with the coke boiling in his system. For the first time it was beginning to sink in that he had made it; that he was no longer Clay

Spurling's son. He was *Bobby Spurling*, head of the company that bore his family name, one of the most influential men in Africa.

The sensation of power was almost dizzying.

The Anaconda was, as it always had been, the last stop of the night. Shortly before midnight the limo pulled up outside and Bobby tottered towards the entrance, where the red velvet rope had already been lifted in readiness.

'*Forgive me, Boss — spare some change?*'

Bobby whirled round indignantly – but he recoiled as he saw the creature that was tugging the sleeve of his silk Versace shirt. It was small and hunched, with some sort of knitted shawl over its head that partially hid a face that had been almost burned away, leaving a mask of purple scar tissue and a pair of lidless, staring eyes.

The creature extended a tin cup clutched in a blackened claw.

'*Please, Boss?*'

'Get this fucking freak away from me, for Christ's sake,' Bobby said, pushing past and into the sanctuary of the club.

Behind him one of the Anaconda's hulking doormen grabbed the creature and threw it unceremoniously into the gutter.

The club manager, a hand-wringing Indian spiv named Khan, shot across the lobby. 'Is everything all right, Mr Spurling, sir?'

'That ... *thing* just asked me for money, Mr Khan. What sort of establishment do you run here?'

'A thousand apologies, Mr Spurling, sir,' Khan grovelled.

Outside, the doorman was kicking the creature as

246

it scuttled away in the direction of an alleyway on the other side of the street. 'Please – allow me to take you to our most special table.' Khan quickly ushered Bobby towards a flight of stairs leading down into the club. 'And please – allow me to provide you with our finest champagne.'

'It's the very least I would expect,' Bobby said, secretly enjoying every minute of this encounter. Such a lapse of security would never have happened in Jo'burg, where the doormen were armed and the beggars had more sense than to badger the customers. But Khan's horrified reaction more than made up for it. It told Bobby what he needed to know – that he was a VIP at last. Looked up to. Admired. Feared.

Untouchable.

The Lebanese dancer had worked the belt buckle free and was now busily undoing his trousers. *Good luck to you*, Bobby thought. He was too far gone. Everything from his waist down was numb. *Was this what it was like to be paraplegic?* He worked the word in his mind as if it was chewing gum.

Pa-ra-ple-gic.

Ple-pa-gic-ra.

He laughed and the girl looked up. 'It tickles you?' she said.

'Oh, it tickles me all right.'

As the girl returned to her fruitless task, Bobby reached for a keypad set in the leather armrest. He jabbed one of the buttons and a TV set lowered from the ceiling. *Jab. Jab. Jab.* MTV. CNN. BBC.

Jab. Kenya TV. A newsreader's shiny head. The

247

mouth moving silently. Words scrolling across the screen. Pictures of politicians in ridiculous suits glad-handing African tribal leaders in ludicrous hats.

'Why the fuck doesn't the sound work, Alan?' he shouted.

'Electrical fault, sir,' said a disembodied voice from the sealed-off driver's section.

Bobby thought for a moment about blowing his top, but decided he simply couldn't be bothered. He was strung out. Stressed out. He needed a large brandy and a couple of Ambiens. He would feel better after a few hours' sleep.

'Where to, sir?' Alan asked, starting the limo's engines.

'My apartment,' Bobby said. Then: 'Wait a minute.'

The girl looked up. Her red lipstick was smeared. 'What is the matter, baby?'

'Go and get me a newspaper,' he said, pointing at a vending machine on the other side of the street dispensing that morning's edition of the *Daily Nation*.

'What?'

'You fucking heard me. Do you need some money?'

'I have money.' The girl pouted, straightened her hair and wriggled out of the car. Bobby watched disinterestedly as she pushed some coins into the machine.

'OK, Alan – let's get out of here.'

'Right away, sir.'

The limo pulled away, leaving the dancer standing shivering in her short dress and Jimmy Choos, cursing him in vivid Arabic.

Presently they reached Bobby's apartment building, a tall adobe structure overlooking the fort.

'Here you are, sir,' Alan said. 'You want me to wait for you?'

'No – I need to lie down,' Bobby said. 'I'll call you when I'm ready.'

'Very good, sir.'

Alan got out of the car and opened the rear doors. Bobby climbed out and, wincing in the sunlight, lurched towards the security gates guarding the entrance to the building from the busy street. The gates swung open and he disappeared inside the compound without looking back.

Alan got back behind the wheel and started the engine. He was at something of a loose end now. Old Mr Spurling, for whom he'd driven for the best part of twenty years, was regular as clockwork when it came to his hours. He would expect the car to be waiting outside the office at six o'clock in the evening, and outside the ranch house at six the following morning. Alan had the impression that young Bobby's hours would not be quite so predictable. He would have to have a word with Mr Roarke about his shifts. And his missus would not be too pleased about the new regime. She gave him enough earache about not being around as it was.

It was indeed a worry. But then at that moment Alan had no idea that on the other side of the security gates Bobby Spurling had already been abducted, and that when the news reached Douglas Roarke he would be out of a job anyway.

54

Harry looked up from his desk. He was not impressed – and for once it had nothing to do with the early hour.

'You have to be joking, old man,' he said.

'You know I'm not,' Jake said sullenly.

Harry jabbed his finger at the ledger in front of him. 'But we have two bookings today. Not to mention the two I had to cancel yesterday. That's—'

'I know, Harry. But there's nothing I can do about it.'

Harry stood and went to the office window. Through it he could peer directly across at the Flamingo Creek Yacht Club on the other side of the river. A young black cleaning girl was polishing the plate glass of the members' lounge window. Outside, on the deck, a gardener was watering sprays of frangipani that spilled down from the wooden roof gables.

'I still don't see why the hell you had to get yourself involved with these people,' he said. 'I mean, who do you think you are? Some sort of bloody crusader?

You're a fishing-boat skipper, Jakey-boy! You drive a bloody boat for a living! For *our* living! If you want to go off saving the planet then fine – but let me know so I can get someone else on board.'

'This is not about saving the world,' Jake said. 'It's about a kid who has been framed for murder.'

Harry whirled round angrily. 'If he's innocent then he should hand himself in.'

Jake stared at his partner. Harry was right, of course. The best chance Alex Hopper had of proving his innocence was to give himself up. Christ, his parents were surely rich enough to afford the calibre of lawyer who would tear these trumped-up charges to pieces. Yet every hour the kid spent on the run made the case against him stronger. Jake of all people knew that.

So why had he helped him? Was it because he felt sorry for him? Or because he had an innate mistrust of the Kenyan legal process to treat him fairly?

Or was it simply because he still regarded himself as a hot-shot cop from London who was still better than everyone else?

Yeah – well the demise of Jimmy Chen had fired a big hole in that particular fantasy. He still had the junkie's blood under his fingernails to prove it.

No, Harry was right. And so was Jouma. It was time Jake started acting like who he really was: Joe Q Public and not the Caped Crusader. This morning he would drive down to Mombasa, pick up Alex Hopper and hand him over to the authorities, making sure not to implicate Jouma in his own reck-less folly. The kid would be pissed off, for sure. But Jake would make sure he got a decent lawyer – and a few nights in Kingorani would do wonders for focusing his mind.

Unfortunately, that still meant rearranging that day's bookings.

'I'll make it up to you, Harry,' he said sheepishly.

Harry glowered. 'I thought *I* was supposed to be the liability in this partnership,' he said.

55

At the entrance to the Ndia Kuu alleyway Jouma pulled a pair of denim workman's overalls over his suit, gripped his torch and thought about an unremarkable-looking tree with edible pods and flowers called the moringa.

'Have you heard of it?' Christie had asked him over the phone that morning.

'I have heard of the moringa, certainly.'

It was eight o'clock and the pathologist had taken the almost unprecedented step of calling him at home – although his phone manner was as infuriatingly opaque as it was face-to-face.

'And what about spirochin?'

Jouma had looked across to the kitchen, where Winifred was fussing over Alex Hopper.

'Will you please get to the point! I am very busy.'

'Spirochin is an alkaloid found in the roots of the moringa tree,' Christie had explained. 'It is a particularly potent nerve agent that can cause temporary paralysis – although in larger doses it can kill.'

'What of it?'

'Traces of it were found in the blood of your man who fell from Fort Jesus. The analysis has just come back from the lab in Nairobi.'

'Traces? You mean he was poisoned?'

'Rendered immobile to be more accurate, Jouma. The effects, depending on the dosage, can last for several hours and take up to twenty-four hours to wear off. You say your man was seen to be unsteady on his feet?'

'The witness thought he was drunk.'

'Well, I would suggest he was most likely suffering the after-effects of being jabbed with a nerve agent. Spirochin is strong stuff. Bound to make you a bit wobbly on your feet.'

Then the pathologist had said, 'I took another look at the body. Not sure how I missed it first time – but just behind the right knee there was a tiny puncture mark. Your boy was injected, my friend.'

It was not often Christie was the bringer of glad tidings – but as he switched on his torch and entered the alleyway Jouma reflected that it was the best news he had heard in a long time.

Beside him stood a burly uniformed constable from central station. The two men looked down at the heavy circular manhole cover.

'Lift it, Nambu,' Jouma said.

The officer hunkered down and, with considerable effort, heaved the cover to one side. Jouma knelt beside him and shone his torch into the circular abyss. He saw a rusting access ladder descending to an equally decrepit metal sewer pipe running cross-ways in the north–south direction of the alley. He wondered what it would be like to look all the way along this pipe, right into the very heart of Mombasa island itself, the way Christie might explore the arteries of a dead patient. What would he see? He imagined it clogged with disease, with malignant, inoperable tumours feeding off it, sucking it of life.

'Wait here, Constable,' he said.

Constable Nambu looked at him in astonishment. 'You don't want me to go down, sir?'

Jouma shook his head. 'This is CID business,' he said. 'I won't be long.'

Tying a handkerchief over his nose and mouth, he gingerly began to descend into the sewer – and it was not long before he felt dank, fetid air against his face.

56

A rat was climbing up Bobby Spurling's bare chest. Its jagged claws were digging into his plump flesh for purchase. Bobby, who was kneeling on a hard stone floor with his hands tied above his head, was keeping as still as he possibly could – which was difficult when every tentative step the rodent took was like someone stubbing out a cigarette on his skin.

His prison was pitch black. Feeling the rat's damp, wiry fur against his body was bad – but what was worse was that he couldn't see it. It could be huge, with enormous yellow fangs. And now it was sniffing at his neck with its icy nose.

Jesus – what was happening to him?

Again and again he played out the events of that morning in his mind. He remembered leaving the club. He remembered the Lebanese girl at the news-paper-vending machine and getting back to his apartment building. He even remembered taking a piss against an orange tree outside the door.

After that, he remembered nothing. Nothing, that is, until he woke up here. Wherever *here* was.

Had he been drugged? Bobby was not averse to using Rohypnol or GHB to spike girls' drinks in order to get them into his bed – but had someone done the same to him? It barely seemed credible.

So what the hell had happened?

The rat climbed up on to Bobby's shoulder. He could hear the obscene smack of its jaws and the waft of its rancid breath. He gagged, but knew that if he was sick it was bound to attract God knows how many of the fucking things from the dank corners of his prison.

Then the rat sank its fangs into his earlobe and he screamed.

'*You should not be afraid,*' said a grating, inhuman voice from somewhere in the darkness. '*Rats much prefer dead meat to live flesh.*'

'Who's that?' Bobby cried out, and the rodent leaped off his shoulder.

'*They are also incredibly hard to kill. Drop one fifty feet and it will survive. Throw it in the ocean and it will swim to safety. Burn down its nest and it will burrow underground to escape the flames.*'

'What do you want? Money?'

'*I don't want your money. Money won't bring back what I have lost.*'

There was a scraping noise and Bobby flinched as a match was struck near his face. A moment later a tumbler-sized oil lantern sputtered to life, and as his eyes slowly adjusted to its weak glow he saw his prison for the first time. He was in what appeared to be a narrow, square tunnel of mould-covered brick. It was high enough for him to kneel, with his head bowed and his hands tied to some sort of hook behind his neck, but from this position he could see only a few feet ahead.

He also realised, with a sickening jolt, that he was naked.

'Where am I?'

A voice from the shadows behind him said, '*Does it matter?*'

Bobby tried without success to rotate his body, but his hands were fixed too close to the ceiling. 'At least tell me why I'm here,' he pleaded.

'*You are here because you deserve to be here. In the darkness. In fear. In pain.*'

Bobby was close to tears. 'I'm sorry ... I'm so sorry.'

'*For what?*'

'For whatever it is I have done.'

'*You don't even know what you have done. You have never cared about the consequences of your actions, because you care only about yourself.*'

He nodded, tears and snot mingling on his face. 'You're right. I am a selfish person. I always have been. *But I can change.*'

'*Can you? Can you really?*'

'I swear it. All I need is a second chance, that's all. Please – you have to give me a second chance.'

For a while there was only unnerving silence. Then someone grabbed his hair and yanked his head back agonisingly so that now he could see straight ahead of him down the tunnel.

'*That's what* she *said too*,' said the voice in his ear, and the stinking breath was worse than any rat.

In the dim light of the lantern, he could see what was hanging from a hook on the ceiling no more than ten feet away, like some grotesque mirror image. It was a body. It was covered in dried blood. And it was very dead.

57

Jouma was five feet five inches tall. The sewer pipe had a diameter of just three feet, making it only just possible for him to crawl on his hands and knees through a good two inches of dark, stinking residue, using his elbows to gain some sort of forward momentum against the sheer metal walls. Time and again his instinct was to sit up, and each time he did he was punished with a painful smack on the back of his head. On more than one occasion the torch dropped into the slime, forcing him to halt his painful progress and rummage for it with his fingers. He could feel cold liquid seeping through the denim overalls and he didn't dare to think of the irreversible damage that was being done to his suit trousers. They may have been through half a dozen previous owners since they were tailored in Jermyn Street in London, but they had lasted Jouma for the best part of five years without so much as a split seam. They did not deserve this abuse for their loyalty.

He had no idea how far he had come, or even in

which direction he was going. In fact, there was only one thought in his mind.

You are in a sewer.

One that is used by over half a million people.

It was quite possible that, any moment now, he could be washed away by a tidal wave of effluent.

Jouma inched his way forward, wedging his feet and his forearms against the metal walls of the pipe. His muscles were beginning to scream now, and his elbows and ankles had already been rubbed raw. Ahead the torch beam showed an apparently endless length of pipe.

This was stupid. He was going nowhere, and he had no idea how much breathable air there was left.

But then he heard a scream.

'*Scream all you want. Nobody will hear you.*'

Bobby sucked in a deep breath in an attempt to control his breathing.

'Who ... who is it?' he uttered, staring at the ... *thing* dangling from its hook like a side of butchered meat.

'*Someone else from my past who thought that begging for forgiveness would make everything all right.*'

'At least let me see you! How can I begin to understand what I've done if you won't show your face?'

'*You want to see my face?*'

'Yes. For God's sake – if you're going to kill me anyway, what does it matter?'

'*Very well.*'

His captor's hands gripped his shoulders and, with one swift tug, spun him round one hundred and eighty degrees on the axis of his bound hands – and Bobby screamed again, this time in agony, as the skin of his wrists ripped open.

But now he could see his tormentor, sitting hunched in the tunnel like the rat that had been crawling on him. And, as one claw-like hand removed the cowl that covered its features, Bobby recoiled. It was a face he had seen, only fleetingly, just a few hours ago outside the Anaconda Club.

'*Forgive me, Boss. Spare some change?*'

Was that what this was all about? he wondered frantically. Because he'd told the beggar to fuck off? Because some bouncer had kicked the shit out of him? If so, the punishment seemed inordinately extreme for the crime. Then he thought about the abomination dangling from its hook behind him, and wondered what *its* crime had been.

'Listen,' he said. He was snivelling freely now. 'Can't we talk about this?'

'*You may have noticed I find talking difficult,*' the creature rasped.

'I'd had a bad day. My old man had just died. I wasn't thinking straight. Normally I always give money to beggars. I'm sorry if you were upset. I am truly, truly sorry.'

The creature stared at him with dark lidless eyes, then laughed. '*You think that is what this is about? A few shillings in a beggar's cup? You are even more arrogant than I thought.*'

Twenty yards further on he found it: a large metal plate that had been riveted to the wall of the pipe, presumably to replace a section of the original that

262

had eroded away. Except, whether by accident or design, most of the rivets were missing. Those that were left loosely held the plate in place along one edge, like the binding of a folder. It meant that, when the sewer was being used, the force of the onrushing effluent would keep the plate pinned to the wall. But, when it was not, there was a small gap where the metal had buckled outwards slightly. It was through this gap that he could hear distant voices.

Jouma tugged, trying to prise the plate away from the wall of the pipe. To his relief he found it was flimsy and opened out enough for him to squeeze his head and shoulders through.

Now he saw uneven brickwork in the torch beam, and, as he lifted his head, a gently sloping, rectangular shaft rising a few feet to a plateau. This tunnel was clearly much older than the pipe; whole sections of its brick lining had collapsed to reveal chisel marks, suggesting it had been physically hewn from the coral on which the island was built. It was also dry and musty, which suggested it had not been used for many years.

The tiny detective wriggled through from the pipe and slumped against the stone. He estimated he had travelled a hundred yards from the manhole, a distance he would cover on foot in less than thirty seconds. Checking the luminous dial of his watch, he saw it had taken the best part of thirty minutes.

Catching his breath he saw that beyond the plateau, where the shaft straightened out, there was feeble light.

★

'*Remember the two pretty flowers by the roadside? Jasmine and Rose?*'

Bobby Spurling's blood froze. 'Oh, God ... '

'*It was such a beautiful morning. Do you remember?*'

'You? But it can't be— '

'*And then you came along and spoiled everything.*'

'I – I can help you. I can get you treatment, anything you need.'

His captor emitted a cackle of derision. '*You can help me? It is because of you that I look like this!*'

'Please don't kill me.'

'*I'm not going to kill you. Not yet. Why should I let you escape so lightly? I want you to think long and hard about the suffering you have caused others.*'

'But I will, I promise,' Bobby gabbled. 'I'll turn myself in, tell the police everything. They'll lock me up like I deserve. Just let me go. I won't tell anyone about you.'

'*But that would require a conscience. And that is the one thing all your money cannot buy.*'

'You have to believe me, I didn't know anything about what happened,' Bobby said, feeling faint as the blood from his wounded wrists flowed down his arms.

'*If it hadn't been for you, none of this would have happened.*'

Bobby stared at the razor-sharp teeth of the knife that had appeared from the folds of the creature's cloak, then he squawked in horror as one of the creature's leathery claws reached out and grabbed his shrivelled scrotum. He felt the cold metal against his skin.

'*How many other lives have you ruined with this? They should have cut it off at birth.*'

264

His vision swam and, although his mouth was open to scream, no sound would come out.

'*Another thing about rats is that they will eat anything. And, once they've got a taste for it, they always look for more.*'

'Please,' Bobby said weakly, and there was a splash as he soiled himself.

Then a voice from the darkness said, 'Police! Stop where you are!'

And Bobby Spurling passed out.

58

Jake drove to Makupa feeling like he was about to deliver the kiss of Judas. He was relieved that when he knocked on Jouma's door neither the inspector nor his wife was at home, because after everything they had done he didn't want them to witness his betrayal of Alex Hopper.

'Hey, man,' the hippie kid said, opening the door. He was much changed from the pathetic specimen washed up on *Yellowfin* the other day. Sleep, soap and water, and Winifred Jouma's home cooking had restored the colour to his face and his shoulders no longer sagged with despair.

But what Jake said next sent him crashing back to square one in an instant.

'I have to hand you in, Alex.'

Fat tears of fear and disbelief filled Alex's eyes and he physically backed away, like a child who has just been informed he has to go to the dentist to have his wisdom teeth removed.

'It's for the best, son,' Jake said, and tried to explain his change of heart. 'I can't just dump you on Jouma.

I've made this my problem, and so I've got to deal with it.'

Alex was having none of it. The tears soon gave way to bitter recrimination. Jake had been expecting it and was prepared to let the boy get it out of his system – but then, as the vituperation washed over him, he suddenly tired of all this shit. He'd done more than enough for this kid. Harry was right. It wasn't *his* fucking problem.

The back of his hand connected once with Alex's mouth and the hippie was immediately silent.

'Get your fucking gear,' Jake said. 'We're leaving.'

As arranged, Evie Simenon was waiting outside central police station when they got there thirty minutes later. She had risked her neck biking it down from Jalawi on the hippies' clapped-out 125 Suzuki. She immediately ran up to Alex and hugged him. Jake was expecting more tears, but the boy was beyond self-pity now. He just stood there looking shell-shocked.

'Do you want to hand him over, or shall I?' Jake asked her.

'I'll do it,' she said.

Jake lit a cigarette and waited on the steps. When Evie emerged from the station, pale faced, he crushed the butt under his shoe.

'You all right?'

She looked at him. 'Why are they doing this to us, Jake?'

'Because you're in their way. And because they're bigger than you.'

She nodded, as if he had finally confirmed something she had always known but never had the courage to admit. Then, abruptly, she stopped and shrieked an obscenity at the clear blue sky. When she looked at him again, there were tears in her eyes. She looked, Jake thought, as if she had finally reached the end of the road.

'You heading back?' he asked her.

She shook her head. 'There are some people I have to see,' she said quietly. 'Campaigners from Nairobi. They say they know people who might be able to—'

'For God's sake, Evie!' Jake exclaimed.

'Well, what do you want me to do?' she snapped, eyes blazing. 'Give up? I'm not like you, Jake. I can't just go back to being a fishing-boat skipper. This is what I am.'

After a while he sighed. 'I'll make sure Alex is treated OK,' he said. 'And he's given me a number where I can reach his parents.'

'Thank you,' Evie said.

And then she was gone.

59

For five hundred years the Portuguese soldiers, Omani Arabs and, in later years, prisoners of the British Empire who occupied Fort Jesus had just one thing in common – and that was the rudimentary sewage system that flushed their shit from the garderobes on the west ramparts along a series of connected stone channels to a spillage outlet in the walls overlooking the harbour. In the late nineteenth century, British engineers modified and expanded this system into a labyrinth of brick tunnels beneath the fort that extended the city's main sewer beyond the city walls. In the 1950s, when the prison was shut down and the fort turned into a museum, its Victorian sewer system was decommissioned, the garderobes became a talking point for tourists and the service entrance to the tunnels, close to the San Felipe bastion, was bricked over and forgotten about.

It had taken a workman with a pneumatic drill less than a minute to break open the seal to reveal, for the first time in fifty years, an access chamber carved from the rock foundations on which the fort was built. The chamber was perhaps five feet square, with a reinforced wooden hatch on the floor through which water would have been poured to sluice the system when it became blocked or the stench became unbearable.

This was the creature's lair.

From here, through the hatch, it was free to roam Mombasa's modern sewer system via the disused tunnels under the fort. It was the perfect hiding place, because nobody knew it was here. After fifty years even the museum curator had forgotten the Victorian tunnels existed.

'It would appear the victims were immobilised with an injection of nerve agent before being bundled into the sewer through manholes,' Jouma said. 'They were then dragged into the tunnels beneath the fort where they were ...'

'Strung up and tortured,' Superintendent Simba said.

'That would seem to have been the plan, ma'am.'

'It worked for the Jalawi nun. And, if it hadn't been for you, I have no doubt Mr Spurling would have suffered a similar fate. But what about Mr Quarrie? I take it the boy this furniture-maker spoke of—'

'—must have been the creature. Old Mr Mukhtar must have seen it as it lured Mr Quarrie into the alleyway. There it injected him and abducted him into the sewer.'

'And the *clank* noise?'

'The manhole cover being replaced.'

'This ... *creature* must be incredibly strong.'

Jouma thought about the tiny, rat-like thing he had seen for a split-second before it scuttled away

270

into the darkness. 'Or incredibly determined,' he said. 'Like Mr Quarrie.'

Having been down in those hellish tunnels himself, Jouma could only marvel at Quarrie's survival instinct. In the pitch black and suffering the debilitating effects of spirochin toxin, the retired RUC man must have nevertheless crawled around in the maze for hours until the faint waft of fresh air led him to a section behind the bunkhouses where clumsy renovation work had caused the Victorian brickwork to cave in. Tearing at the hard-packed rubble with his fingers, Quarrie had somehow managed to burrow his way to freedom.

It was almost unbearable to imagine him staggering on to the ramparts, calling for help that never came, before losing his footing and plunging to his death.

'What are we dealing with here, Daniel?' Simba sighed.

'I don't know, ma'am.'

The two detectives peered down into the access chamber. From what they could see, the creature's needs were few. A blanket, a little bread and dried meat, a skin of water and a litre of kerosene for the lamps. There was also a raffia bag stuffed with dried herbs and bark, as well as earthenware finger pots containing various glutinous and pungent potions. Scientific tests would confirm the nature of these substances, as would toxicity tests on the blood of Bobby Spurling. The rat-eaten remains of Sister Gudrun were too far gone for anything other than a quick and decent Christian burial.

'How were the victims chosen?' Simba asked.

'There is no clear link between them,' Jouma

admitted. 'I would suggest that to solve that riddle we must first find out the creature's identity.'

'The Spurling boy did not recognise his captor?'

'He is still in a state of profound shock, ma'am.'

Simba looked at him, and there was concern on her face. 'And what about you, Daniel?'

Several hours had passed since he had stumbled upon Bobby Spurling in the tunnel, and Jouma was still wearing his filthy overalls. There had been no time to change, no time to even *think* about what had happened – which was a good thing, because it had kept him from dwelling on what he had confronted in that hellish underground torture chamber.

The image of Bobby Spurling, naked and blood-ied in the guttering kerosene light, and suspended at an excruciating angle from a hook in the ceiling of the tunnel, was one that kept trying to sear itself on his brain. But Jouma knew he could not let it, other-wise it would drive him mad.

Down there, in the darkness, he had focused solely on the practicalities. The creature that had done this to Spurling, and to the horribly mouldering corpse suspended just a few yards further along the tunnel, had disappeared into the darkness, agile as a rodent in the confined space. It would not be back, of that Jouma was sure. Not now that its sordid killing ground had been discovered.

But that still left the problem of getting Bobby Spurling back along the sewer to safety.

The slightest touch set him off into paroxysms of frantic screaming, and Jouma had realised why the creature had chosen to first paralyse his victims. It took several minutes to convince the boy he was safe, many more to reason with him that the only way out of the tunnel was to crawl back along the sewer Jouma had come. Somehow the inspector managed to urge Bobby inch by inch to safety, the boy whimpering with pain from his wounded wrists and from the chafing stone and metal against his bare skin. When they finally arrived at the manhole exit what seemed like a lifetime later, and were hauled above ground by the horrified Constable Nambu, Jouma had never tasted anything as sweet as the ripe, stinking air of the alleyway.

After that Jouma had been a spectator as a hastily assembled task force, armed with sanitation department plans and the most up-to-date archaeological diagrams of the Fort Jesus tunnel system, systematically set about scouring the sewer systems for anything else that may be lurking there. It was they who had discovered the creature's lair, they who had traced the last, desperate movements of Lol Quarrie. And it was they who were now bringing Sister Gudrun's ravaged corpse to the surface.

'I take it this exonerates Abdelbassir Hossain, ma'am,' Jouma said.

Simba's shoulders sagged slightly, as if it was a question she had been waiting for and dreading at the same time.

'Completely,' she said quietly.

'And Mugo?'

She stared down into the terrible pit where the creature's scant belongings lay like exhibits in the Fort Jesus museum. 'Mugo is my problem, Daniel,' she said. 'The creature is yours.'

60

In a room in a private hospital less than half a mile away, Bobby Spurling was sitting up in bed with both wrists encased in gauze bandages.

'What is the point of a security division, Mr Roarke, if it can't even keep the chairman of the company safe?' he demanded, his voice rising close to hysterical.

It was a question he had been expecting yet Douglas Roarke, standing with his shoulders pinned back and his eyes fixed on the medical chart at the foot of Bobby's bed, had no answer.

'You will, of course, have my resignation on your desk first thing in the morning, Mr Spurling, sir.'

'Resignation? I don't want your fucking resignation! Don't you understand? That fucking *thing* is still out there. My life is in danger. *It was going to cut my balls off for the rats to gnaw on!*'

'There is a guard on your door and I have tripled your security detail,' Roarke said. 'Nobody will be able to come within fifty feet of you, night or day, without us knowing about it.'

'I don't *want* a tripled security detail!' Bobby shouted. 'I want that freak liquidated! Have you got any idea what would happen if the police found it alive? If it told them what it knows?'

'Of course, Mr Spurling, sir.'

Bobby shook his head in disbelief at the last twenty-four hours of his life. 'I had to play catatonic to get out of talking to the police today,' he exclaimed. 'But they'll be back. And it won't take them long to work out the connection.'

'I can assure you they won't, sir,' Roarke said.

'Then you'd better sort this mess out right away, because I'm getting out of here – and I don't intend to spend the rest of my life looking over my shoulder, understand?'

Roarke understood perfectly. Five years he had been head of the division. Five years of frustration, bowing to old man Spurling's conservative instincts. Now that he had his big chance to prove himself – to prove that his philosophy was the only way forward – he was damned if he was going to blow it.

What *did* concern the security chief, however, was that that no sooner was Clay Spurling dead than everything he touched seemed to turn to shit. It was, he reflected unhappily, a truly absurd run of bad luck. He shook his head. *Christ!* His job was fighting fires – but right now it seemed that every time he stamped on one flame another blew up in his face.

As his SUV swept him away from the hospital, he looked across at the police vehicles and ambulances still parked outside Fort Jesus, where they'd been ever since Bobby had been manhandled, naked and bleating, from the disused sewers beneath the fort. The abduction was a headache, make no mistake, and one which could yet come back to bite him in the arse. But at least it had helped to briefly take his mind off other pressing concerns piling up in his in-box.

Like his plan to discredit the Flamingo Creek hippies, it would have worked like a fucking charm had the men he had instructed to carry out this simple task not failed so dismally. And they had the nerve to call themselves experienced ex-soldiers! His own grandmother could have made a better fist of killing a defenceless old man and an unarmed kid.

To make matters worse he'd learned that someone had been sniffing around Jimmy Chen yesterday. Was it a cop? If so, why was he so interested in Jimmy? *More to the point, what had that junkie fucking slope told him before he'd been so conveniently flattened by a truck?*

Roarke shook his head. There was no point getting paranoid. What was required was cool, rational problem solving. As soon as he got back to the office he would put one of his crack operatives to work finding out just who this bozo was. Then he would order another of his best men to take care of the problem of William Fearon, the fat company CEO who was threatening to cause all sorts of inconvenience to the company if he didn't get his way.

The SUV moved forward in the traffic then stopped again, and, as it did so, Douglas Roarke angrily jabbed a number into his cell phone. *What was the point of waiting to get back to the office?* It was time for action. The sooner he started solving one set of problems, the sooner he could concentrate on the next.

61

In Mombasa they say that if you are a rat you are never more than five feet from a human being. Others who are less charitable point out that there are two type of vermin in the city – those with four legs and those with two.

Detective Constable David Mwangi would never have known that a whole sub-species of Mombasan society was living beneath his feet had Jouma not enlightened him. He would certainly have had no idea how to tempt them to the surface.

'Think of it in terms of fishing,' Jouma said, dropping a hundred-shilling note into a storm drain on the corner of Nkrumah Road and Ndia Kuu Road, a few hundred yards from Fort Jesus. 'Bait your hook with an appetising morsel, and you will soon catch something.'

Mwangi looked at his boss. Considering the unspeakable ordeal he had been through that day, Jouma seemed remarkably upbeat. *Chipper* almost. But perhaps that was the only way to deal with such dreadful events. That and police work. And Jouma had been quick to remind him that, even though the unfortunate Sister Gudrun's body had been found, the mystery of her disappearance was far from over.

The inspector knelt and used a stone to secure a second hundred-shilling bill on the lip of the drain so that it dangled invitingly over the hole.

'Now we wait,' he said.

They did not have to wait long. Barely a minute had passed before a thin hand emerged from the gutter. As the fingers closed around the bill, Jouma's foot stamped on it, pinning it fast. There was a howl of pain that seemed to come from the very bowels of the earth.

'Pull him up, Mwangi,' Jouma said.

Aware that people were stopping to stare, Mwangi reached down and with both hands reached into the drain. He grabbed an arm and began pulling.

'Be careful. They can bite.'

Jouma lifted his shoe and between the two of them they hauled their wriggling catch out of the storm drain and on to the street. It was a small boy, no more than six years old and thin as a pencil. He was wearing a T-shirt and hand-me-down jeans two sizes too big for him.

'What is your name?' Jouma asked him.

'Fuck off.'

'I will ask you one more time. If you persist with shouting obscenities I will send you to the correctional house at Likoni.'

'You can't do that. I have done nothing wrong.'

'I am Detective Inspector Daniel Jouma of Mombasa CID. I can do anything. Now – what is your name?'

The boy mumbled something.

'Louder, boy. I did not hear you.'

'Geoffrey.'

'Geoffrey what?'

'Geoffrey Kono.'

'And who do you work for?'

'Fuck off!'

'Sergeant Mwangi, I want you to take this boy to the correctional facility at Likoni immediately.'

'Mr Tumbai,' the boy sighed.

Jouma winked at Mwangi. 'They *all* work for Mr Tumbai,' he said. 'Mr Tumbai is probably one of the biggest employers in Mombasa.' He turned back to the boy. 'Very well, Geoffrey Kono. I want you to tell Mr Tumbai that I wish to see him at the central police station in one hour. Tell him that, if he is not there, then I will personally come down into that drain to look for him. Tell him that Mombasa Police are very keen to crack down on shoplifting and pickpocketing in the Old Town, and out of sight does not mean out of mind. Do you understand?'

'Yes.'

'Yes what?'

'Yes, sir.'

Jouma released the boy and he disappeared back into the drain.

Mwangi looked shell-shocked. 'The boy *lives* down there?'

'Mwangi,' Jouma said, 'you have no *idea* how some people live in this city.'

62

One hour later Early Tumbai, the king rat of the Mombasa sewers, sat in the interview room and regarded Jouma with an air of supreme indifference. According to his lengthy police record he was forty-five years old, but he looked twenty years older. He had a shaven head and bad skin. He was dressed in army-issue combat fatigues and was wearing an expensive pair of sunglasses – stolen to order, no doubt – to protect his weak eyes from the single sodium tube on the ceiling. He stank of damp earth and decay.

'You're looking well, Mr Tumbai,' Jouma said.

Early smiled. He had two teeth, and even these clung to his gums in a state of imminent collapse. 'Just tell me what you want.'

'I want to know who has been dragging people into the sewers and killing them.'

Early did not flinch. 'Why are you asking me?'

'Because you know every inch of those sewers and every person who lives down there. And because, if you don't tell me, I will have to assume you are implicated in these murders.'

Early Tumbai rolled his eyes behind the expensive lenses. 'Why is it that whenever a body is found in the sewers it is somehow my fault? Do I accuse *you* of murder every time someone is found dead on the surface?'

Jouma stared at him. It was a fair point. Early's sewer rats had a bad reputation precisely because of where they chose to live. In fact, most had retreated underground because they were too poor to live above it. In the sewers there was no rent, and excrement wasn't the only commodity that was flushed down its network of pipes.

'The person I am looking for appears to have suffered burns,' he said.

'What sort of burns?'

'Very bad burns,' Jouma said. 'Most of his face has gone.'

'Sounds nasty. But I have not seen anyone fitting that description.'

'The person I am looking for has also been hiding in the tunnels under Fort Jesus.'

'Those tunnels have not been used for years,' Early pointed out.

'I know.'

'You sure you are not trying to trick me, Inspector Jouma? Because I do not like to be tricked.'

'This is no trick, Mr Tumbai,' Jouma said. 'This is deadly serious.'

Early sighed. 'Very well. I will make some enquiries. But I do not promise anything, and I do not expect to be persecuted. In fact, these enquiries will most certainly affect my normal business . . . '

He held out his hand expectantly.

Jouma took it and shook it vigorously. 'I commend your public-spiritedness, Mr Tumbai. I shall be certain to tell my superintendent how helpful you have been.'

Jouma left the station and returned to his Fiat Panda, which was parked untidily on a kerb nearby. Bringing Early Tumbai in for questioning was a legitimate move, but he doubted it would advance the investigation one iota. If the king rat knew anything he would have coughed up the information, because his primary concern was keeping the police off his back. But at this stage any possibility was worth exploring, because the key to this case was finding out the identity of the creature.

At least, he reflected, there was one ray of light to be had in this dark, dark day. Indeed, despite his ordeal there was a spring in Jouma's step as he approached the forbidding entrance to Kingorani jail.

But the moment he stepped through the heavy steel doors into the floodlit concrete yard, he knew something was wrong. He saw it in the faces of the *askari* at the guardhouse and in the averted gaze of the corporal who led him, not to the secured holding wing where Abdelbassir Hossain was being held, but to the office of the prison warden.

'Inspector Jouma,' the warden said, shaking his head. He was a careworn man who had been through this same scenario a thousand times and had long learned to disassociate himself from it.

'When?' Jouma demanded.

The warden gazed at the grey, utilitarian carpet at his feet. 'He was found fifteen minutes ago.'

'How did it happen?' Jouma said.

'I assure you all precautions were taken, Inspector. But it would appear he simply . . .'

Jouma felt the energy seep out of him. 'Where is he now?'

'He is still in his cell. The prison doctor is examining the body.'

'Take me there.'

He followed the warden across the compound and into the sooty, stinking prisoner wing.

'I gave express instructions that he was to be placed on round-the-clock surveillance,' Jouma said.

The warden shrugged, as if to say '*What did you expect?*'

The two men walked on, each step taking them deeper into the prison. Presently they came to Abdelbassir Hossain's cell. A large pool of dark blood had soaked into the dirt floor and oozed between the bars and into the corridor. The boots of panicked men had trailed it almost as far as the metal security door at the far end.

The dockhand was lying on his back. His face was covered in fresh blood, as was his filthy prison-issue uniform. The prison doctor, a bibulous white sawbones from a downtown surgery, was kneeling over the body and he looked up as Jouma stepped into the cell.

'What happened?'

'You wouldn't believe it if I told you, Inspector.'

'Try me.'

With a grunt and a cracking of arthritic knees, the doctor got to his feet. Jouma could now see that, while one of Hossain's sightless eyes was open and fixed on the ceiling, the other was little more than a dripping bag of bloody fluid seeping from its socket.

'Took me a while to work it out, I have to say.'

The doctor had moved across to the wall opposite the cell bars. Against the wall was Hossain's bunk, and above this was a window made up of thick mosaic squares of translucent glass that allowed watery light to pass into the cell. The doctor pointed at the window, where, upon closer examination, one of the glass cubes was stained with blood.

'The poor chap deserves full marks for ingenuity at the very least.'

Jouma stepped up on to the bunk for a closer look at the window. Now he saw it: a six-inch needle of rusted metal which had been prised from the window frame and bent so that it stuck straight out.

'It penetrated the left eye and went straight into his brain,' said the doctor. 'Normally that would be sufficient to kill him – but the damage to the eyeball suggests that it didn't work first time. I'd say he had two, maybe three attempts before he struck lucky.'

The inspector felt sick. *Struck lucky?* He looked down at the body of Abdelbassir Hossain and wondered just what level of despair and hopelessness could possibly drive a man to end his life in such a way. But then anger welled up inside him again, and instead of the Moroccan dockhand's face all he could see was the grinning visage of Oliver Mugo announcing his triumph on live television – and in doing so condemning an innocent man to death.

Day Seven

63

William Fearon, until very recently CEO of Spurling Developments, was woken by the sea breeze flapping the bedroom curtains, the sun playing on his face, and his lover's hand gently massaging his erection. He smiled blissfully and rolled on to his side.

'Hello, you,' he said.

'*Hola, papa.*'

The boy's name was Isidro and he was a twenty-two-year-old barman at an Old Town strip club called the Baobab. Meeting him had, for Fearon, been the only pleasant thing about his visit to the club eight months ago. Drug-addled whores wrapped around metal poles did nothing for him – but he had been in the business long enough to know that the client was always right. And on this occasion the client happened to be a provincial government official with the final say over a lucrative tract of land for sale south of Malindi. While the official gawped, Fearon ordered overpriced champagne and fell in love.

Isidro expertly brought the older man to orgasm,

then slinked off to the shower leaving Fearon wheezing and wishing he was thirty years younger and a hundred pounds lighter.

'What time do you start work?' he called

'One thirty,' Isidro shouted over the thunder of water.

'But it's not even nine.'

'I want to hit the shops first.'

'I'll give you a lift if you like.'

The boy returned to the bedroom, rubbing his lustrous black hair with a towel. Fearon propped himself on one arm and allowed his gaze to linger on the taut, dripping muscles of Isidro's abdomen.

'Maybe we could have lunch together.'

'You know something, *amado*?' Isidro said, examining himself in the full-length mirror on the wardrobe door. 'I think I liked you better when you had a job. You weren't in my face so much.'

'I still have a job,' Fearon reminded him.

'Yeah? Then how come you don't go there no more?'

'It's a long story.'

Isidro wriggled into a pair of faded denim jeans. He turned and smiled coquettishly. 'Well, I hope it finish soon. I don't like to see you all tensed up like this. I want my big happy *papa* back.'

'Come here.'

The boy went across to the bed and stood obediently as Fearon ran his plump fingers across his chest and down to where a thick line of hair trailed from his navel into the open buttons of his jeans.

'You really are quite exquisite.'

Isidro giggled and bent down to peck the older

man on the cheek. 'You should get up, *amado*,' he said, pulling on a white sleeveless T-shirt and a pair of espadrilles. 'Go somewhere nice for the day.'

'Do you *have* to go to work?' Fearon said, flopping back on to his pillows.

'Well, *one* of us does, baby.' With that Isidro fastened his leather belt – the one with the metal American eagle buckle that Fearon had bought him on their Easter trip to Disneyworld – and left the room.

Of course he was right, Fearon thought, staring at the ceiling fan that revolved lazily above his head. The situation with Bobby Spurling was no excuse for torpor, even if the matter was in the hands of the lawyers. After twenty years at the coal face, maybe this *was* an opportunity to broaden his scope a little. It was only after taking a small step backwards that he realised how institutionalised he had become working for Spurling Developments. Twelve- and even fourteen-hour days had become the norm. Apart from Isidro he had no life outside the company – and their relationship only prospered because both men worked unsociable hours.

Becoming chairman of the board had always been his ambition, but the more he thought about it the less he was sure that it was what he really wanted, especially now. His legal team had warned him that wresting control of the company from Bobby Spurling could take months, if not years. And then what? He was fifty-seven now. At best he was looking at another eight years before he retired. Eight more years of stress and sixty-hour weeks – assuming, of course, that he lived that long. Or the three million dollars Cyril Craven had offered him to go quietly?

He wanted ten, but knew that was being ambitious. Three was well below the five he was prepared to accept – but even so with that sort of money he and Isidro could go anywhere they wanted. They could spend all day in bed if they so chose.

Fearon heaved himself out of bed and into a silk kimono. He padded from the bedroom into the kitchen and poured himself a cup of coffee. Somewhere in the house something was banging and he followed the noise through to the lounge. The room was spacious and light, one wall made of glass to allow an unobstructed view of the ocean. The sliding door on to the balcony was open, and the wind was catching the slatted wooden blinds.

'*Isidro!*' If he had told the boy once he had told him a thousand times about closing the door behind him when he left. This part of Shanzu beach was highly exclusive and reserved for only the very rich – which made it a perfect target for robbers. As the local neighbourhood watch representative always said, an open door was an open invitation.

Fearon slid the door closed and locked the latch. Then he turned and saw Isidro sprawled on the white leather sofa with a kitchen knife sticking out of his chest. He had barely registered this when someone came up behind him and pulled a piece of clear plastic clingfilm over his face. Then he felt himself being manhandled towards the bedroom. He tried to cry out, but he couldn't even breathe.

As his brain shut down, the last thing William Fearon saw through the fogged plastic was an American eagle. *It was so shiny and pretty – and didn't Isidro have a belt buckle like that?*

64

A man was wandering along the track towards the boatyard. He was African, scruffily dressed and wearing a frayed straw hat. He also seemed unsteady on his feet and, as he approached, even Harry smelled the unmistakable waft of stale booze on his breath.

'*Jambo*,' he said and stared glassily at the Englishman. 'My name is Mathenge. Baptiste Mathenge. I am looking for a gentleman by the name of Mr Moore.'

Harry shrugged and called across to *Yellowfin*, where Jake was busy loading up for that morning's excursion with a party of Ernies from the Casuarina Hotel just south of Mida Creek.

'I'm Moore,' he said, jumping up on to the jetty a few minutes later.

Baptiste Mathenge swayed noticeably and offered his hand, partly out of greeting and partly in the interests of keeping his own balance.

'*Jambo*,' he said. 'I have been asked to pass a message to you.'

'A message from who?'

'He was a big Masai. An old man, I guess. Knocked on my door this morning. I never seen him before, but he said his boss knew me. Then he gave me ten dollars, told me to give you the message. But first I am to give you this, Mr Moore. The Masai said then you would know who it was from.'

Jake and Harry exchanged glances as the visitor rummaged in the pocket of a grubby pair of cotton trousers. Even though it was early it was clear Mathenge had already spent most of his ten dollars on hooch.

'Ah!' Mathenge said with delight and relief. 'I have found it.'

And there, like a shiny bauble in the palm of a children's magician, was the copper-jacketed cylinder of a .300 Winchester Magnum cartridge.

On a low ridge overlooking the boatyard, a US Navy Seal-trained sniper, rendered invisible by a camouflage suit and the ability to remain motionless for several hours at a time, trained the telescopic sights of his rifle on the back of Baptiste Mathenge's head.

'I have the shot,' he murmured into a throat mike.

A hundred yards away, hidden by the undergrowth, Special Agents Bryson and McCrickerd silently watched the encounter through high-powered binoculars.

'Stand by, Sentinel,' Bryson whispered presently.

He looked at McCrickerd, squatting beside him in the tall, thick grass. The younger man shook his head. Bryson nodded in agreement. Whoever the visitor was, it was clear he posed no threat to the target.

He was not the Ghost.

'Stand down, Sentinel.'

'Roger that,' the sniper said.

Bryson removed the receiver bud from his right ear and rubbed the irritated skin. It was now almost thirty-six hours since the encrypted conversation between the Ghost and his employers had been intercepted by GCHQ, and Dean Hoffman's breathless message from Washington.

'Looks like the sonofabitch had packed his bags and was ready to go,' Hoffman had said, the excitement rising in his voice on the secure line from the J Edgar Hoover Building. 'But they've given him a new target.'

A new target? Jesus, Bryson thought. But he could have been away scot free, his job done, the FBI investigation in tatters.

'Who is it?'

When Hoffman told him the name of the decrypted intercept he'd been surprised. But then the more he thought about it the more it made sense. Harry Philliskirk had, unwittingly, worked as a courier for Patrick Noonan's crew. He'd had direct contact with Conrad Getty, Noonan's man on the ground. And when it came to severing all ties to its operatives and those connected with them, the organisation had shown itself to be utterly ruthless.

'We're on to the originator now,' Hoffman said. 'The bastards have made a mistake, Clarence. *They've finally made a mistake.*'

Bryson had acted fast to establish surveillance positions in the vicinity of the Brits' boatyard at Flamingo Creek. Within hours they had been reinforced by Sentinel and a jungle-trained spotter and close-quarters specialist codenamed Tradecraft, who was presently up a tree in a nearby sector. Both men had been choppered in from Mogadishu, where they were attached to an ongoing CIA field operation against Somali pirates.

Even Bryson was impressed by the level of interagency cooperation on this one. But then the intercepts were the first solid intel they'd had about the Ghost and the people who had hired him to do their killing.

The Ghost was coming back? It was a hell of a risk.

Is he taunting you, Clarence?

65

It was well past eight when Jouma rose that morning, which was late for him. But Winifred had gone to spend a couple of nights with her sister on the north shore and in her absence the inspector had taken the opportunity to set his alarm clock thirty minutes later. In truth, he had almost considered switching it off entirely and spending the day in bed.

It was not so much the manner of Abdelbassir Hossain's death that had sickened him to the core, but that it should have happened in the first place. He felt somehow culpable, as if he had not done enough to prevent it. Jouma knew that there were those in the department, Simba included, who were hailing him as some sort of hero for his actions in the tunnels beneath Fort Jesus yesterday.

If that was the case, then he was also the biggest fraud.

As the apartment began to shake with the morning rush-hour traffic, Jouma stared at the ceiling, his mind whirling, and he realised that he was no good at brooding. He sighed and got out of bed, making sure to make it neatly after him.

He performed his ablutions in the bathroom mirror and considered his schedule for the day. First, to Mama Ngina Drive to liaise with Mwangi about the Gudrun investigation and, no doubt, discuss Abdelbassir Hossain's suicide with Simba. After that, he would return to Fort Jesus to see if the teams working underground had come up with anything of interest overnight. Next, he would go to the hospital to check on the condition of Bobby Spurling. The boy, he was convinced, held the key to the abductions. They were too wildly random to be anything other than planned – *but what was the connection?* To have one of the victims still alive to tell the tale was a huge bonus. It was just frustrating that Bobby had been too traumatised to talk.

Cheered somewhat by the simple act of planning his morning, Jouma dressed and opened the front door.

Like a squatter who refused to go away, Jake was sitting against the crumbling concrete wall of the stairwell. 'Guess who?' he said. The inspector's mood disintegrated instantly.

'Ah, sir – this is Tradecraft.'

'Go ahead.'

'I've got movement in the north-east quadrant.'

'What sort of movement?'

'There's someone out there, sir.'

Bryson felt his heart begin to pound. The north-east quadrant was an area of forest behind the workshop. For a blissful moment he forgot all about his stiffened muscles and screaming joints – the result of too many hours on field surveillance and too many years sitting behind a desk.

'Stand by – we're on our way. Sentinel?'

'Moving to Position Two, sir,' the sniper said.

Bryson and McCrickerd were downriver of the boatyard, facing directly on to the workshop where at that moment Harry Philliskirk, the assassin's target, was in the office rearranging his decimated bookings ledger. An hour earlier they had watched the visitor in the straw hat totter away and Jake jump into the Land Rover and drive off in the direction of the highway. The two FBI agents carefully left their position and circled round towards the rear of the ugly breezeblock building. Each man had drawn their standard-issue Glock 22 automatic.

Tradecraft was hunkered down behind a thorn bush, his position giving him a clear view of the tangled wilderness of mangroves and vines to the rear of the workshop. He was a rangy African with an almost supernatural ability to blend into his surroundings. His vision was equally outstanding. Even when they followed his outstretched finger it still took Bryson several moments to see the figure creeping through the undergrowth towards the building.

Christ almighty . . .

'The guy said his name was Baptiste Mathenge,' Jake said. 'Claimed he used to work as a driver for Spurling Developments but got the sack. I swear I would have told him to sling his hook as well – but then he gave me this.'

They were in the kitchen drinking finest English

breakfast tea from a china pot. By the expression on Jouma's face, Jake could tell he did not like wasting it on those who did not appreciate it.

Jouma glanced at the copper cylinder in his hand. 'What is it?'

'It's a .300 Winchester Magnum cartridge. A high-velocity hunting shell. The guy I went to see the other day at Spurling Developments had one on his key ring. His name is Frank Walker, he's the chief operations manager for Coast Province. He was Mathenge's boss.'

'I don't understand.'

'Walker wants a meet. Today. Apparently he has some important information about the company.'

'Why you?'

'I guess he's done his research,' Jake said. 'He obviously knows about my connection to you. He wants you to come along as well.'

Jouma raised his eyebrows over the rim of his teacup. 'Me? What has this got to do with me?'

'He says he's got information about Bobby Spurling.'

The intruder's face was partially covered with a shemagh Arab scarf, but enough of it was exposed to identify him as a white male. He stood five feet seven and weighed in at maybe one hundred and forty pounds, although his slight frame was cloaked in a bulky field jacket. He was moving slowly and deliberately, ensuring that his footsteps made the minimum impact or noise.

'Sentinel?' Bryson muttered.

'I'm in position and I have the shot, sir.'

'Is he armed?'

'Unable to confirm, sir.'

Bryson stared until he felt his eyeballs were about to pop out of their sockets. The intruder was at the workshop, his gloved hands on the sill of one of the rear windows.

Sentinel: 'Be advised I have a clear shot.'

Decision time, Clarence. Stick or twist.

Jouma could not believe what he was hearing.

'Do you have some sort of mental disorder that compels you to involve yourself in matters which do not concern you, Jake? First the Jalawi boy and now this?'

'Hey! I'm sorry about taking Alex without letting you know,' Jake protested. 'But I left a note for your wife.'

'Winifred does not *open* letters,' exclaimed Jouma. 'She leaves that to me. By the time I got home last night she was beside herself with worry.' He shook his head and, in a further fit of pique, rattled his cup in its saucer. 'After the day I had yesterday, a frantic wife was the last thing I needed.'

Jake had to concede that the inspector had had a hell of a day. Listening to him recounting the ordeal in the tunnels was horrific enough, but he had gasped hardest when he heard Jouma's theory about the hours leading up to Lol Quarrie's death. It was sobering to think that, while the pair of them were toasting auld acquaintance in an Algerian restaurant in Government Square, half a mile away some poor bastard was digging himself out of his own grave.

'I thought you might be interested in what Walker

had to say, that's all,' he said. 'But I appreciate you've probably got other things on your mind. I'll go and see him myself.'

Jouma emitted a low groan and slumped in his chair. 'As it happens, I *am* interested,' he said. 'Where is the meeting? Mombasa? That's where Spurling headquarters is.'

'No,' Jake said. 'And there's the thing. You see, it seems Walker doesn't work for Spurling Developments any more. In fact, when I called his office to check this morning, I was told he had quit his job and gone back to Glasgow.'

66

'Are you a religious man, Constable Mwangi?'
Christie the pathologist asked.

'I used to go to Sunday school.'

'Then I don't suppose your studies will have
included the Gospel accounts of the Crucifixion.'

'I seem to remember singing "Little Donkey", but
that's about as in-depth as we got.'

Christie nodded as, with a flourish, he pushed
open the heavy swing door to the autopsy room and
marched inside. 'Then observe as the words of the
disciples are made real.'

Sister Gudrun was lying face down on the metal
examination table. Getting the body straightened had
taken the collective efforts of three morgue assistants;
she had stiffened into the position in which she had
been kept in the tunnel – knees bent, hands up
behind her head, as if in some bizarre form of prayer.

'Look at these marks,' Christie said.

Now that the dried blood had been washed from
the nun's wizened back, Mwangi could see that it
was criss-crossed with welts. Some had gouged the

skin, others were barely a shadow. On closer examination there seemed to be a definite pattern to the marks.

'She was whipped?'

'Well, there is whipping, and there is scourging. This is most definitely the latter.'

'Scourging?'

'A particularly nasty form of punishment favoured by the Romans. The device they used was called a *flagellum*. Essentially it was a whip with braided leather thongs.'

The pathologist went across to his briefcase lying open on an instrument stand in the corner of the autopsy room. From it he removed a red-covered edition of the Gideon's Bible.

'Borrowed it from the hospital chapel of rest,' he explained with a shudder. 'Just in case you thought I was some sort of weirdo evangelist.' He opened the book and flipped quickly through its onion-skin pages. 'Mark, Chapter 15, verse 15,' he said, clearing his throat. '*And so Pilate, willing to content the people, released Barabbas unto them, and delivered Jesus, when he had scourged him, to be crucified.*' He closed the book and returned to the body. 'In keeping with Jewish law of the time, the number of lashes was kept to thirty-nine. I have counted thirty-nine lesions on the deceased's back.'

Mwangi looked at him. 'You are suggesting Sister Gudrun was *crucified*?'

'No, Constable Mwangi,' Christie said, rolling his eyes. 'Scourging was merely the aperitif. The crucifixion came later – assuming the poor sod lived long enough. Depending on the severity, scourging was often enough to cause fatal blood loss and circulatory shock.'

'And this is what killed her?'

'She was an old woman. From what I can deduce from the intensity of the blows, even a strapping fellow like you would have done well to survive an assault of this ferocity.'

67

Just three miles south of Mombasa, on the highway headed for the Tanzanian border, the driver of a refrigerated truck containing fifteen thousand frozen chicken carcasses and travelling at over eighty miles an hour had failed to notice one of the many unmarked speed bumps that had been laid across the road when it had received an expensive and highly publicised resurfacing a couple of years earlier. The impact shattered the front axle of the vehicle and caused the rear doors to explode outwards, spilling the frozen chickens across the highway as the truck slewed into the opposite lane. While nearby residents and opportunist motorists did their best to scavenge as many of the chickens as they possibly could, there were so many birds that it would take them several hours to clear them all. In the meantime, the road was completely blocked and would remain so for most of the day.

As the Land Rover sizzled in the southbound traffic jam, Jake wondered if there was any hope for a country that considered a thoroughfare no wider than an English B road to be a major intercity artery. But, as the man ahead of him in the queue calmly loaded rapidly thawing chicken carcasses into the boot of his car, in truth his mind was elsewhere.

When, presently, Jouma said, 'Have you considered the possibility that this could be a trap?' he realised they were thinking the same thing.

'Why should it be? What have I ever done to hurt Walker?'

Jouma mentioned the name of Alex Hopper. 'If the company was indeed behind the murder of Gangra, then they may well regard you as a threat.'

'If they were, then you're assuming Walker knew about the conspiracy.'

'You are assuming he did not.'

'Then why is he dead? And why did he ask for you?'

A smiling face appeared at his window. It belonged to a well-dressed black man in a suit and tie.

'Excuse me, sir,' the man said. 'My name is Mr Moses Saba. I am the driver of the car behind. Please, take one of my business cards.'

Jake looked at the card. In embossed print it read: MR M SABA – ENTREPRENEUR. In his rear-view mirror he saw a rusting, shit-coloured Citroën 2CV.

'What do you want?'

'I couldn't help noticing that there are a number of unclaimed chickens under your car,' Saba said. 'I wondered if you intended to claim them.'

'I have no intention whatsoever.'

'Then I wonder if you would object if I took them?'

Jake looked into Saba's expectant eyes. 'Be my guest, Mr Saba,' he said. 'We're late for an appointment.'

He started the engine and, ignoring the blare of outraged horns, swung his car on to the dirt verge and continued south. There was only one way to find out the answers to the questions that troubled them both.

68

Brother Willem of the Reedemed Apostolic Gospel Church arrived at the mortuary of Mombasa Hospital accompanied by Sister Constance and Sister Florence. When the curtain went back to reveal the prepared body of Sister Gudrun the two nuns gasped, but it was Willem who gripped hold of their arms as if he was about to fall. He was no longer the strident figure that Mwangi had met that first day at the Jalawi mission. He seemed crushed, as if the confirmation that Gudrun was dead had realised some terrible suppressed fear.

Mwangi had rehearsed his lines a hundred times, to the point he was almost confident about his onerous task.

'May I on behalf of Coast Province CID pass on my deepest condolences to you and your Church.'

'Who would do such a thing?' Willem whispered.

Thirty minutes later Mwangi was in the hospital canteen, waiting to take delivery of Christie's written autopsy report, when he saw Sister Constance and Sister Florence nervously peering round the door.

He waved them across and they sat, fidgety and, he sensed, *frightened*.

He offered them tea but they shook their heads.

'Where is Brother Willem?'

'He has returned to Jalawi,' Constance said. 'We told him we had things we needed to buy in Mombasa. Women's things.' She was clearly bursting to ask him something. 'Is it true?' she hissed urgently. 'About Sister Gudrun?'

'Is what true?'

'That she was – *whipped to death*?'

'Whatever gives you that idea?'

'Florence's brother is friends with the sister of one of the ambulance drivers.'

Mwangi sighed. Such was the extent of the grapevine around Mombasa, he would not be surprised if the whole of Kenya knew about Sister Gudrun's scourging by now.

'*Is it true?*'

'Yes,' Mwangi said. 'It's true.'

The two nuns crossed themselves.

'There is nothing to worry about, Sisters. You are perfectly safe.'

Constance stared at him. 'You don't understand,' she said.

'I'd heard stories from nuns I met at other missions. How Gudrun would punish them for their sins just as Jesus was punished. They said she used a switch from a neem tree, because the bark was soft and its medicinal properties would help ease the stinging – but that it was just one of her sick jokes because she always hit you thirty-nine times, just like the Roman soldiers hit Jesus.'

Thirty-nine times, Mwangi thought. *The number of strokes Christie had found on the old nun's scourged back.*

They had moved from the hospital canteen to the privacy of the chapel.

'I never really believed what they said,' Constance continued. Beside her, Florence sat almost quivering with apprehension. 'I thought they were just trying to scare me – you know, the naïve new girl straight off the boat, that kind of thing. But it didn't stop me being terrified of her. Everybody was terrified of her, even Brother Willem.'

'Did she ever hit you?' Mwangi asked.

'No.'

'Then perhaps you are right. Maybe these are just stories.'

'They are not stories, Constable Mwangi.' She looked at Florence. 'Before she was a nun, Florence was at the Church orphanage Sister Gudrun ran at Majimboni, near the Tanzanian border. Show him.'

Head bowed with shame, Florence reached behind her head and began unbuttoning her heavy cotton robe. Carefully pulling it down from the neck she turned so that Mwangi could see a line of ugly weals raised on the chocolate skin of her back.

'Thirty-nine strokes,' Constance said, gently caressing the young girl's wounds. 'Maybe you would like to count them yourself, Constable Mwangi.'

Mwangi felt his eyes prickle with both anger and compassion for this young girl. 'Why didn't you tell me this before?' he demanded.

'Because she was not dead!' Florence exclaimed. '*Because she might have come back!*'

309

69

The rendezvous was a car park overlooking the beach at Black Cliff Point, ten miles further south on the Likoni–Ukunda highway. According to Walker's message they were to be there at noon. Thanks to the spilled chickens back up the road, they had made it by the skin of their teeth.

'Now what?' Jouma said.

Jake shrugged. 'Now we wait.'

After thirty minutes an olive-green Jeep pulled up in the car park. A tall African in safari attire climbed out and approached the two men warily. He was aged anywhere between fifty and seventy, white haired with a face like wind-blasted sandstone.

'You are Mr Moore?'

Jake nodded. 'And this is Inspector Jouma of Mombasa CID. As requested.'

There was another pause, then the African nodded. 'I am Malachi,' he said. 'Leave your vehicle and come with me.'

They drove south for a further twenty miles. At the

town of Mwabungu, Malachi turned inland towards the vast tracts of forested highlands that made up the Shimba Hills reserve. The road gradually thinned to a red dirt track that followed the southern perimeter of the reserve. The track was rarely used except by park rangers, and meandered from the steeply cut, forested valleys of the western foothills to the open grassland of the plains.

'I take it Mr Walker did not make it back to Glasgow,' Jouma said.

Malachi said nothing, and gave no indication that he was in the mood for conversation. The two passengers in the Jeep contented themselves with this private safari, staring in amazement at wildlife that seemed close enough to touch. Jake's livelihood was the sea, and to his shame he had never even bothered to venture inland. He had seen plenty of cheetahs, lions and leopards on TV documentaries, but never in real life. Dozy in the growing heat of the afternoon sun, the great predators lounged in the shade of flat-topped acacias and croton bushes and watched disinterestedly as the Jeep rattled past.

For Jouma, brought up in the foothills of Mount Kenya, the landscape was much more familiar. Yet it had been a long time since he had seen further than the concrete and steel of the city, or smelled anything other than petrol fumes and decay.

Their destination was a bivouac situated in the lee of a low hill overlooking the plains. It consisted of a couple of bush tents either side of a circular, stone-ringed fire. There was a camping table with a thatched canopy to keep out the sun. As Malachi killed the engine, Jake and Jouma exchanged glances because this truly was the middle of nowhere. Ten miles to the east were the rolling ridges of the Shimba Hills, but in every other direction the plains stretched out unbroken to the horizon.

Jake looked around. 'Where's Walker?' he asked.

70

All morning there had been a chill breeze blowing over the plains. But it had gone now, replaced by thick, soporific heat.

This was the hunter's time.

There. In the shadow of a croton bush the reedbuck stiffened and lifted its head, its long ears erect like antennae. Three hundred yards away, Frank Walker put his eye to the scope on top of his Interceptor hunting rifle and for a moment the animal was caught in the sights like the subject of a wildlife photograph. He eased a .300 Winchester Magnum cartridge into the breech and silently slid the bolt.

Easy now . . .

The reedbuck's huge, glossy eyes were staring directly at him, but Walker knew he couldn't be seen. Malachi had taught him well. Stay upwind. Become one with the land. He pressed the stock hard against his left shoulder and his finger closed around the trigger.

Easy now . . .

At the age of twenty, and never having been

further than northern Europe in his life, Walker arrived at the Spurling reserve with nothing but the clothes on his back and a willingness to work hard. Within a year of hammering fence posts he had been promoted to ranger, learning his trade under Malachi. Within five he was the wise old Masai's deputy. His life could not have been better. If he'd done nothing else but live and work in the vast open spaces of the reserve, Frank would have died a happy man. But Clay Spurling had other plans for him.

Frank had never fully understood why the old man had singled him out. After all there were others, better qualified, time-served rangers on the payroll who deserved promotion more than he did. Maybe it was because of the way young Bobby had latched on to him. *Aye, now there was an irony.* The kid who had idolised him the way Frank used to idolise his heroes at Celtic Park on a Saturday afternoon was now the bastard who had ordered his execution.

Be still . . .

The optimum kill zone for an animal the size of a reedbuck is an area of about nine square inches just behind the shoulders. From three hundred yards, Walker's bullet ripped apart the animal's heart and lungs and punched an exit hole just above its right shoulder blade. Nerve impulses and ancient instincts made it bolt for thirty yards through the low grass, but it was already dead before it collapsed to the ground.

The report from the powerful rifle would have carried miles, beyond the bluff to the east and as far as the Spurling ranch nestled in the valley. But the big house was empty now.

Thanks to Bobby . . .

Even as a wee boy there had always been something odd about Bobby Spurling: a mad glint in his eye. And as he grew older the kid reminded Frank so much of the braggarts and bully-boys he had despised in the schemes of Glasgow; the kind who thought they were untouchable because their auld boy was head man in Ruchazie or Easterhouse. And, just like those battle-scarred, stupidly sentimental old men, Clay Spurling had a blind spot when it came to his son. In Clay's eyes, Bobby could do no wrong and he was happy to indulge the boy with sports cars and penthouses and an allowance big enough to fund as much coke and as many whores as he wanted.

But he was not stupid. Five years ago Clay had appointed Frank as operations chief for the coast region, and Frank, reluctant to spit in the old man's face, had taken the job. At the time Bobby, then eighteen, had too many other things on his mind to give a shit about an internal appointment. He was off to England, ostensibly to study, but in reality to lead a playboy's existence on his daddy's shillings. At the age of twenty-one, when he returned to Mombasa from gallivanting around Europe, expecting to walk into a high-ranking job in the family business, Bobby discovered to his horror that Clay had decided to send him to work as a deputy foreman at a building site in Lamu. It was so he could gain experience, Clay told him, to show the rest of the company there was no nepotism in the Spurling family.

Bobby hadn't seen it that way, of course. To him it was a humiliation. And deep in that twisted mind of his, Bobby blamed Frank for turning his father against him.

Away to the east Frank could see the dust cloud boiling up behind the wheels of Malachi's Jeep. His guests were on their way. By the time he got back to the bivouac the old warden would have filled his battered coffee pot and a fire would be burning. He doubted whether Jake Moore or his detective friend Daniel Jouma would appreciate such rudimentary hospitality, but to Frank Walker it was pure heaven, the life he had always wanted.

But now Clay Spurling was dead, and Bobby had killed him – and, as long as that injustice remained, the Scotsman knew that he could never truly be content.

Sliding his rifle over his shoulder, Walker set off for the bivouac.

71

Superintendent Elizabeth Simba had spent much of her detective career in the service of the moneyed white élite of Nairobi, so she was no stranger to the sort of security-gated and *askari*-patrolled paranoia in which the residents of the Whispering Pines at Shanzu beach enclave lived their lives.

'Who found them?' she asked, stepping through the sliding window of one of the more expensive beachfront villas.

'The maid.'

'Do we know who they are?'

'The one on the sofa is Isidro Velazquez. Mexican national. Works in a bar in the Old Town.'

'And the other one?'

'William Fearon. CEO of Spurling Developments.'

Simba thanked the uniformed sergeant and complimented him on his professionalism. It was indeed rare. Not only had he elicited the salient details of the victims, but he had also sealed off the crime scene from the usual invasion of blundering boots.

Isidro Velazquez, judging by his wide eyes and startled expression, had died the instant the kitchen knife had been plunged into his chest. A cursory check confirmed that one knife was missing from a set of five in a wooden block by the stove. The room was disturbed, chairs out of place, lamps upended, shards of broken glass on the carpet.

William Fearon was on his knees in the bedroom, his upper body leaning forward at an angle of forty-five degrees, his silk kimono hanging open to expose a vast blotchy-white belly. A thick leather belt with an elaborate eagle buckle was pulled tight around his fleshy neck. The other end was tied to the handle of the wardrobe. Drawers had been pulled open and clothes were strewn across the floor. There was an open suitcase on the bed and Velazquez's passport on the nightstand.

'So what do you think, ma'am? It looks to me like they had quite a tiff.'

The sergeant, a veteran in his late forties, had followed her to the bedroom, which was in normal circumstances a breach of protocol. But on this occasion Simba was pleased to have his company. After everything that had happened in the last twenty-four hours she was in need of at least one fellow officer who thought she was worth talking to.

'Are you married, Sergeant?'

'Yes, ma'am.'

'And do you and your wife ever fight?'

He smiled. 'Like cat and dog, ma'am.'

'Has she ever threatened to leave you?'

'Several times. And I her.'

'Have you ever been tempted to kill your wife

with a kitchen knife, then hang yourself with a belt?'

'No, ma'am. No marriage is worth that.'

'Precisely,' Simba nodded. 'Which is why the person who killed these two men has clearly never been married.'

In his office in central Mombasa Douglas Roarke turned on the TV news. The murder-suicide of William Fearon and his barman boyfriend was lead item.

At least *something* was going according to plan at last, he thought sourly.

In his office on the next floor up, Cyril Craven was also watching the television. He saw William Fearon's beach house hidden behind palm trees and tall security gates, and two corpses in body bags being wheeled into a waiting ambulance. Words were scrolling across the bottom of the screen, but they were just a blur. Now there was a pretty young reporter talking into a microphone outside the house, but Craven heard nothing but the sound of blood thumping in his ears.

Jesus Christ Almighty, he had done it. That mad, murderous bastard Roarke had actually gone and done it.

He had killed one of their own. The purge had begun . . .

Craven had always been pragmatic; he existed on the very limit of the law and quite often on the other side of it, and he knew that if things went wrong there would be no time to go home and kiss his wife goodbye. Which was why, for the last twenty years, he had kept a suitcase of clothes at the office for just this occasion. His passport was in his desk drawer, and his contacts at Kenya Airways could provide him with a ticket to any destination. All it would take was a phone call.

'Initial reports suggest the deaths of William Fearon and Isidro Velazquez were not the result of a robbery, but a domestic incident that got out of hand and ended in tragedy,' the pretty young TV reporter said into the camera lens.

A domestic incident! Oh bravo, Mr Roarke, Craven thought – because there was only one person he knew who could engineer a double murder to look like a lovers' tiff, and he was on the next floor down. And suddenly the lawyer realised that, wherever he went in the world, the same domestic incident would be awaiting him.

He was a dead man walking.

There was another face on the TV screen now. Square-jawed and short-haired – it took Craven a moment to realise that it was a woman.

'Tragic ... circumstances ... sympathy ... well-respected ...'

The name that flashed up on the caption was *Superintendent Elizabeth Simba, Coast Province CID.* Craven scribbled the name on a yellow legal pad.

'Maureen,' he said to his secretary through the squawk box on his desk. 'Cancel my appointments for the rest of the day, would you? Something's cropped up.'

'Of course, sir. May I ask when you'll be back?'

'Oh, I'm not going anywhere. There's some paper-work I need to finish.'

'Very well, Mr Craven.'

Poor deluded girl. So oblivious to the carnage that was about to take place.

'One more thing, Maureen.'

'Yes, Mr Craven.'

'Do you think Mombasa CID have email yet?'

It was a short distance from Shanzu to the Tamarind restaurant in Nyali. When she found them, Mugo and Obbo were midway through a convivial luncheon of oysters mambrui on the dhow that was moored to the restaurant's jetty.

'Superintendent Simba – do come and join us!' Mugo said. A long strand of cheese gratin connected one of the dainty oyster shells to his slobbering bottom lip.

'I take it you have heard about Abdelbassir Hossain, Detective Inspector Mugo?' Simba said.

Mugo smiled at Obbo, who was delicately spooning chilled lobster bisque into his mouth. 'Frederick?'

'There was a rumour about him,' the mayor's fixer said noncommittally. 'Why? Is it true?'

'Yes it is.'

Mugo seemed utterly unconcerned. 'Clearly the man could not live with his guilt,' he said. 'Now why don't you sit down, ma'am? Join us! Have some wine! Is this not a cause for celebration?'

On the other side of the creek the unsightly concrete edifice of Mombasa Hospital clung to the island like a parasite. Simba had heard that at night, under cover of darkness, barges came round the headland laden with wooden coffins from the timber factories in Chamgamwe. While diners stuffed their faces with gourmet food and expensive bottles of wine on the dhow, less than two hundred yards across the water the empty coffins were being unloaded into basement storage rooms while full ones – containing the bodies of the poor and the unknown – were stacked on to the barges for transport to the municipal crematorium downriver at Likoni.

It was here that Abdelbassir Hossain would be taken once his body had been examined and an autopsy report into his death written up. Perhaps, Simba thought, his coffin was already waiting for him in the hospital basement.

Most likely it had been waiting for him before he killed himself.

'You really should try these oysters, Superintendent,' Mugo said. 'They are quite exquisite.'

'I expect you have not heard about the body that was found in the sewers under Fort Jesus yesterday,' Simba said.

Mugo extended his arms. 'Please enlighten me, ma'am. Is it another murder case you wish me to solve for Coast Province CID?'

Simba enlightened him. It took several minutes, and during that time the solitary oyster in Mugo's hand remained uneaten.

'This proves nothing,' Obbo said, his eyes darting frantically.

'It proves that Inspector Mugo's investigation was flawed and incompetent from the very beginning. It proves that the charges against Abdelbassir Hossain were premature, without reasonable grounds, and led at least indirectly to his death. I have no doubt at all that, when my report reaches the desk of the Commissioner of Police in Nairobi, Inspector Mugo will be lucky to find a job washing squad cars.'

The oyster in Mugo's hand slid from its shell and flopped into his lap.

'The one thing I cannot prove,' Simba continued, 'is that this whole case was unduly influenced and therefore tarnished by the reckless interference of the mayor's office. I obviously have my opinions, but I shall let the Director of Public Prosecutions decide whether there is a case to answer.'

Now it was Obbo's turn to be speechless. In one of the pockets of his expensive suit, a cell phone started ringing.

'I expect that will be the mayor, Mr Obbo,' Simba said. 'You should answer it – I believe he will be in need of a good public relations man very soon.'

72

Brother Willem knelt at the altar of the church he had built and prayed to God Almighty to spare his wicked soul. But no matter how hard he prayed, he knew that no one was listening. God had run out of patience with sinners like him. Now He was taking his revenge.

Gudrun was dead.

Part of him had hoped that the old bitch had simply run off, and that he would eventually receive a gloating letter from Monte Carlo or Martinique. And he wouldn't have minded, because it would have brought an end to the police investigation into their affairs. But extravagance was never Gudrun's style. In his heart he'd known the truth from the minute she had disappeared. She had pushed someone too far with her demands for money – and it had cost her life.

Now, he was convinced, it was about to cost him everything.

As he knelt in the gloomy surroundings of the church, Willem contemplated the pay-off that Spurling Developments had promised them. It was more money than they had ever imagined possible. But were these the thirty pieces of silver that had finally plunged them over the abyss into eternal damnation?

When the police found out that he and Gudrun were due to split one million dollars between them, there was only one person they would suspect of her murder.

It was ironic, he reflected. Up until a few years ago he had actually been questioning his faith. In a no-mark Dutch town like Delft, where he preached at the local Lutheran church to a congregation in single figures, it was not hard to wonder if it was worth carrying on. Had he simply gone with his instinct and quit the Church, none of this would have ever happened.

But then he had seen the advertisement in the diocesan magazine: volunteers required for missionary work in Africa. Suddenly he knew that if he was ever going to rekindle his belief in a compassionate God then this was the chance he had been praying for.

Three months later, assigned to a mission in a tiny village close to the shores of Lake Victoria, Willem had his moment of epiphany, in the house of an expat Dutch businessman who had made his millions from mineral exports. His wife, a woman of faded, menopausal glamour whose life revolved around spa treatments, hot-tub parties and long-distance phone calls to her grown-up children back in the old country, looked at him with pleading eyes and said, 'A school for the orphans? How much do you need, Brother Willem?'

And Brother Willem, who knew that a functional village school would cost no more than five thousand dollars to build and equip, had looked the sad, filthy-rich matron in the eye and said, 'Ten thousand dollars, madam.'

After that, it was easy. New churches, schoolrooms and community centres began springing up in villages across Nyanza Province. Almost every month there was another grand opening ceremony, with some grinning, guilt-ridden nabob cutting the ribbon to open a building named after them. They never checked the figures, because to do so would be to impugn the integrity of the Church. But in any case money was not the issue – what counted was that their charity helped them forget how they had become rich by exploiting the poor in the first place.

Meanwhile, Brother Willem's secret bank accounts began to swell with the money he was skimming from each development. It was ridiculously easy. So easy, in fact, it never once occurred to him that someone might have had the idea before he did.

O my God, I am heartily sorry for having offended you, and I detest all my sins because I dread the loss of heaven and the pains of hell; but most of all because they have offended you, my God, who are all good and worthy of all my love.

The door to the church burst open, flooding the interior with light. Willem screwed up his eyes as a tall silhouetted figure approached rapidly. Hands grabbed the front of his robe and shoved him backwards towards the rudimentary wooden altar, spilling candlesticks and a stack of prayer books on the floor.

'You haven't been entirely truthful with me, Brother Willem,' Mwangi said, his face just inches from the priest's.

'I didn't kill her,' Willem squealed. 'I swear to God I didn't kill her!'

326

73

'Dr Livingstone, I presume,' Jake said drily as Frank Walker walked into the encampment.

'I can assure you that Livingstone was a far worthier Scot than I will ever be, Mr Moore,' Walker said. He laid his gun and his rucksack against one of the bush tents and sat down on a collapsible camp chair. 'You got my message, then?'

'Your secretary said you were in Glasgow.'

Walker smiled thinly. 'Is that what they're telling people? I suppose it's better than telling them they put a bullet in the back of my head.'

Jake looked surprised. 'And there was me thinking you were a company man through and through.'

'Oh, I was,' Walker said, rubbing a ridge of raw, swollen flesh under his eye. 'But me and the new boss have never seen eye to eye.' He looked up. 'You must be Inspector Jouma.'

'I do not appreciate mystery tours, Mr Walker,' Jouma told him sternly.

'Sorry about the cloak and dagger routine. But I have to take precautions these days.'

Malachi appeared with a battered coffee pot and a hexamine heating block. He lit the block and went and sat in a folding chair outside one of the tents.

'Your friend is not much of a conversationalist,' Jake said.

Walker waved his hand at the countryside spread around them. 'There's not much call for conversation out here.'

Jake breathed in the warm, pungent air. 'So this is the Spurling reserve. And not a hotel in sight.'

Walker smiled. '*Touché*. But you shouldn't believe everything Evie Simenon tells you. I could argue all day about the thousands of dirt-poor Kenyans who have benefited from Clay Spurling – and I'm including those penniless farmers up at Jalawi village as well. But that's not why I asked you here.'

'So why *did* you ask us here, Mr Walker?' Jouma said impatiently. 'If there is something you have to say regarding an ongoing investigation, why not come straight to the police in the first place?'

'I'm tarnished goods, Inspector,' Walker admitted. 'There are too many things I've done that could earn me a stretch inside – and I don't intend to let some clever-dick barrister tear me apart in the witness box. You can listen to what I've got to say or you can walk away. Either way after today you won't see me again.'

'Then please begin, Mr Walker,' Jouma said. 'I am all ears.'

The coffee had boiled. Walker poured three cups then sat back in his chair and told them his story.

74

It is a warm May night, nearly two years ago now. The old man is away on business, so the party kicks off at the ranch, just to spite him. The usual crew are there: Bobby and his rich boy pals from Mombasa. There is booze and cocaine, just for preliminaries, just to get things warmed up.

And of course there is the babysitter.

'Keep an eye on him while I'm out of town, eh, Frank?' Clay had told him. 'Make sure he keeps his nose clean. I'd get Dougie Roarke to sort it out, but I don't want the kid to think he's under house arrest. He likes you, Frank. You're on his wavelength. You don't mind, do you?'

'Come on, Frank! If you won't have a toot then at least have a fucking drink!'

But what Clay doesn't know is that Bobby hates his guts. That braying voice cuts through him.

'I prefer not to when I'm driving, Bobby.'

'Dah – you're such a pussy. I thought you guys from Scotland were supposed to be party animals.'

In fact, Frank would rather swallow razor blades than drink with these arseholes. If it wasn't for Clay he would tell them all to fuck off – but not before he had given them

329

a lesson in manners and respect they would never forget.

Especially Bobby.

'He's a wild one, Frank, but he's a good boy at heart,'
the old man had said. 'Keep an eye on him for me, will
you? Keep the little sod out of trouble.'

So Frank sits and takes their snide comments and supe-
rior attitude until at last they decide it is time to go out.

'There were four of them in the back of the car that
night, with yours truly as the chauffeur for the
evening. Of course they ended up at the Anaconda
Club – it was their usual haunt, the only one that let
them behave like animals. And of course, once we're
in there it's the usual shit: "Get the drinks in, Frank",
"Go and score us some coke, Frank", "Tell those
floozies to come over here, Frank".

'And when I'm not waiting on them I'm standing
like some fucking bodyguard for Bobby and his pals.
Every fibre of my being is screaming at me to get the
fuck out of there and leave them to it, because I
remember guys just like me in the pubs and clubs of
Glasgow and how I used to think they were
subservient wankers, the lowest of the low.'

It is five the next morning when the party ends. The night-
club is a stinking repository of empty glasses and
overflowing ashtrays. The drunks have fallen asleep at their
tables. Frank finds Bobby semi-conscious in a toilet cubicle,
hoovering cocaine from the cracks in the cistern. He guides
him outside and into the back of the limo.

'Home, Frank,' Bobby says, giggling 'and don't spare the
horses.'

As they head south the sun is rising over the calm ocean.

'We were only a few miles from the ranch. Bobby had been asleep most of the way, which was a blessed relief, and I was just counting down the miles, thinking about the long hot bath I was going to have as soon as I got back to my digs. Then he wakes up and starts shouting that he needs a piss. The road was empty so I just pulled over to the side and let him out.

'Even now I keep thinking that if I'd just kept on driving for another couple of minutes none of this would have ever happened and that poor lassie would still be alive.'

She appears from nowhere, like a mirage or a heat haze. She is sixteen years old, already tall and lean-limbed in the way of all Masai women. She wears a colourful cotton kikoi *wrapped around her waist. One hand supports the heavy plastic water container on her head, the other rests lightly on the shoulder of a younger girl, thirteen or fourteen years old. They are laughing as they walk side by side along the side of the road.*

It is a snapshot that will remain seared in Walker's mind, just as he will never forget the events that follow.

'Look at this, Frank,' Bobby calls from the tree where he is pissing. He has spotted them. 'We have company!'

Frank can smell danger. It seems to emanate from Bobby Spurling like sweat and alcohol. The older girl can sense it too. She is fifty yards away but suddenly the laughter dies abruptly as she stops. Her fingers grip the younger girl's shoulder.

'Jambo, mama!' Bobby exclaims, zipping up his flies and staggering away from the tree towards them. He

331

spreads his arms in welcome, but the smile on his face is that of a hungry jackal. 'And how are you this fine morning?'

'I knew what was going to happen. I'd seen him like this before – the leer on his face, the King of the World swagger, the coke and the booze in his veins. He was an animal, a fucking predator. And that poor lassie was his prey.'

Walker gets out of the limo.

'Come on, Bobby – let's get you back to the house, eh?'

Bobby's eyes are fixed on the girl's anxious face. 'What's the hurry, Frank? I'm just wishing this delightful young lady a good morning. What is your name, sweetheart? Jino lako nani?'

'Jasmine,' the girl tells him.

'And who's this, Jasmine?'

'She is my sister.'

'Sister, eh? And what is your name, young lady?'

The girl shrinks behind the folds of her sister's kikoi.

'Let's go, Bobby. Let's leave these ladies to their business, eh?'

Bobby twists his head and glares furiously at Walker. 'What is your fucking problem, Frank? I am trying to have a fucking conversation.' He turns back to the little girl. 'I asked your name.'

'Rose,' her sister says. 'Her name is Rose.'

'Jasmine and Rose! You hear that, Frank? A pair of beautiful flowers.' Bobby staggers slightly as he smiles at Jasmine. 'I wonder if you are as fragrant as your name suggests?'

She recoils as he lurches towards her, but quick as a flash he has grabbed her upper arm. The container falls from her head and lands heavily, spilling water on the dirt.

'Don't run away, pretty Jasmine,' he says. 'All I want is a sniff.'

Frank's stomach roils as Bobby pulls the girl towards him and buries his face in her neck. 'That's nice,' he mumbles, and, still gripping her, his free hand moves between her legs and squeezes. 'So nice.'

'Jesus Christ, Bobby!'

Frank tries to pull him away, but Bobby turns on him like a wild animal. His flailing elbow connects with Walker's chin and the Scotsman falls to the ground. As he comes to his senses, Frank is aware of the high-pitched screaming of the younger girl. He looks up and sees Rose desperately pummelling Bobby's legs as he drags her sister into the trees at the side of the road.

'I couldn't let her see what that bastard was doing to her sister. I grabbed her, put her in the limo. Locked the doors. Then I went looking for him.

'I found them – *him*. He had her up against a tree, trousers round his ankles. She wasn't crying out any more. She was just staring at me with these blank eyes. I don't even know if she could see me. Next thing I know I've got this stick in my hand, a tree branch or something, and I'm pulling him off her by the scruff of the neck, like he was a fucking dog on heat. And I remember his face: all bulging eyes and spittle coming out of his mouth. And I fucking hit him as hard as I'd ever hit anyone before. And I kept hitting him, even when he was down and helpless – and by Christ if it wasn't for his old man I would have killed him right there and then.'

75

Jake drank hot, thick coffee and wished he had something stronger to pour in it. The reassuring kick of alcohol might just help him to get his head around what Frank Walker had just told him.

The sickening rape.

The even more sickening postscript.

'Please continue, Mr Walker,' Jouma said. The inspector, he knew, was trying to remain professional. But the way his lips were pursed betrayed how hard he found it to suppress his anger and revulsion.

'There was no way I could just sit there and let Bobby get away with it,' Walker said quietly. 'Not this time. So I told Clay. Told him he had to shop Bobby to the police, for his own good. The kid was out of control. He could have *killed* that girl.

'But I was naïve. I didn't understand that people like Clay Spurling don't go to the police – if they've got a problem they sort it out themselves. Bobby got a good hiding, one he wouldn't forget. Then he was sent away to Jo'burg. Dougie Roarke said it would be best until the heat died down.'

'What about the girl?' Jouma said.

'Clay offered her money to keep quiet. Said he'd buy her old man a new farm and make sure her sister Rose got a first-class education. But Jasmine was a bright kid. University material. She wasn't like the other village girls who would have just rolled over. And she wasn't going to let Bobby get away with what he'd done.'

'She went to the police?'

Walker nodded.

'Don't tell me,' Jake said, feeling a wave of terrible inevitability approaching. 'The local police chief was best buddies with Clay Spurling.'

'No.' Walker's battered face was impassive, but Jake could sense the turmoil behind the mask. 'He was best buddies with Douglas Roarke. And that's what signed Jasmine's death warrant.'

Douglas Roarke. The faithful rottweiler.

Frank cannot understand why Clay has promoted him to the head of the Security Division. Nobody can. The guy is a knucklehead, a jumped-up Mombasa doorman with ideas way beyond his station. Maybe Clay wants to show the rest of his employees that with hard work and loyalty it is possible to climb the company ladder – but giving a thug like Roarke a position of power is just asking for trouble.

He arrives at Frank Walker's digs in Mombasa late one night, about a week after the incident. With him is a second man that Frank doesn't know. The second man wears a blazer and tie. His flannels are ironed to perfection, his shoes are like mirrors. He is introduced as Lol, an old friend. Lol nods. He says nothing but he has Polis running through him like the writing on a stick of Blackpool rock. Walker can smell it a mile off.

'Where does she live, Frank?' Roarke asks.

Frank has a bad feeling about this. 'Why do you want to know?'

'Just tell me where the girl lives.'

'Her father has a farm a few miles south of Lukore.'

'Is it remote?'

Frank nods.

Roarke unfolds a map of the Shimba Hills reserve. 'Show me.'

Frank points to the town of Lukore, south of the park perimeter, then traces his finger down towards the blue scribble of the Ramisi river, which runs east from the Shimba foothills to the coast.

'Good,' says Roarke. 'Got that, Lol?'

'Got it.' *An Irish twang. Harsh. From the north.*

'What are you going to do?' Frank asks. *He is feeling really skitterish now.*

Roarke winks. 'I shouldn't worry about that, Frank.'

'Does Clay know about this?'

'My job is to make sure that Mr Spurling is able to run the company without distractions,' *he says.*

The three men walk outside into the oppressively sultry night air. Somewhere to the north is the sound of thunder.

'I'm not happy about this,' *Frank says.*

'Well, just remember this, Frank,' *says Douglas Roarke, climbing into a top-of-the-range 4X4.* 'You were there when Bobby fucked that girl. But instead of going to the police you went straight to Mr Spurling instead. That makes you an accessory. It makes you as guilty as that little prick.'

★

Jouma leaned forward. 'Quarrie and Roarke knew each other?'

'Call it a shared love of the turf,' Walker said. 'One of Security Division's duties was to look after Clay Spurling's precious horses when they were running at meets. Roarke also ran a little bookmaking syndicate on the side. Lol was big into the gee-gees, but he wasn't much of a tipster. He ended up owing Roarke fifty grand. Rather than break his knees, Roarke offered Lol the chance to clear his debts with a one-off job.'

Jouma gasped. Had he heard right? Was the man whose death he had so diligently investigated little more than a thug for hire?

'A few hundred yards north of here you'll come to the Ramisi river,' Walker continued. 'Follow it east towards the hills for five or six miles and that's where the girl lived with her sister and her old man. Malachi was out in his Jeep that night, checking the perimeter for poachers like he always did. He saw the flames. But by the time he got there, the place was all but gutted.'

'What are you talking about?' Jake said.

'Roarke's plan to make things go away. That night, after they'd been to see me, Lol drove to the girl's house and poured gasoline over it. Then he lit a match. The one-off job. His slate wiped clean. Houses round here are made of straw and wood. The poor bastards didn't stand a chance.'

In the dark, and on treacherous, unmarked tracks, the best anyone else could have hoped for that night was to get hopelessly lost.

But Malachi knows this terrain like he knows the contours of his own face. He was born in Lukore, grew up in a tin shack on the edge of the town, learned from nature and from generations of knowledge passed down by word of mouth from father to son. He knows where the flames are coming from and how to get there. Even so, it takes him almost twenty minutes to get there in his Jeep.

Too long.

The wood and thatch house is ablaze, the flames reaching fifty feet into the night sky, the glowing sparks hundreds of feet higher. He jumps out of his vehicle, runs towards the building, but the heat is too intense. He feels his skin of his hands instantly start to burn as he brings them up to protect his face.

Above the roar of the flames and the whipcrack of incinerating wood, Malachi can hear the panicked shrieks of goats and pigs in an adjacent corral. He stumbles across to the pen and kicks a hole in the log fencing. The terrified animals bolt, knocking him over in their rush for the safety of the surrounding forest. Winded, Malachi lies on the stinking straw and watches the sparks fall like rain all around him. Out of his sight, there is a crash as the beams supporting the house cave in. Soon afterwards, with nothing left to consume, the flames die down and all that is left is a perfectly formed rectangle of embers.

It is then that he hears the sound of whimpering.

At first he thinks it is a goat that has been unable to escape from the corral. Even when he sees the charred, smoking body lying in the dirt near the ruins of the house, he believes it to be an animal of some description — a dog, perhaps — that has been caught in the conflagration. The fact it has managed to escape the flames and crawl even this far is amazing. For it still to be alive is a miracle — although *the ranger knows it cannot live for much longer.*

He goes to his Jeep and gets his hunting rifle. As he raises the weapon and aims it at the creature's head he mutters, 'Baba yetu uliye mbinguni, Jina lako litukuzwe', *the Lord's Prayer, the only one he ever learned. And as his finger tenses on the trigger the creature lifts its arm and, to Joshua's astonishment, he sees a human hand attached to it, seared skin hanging from the tiny fingers.*

'It was Lol's only mistake. He never bothered to hang around to check. He just assumed they were all dead. But they weren't.

'Rose had gone round the back of the goat shed to spend a penny. She saw it all. Heard the screams. Saw that *bastard* standing there with his rifle, just in case one of them managed to get out of the house.

'When Lol had gone, she tried to help them, even though they were already dead. But of course she got too close. Her nightdress caught fire. God only knows how, but the kid had the presence of mind to throw herself in the water trough. Even then, if it hadn't been for Malachi she wouldn't have survived.'

Even as he smears her fire-blistered body with a healing balm of neem tree pith mixed with honey and crushed aloe leaves, Malachi knows that the girl will die. No one can possibly survive such terrible burns. Especially not a young girl. Not that she looks anything like a girl now. She barely looks human. Her features have melted, her limbs have shrivelled. What skin remains hangs from her bones like skeins of charred fabric. But as long as he can see her heart pulsing against her ribs, and as long as he can hear her wheezing breaths, Malachi will do what he can for her.

When he has finished tending to her, he carefully lays her down on a bed of soothing lavender, garlic and eucalyptus leaves and goes outside. What happens now is up to God alone. Part of him hopes that He will come for her in the night and spare her the agonies to come.

But the next morning, when he goes inside to say a prayer for the dead, he discovers to his astonishment that she is still alive.

'Later on they found two bodies in the house, but they didn't have anything like forensics to prove that it was arson. They assumed a spark from the fire had caught in the roof. It happens all the time. Folk in Lukore who knew the farmer said they were sure he had two daughters, but there was no sign of Rose. The cops decided she must have run off. Some of them even reckoned she had started the fire. Anyway, they soon lost interest.'

Spring becomes summer, and summer becomes autumn. Hidden from the world in the ranger's remote house in the foothills of the Shimbas, Rose clings tenaciously to life. Malachi tends to her as best he can. He covers her body with maggots to clean the necrotic flesh, and tends her raw, weeping skin with herbal unguents until scar tissue forms and nights pass without the sound of her screaming with pain. He tells no one of her existence – no one, that is, except his friend Frank Walker.

'Where is she now?' Jouma asked. He was almost rigid with horror at what he had heard.

'As soon as she was strong enough Malachi took her to the orphanage at Majimboni,' Walker said. 'He said he'd found her after a forest fire. They took her in.'

'When was this?'

'A year ago, give or take.'

'And you have seen her since?'

'No. If Roarke even suspected Rose was still alive he'd have her rubbed out in a second. But she's safe now. That's all I need to know.'

'Why the fuck didn't you tell the police about this?' Jake demanded. 'Why now?'

Walker's expression hardened. 'I told you. Because it would have made no difference.'

'Jesus!'

Jake looked across at Jouma, but the inspector was lost in dark thoughts of his own.

He had seen her, down there in those terrible vaults beneath the ground.

Rose. The little girl who loved her sister.

The creature who killed without compassion.

'Wherever you think Rose is, Mr Walker, I'm afraid you are mistaken,' he said.

Walker looked at him in puzzlement and was about to say something when Malachi stood sharply from his chair and came across to the table, a hunting rifle gripped lightly in his hands.

'What is it?' Walker asked him.

'Something . . .' the old ranger muttered, his eyes scanning the horizon. 'Something . . .'

There was a crack – but by the time they heard it a soft-pointed bullet travelling at twice the speed of sound had already penetrated Malachi's head and blown his skull to small fragments. Jake, who was still squinting at the puff of smoke rising from the grass a hundred yards away, didn't even know that they were being shot at until Walker grabbed his arm and pulled him to the ground where Jouma had already flung himself. There was a noise like a wasp and a fist-sized bite appeared in the table above his head. There was a pain in his arm and when he looked down he saw that the bullet had taken a chunk of flesh from just above his elbow.

'What the hell's happening?' he cried out.

'Unfinished business,' Walker said grimly. He looked across at the Jeep. It was no more than fifty yards away, but he knew that they would be dead long before they reached it. 'I hope you can run, gentlemen. Because next time he won't miss.'

76

Tom Beye looked peevishly at the telescopic sight on the barrel of his Mauser 03 hunting rifle. Twice he'd had Frank Walker in the cross-hairs, and twice he had been undermined by a faulty scope. As a result his only kill was the flea-bitten Masai ranger – and, while this was personally gratifying, it was not what he had intended.

Nobody knew that Walker and the scrawny Masai pig had bushwhacked him and left him to walk fifteen miles back to the highway the other day. *And nobody would know*, especially not Mr Roarke, because Tom Beye had vowed on that long march across the plain that he would return and kill Frank Walker.

It had been dark last night when Beye set off from Mombasa. He had camped under the stars and then, shortly before first light, he had taken his gun and gone hunting for his quarry on foot. Malachi was not the only one trained in bushcraft, he thought to himself. His own father had been a hunting guide in the Mara – and had crime not been infinitely more profitable, Beye would have followed him.

Finding the bivouac had been easy; keeping down-wind and blending with the contours less so because he was a big man and even in his camouflage suit he presented a large area to conceal. But he had done it. And had it not been for his damn gunsights he would have bagged his prey.

Beye was not unduly concerned, however. The big African stood up from his concealed firing position in the long oat grass and watched Walker and his two friends running in the direction of the river. With his rifle at hip level he strode the short distance to the bivouac where Malachi lay sprawled on the ground. Bits of his head were sprayed against the rough canvas of one of the bush tents. Beye spat on the corpse, then reached down and picked up the ranger's rifle. It was an old-style Winchester, cumbersome and heavy compared to the sleek steel and polymer Mauser. But it was still lethally effective. It could come in useful. Beye slung the weapon over his shoulder and climbed into the abandoned Jeep.

The three men, unarmed and on foot, knew their only chance of survival was to reach the river north of the bivouac. But to get there meant crossing an expanse of open rolling grassland before the ground fell away sharply to the muddy riverbank less than a quarter of a mile away.

Jake heard the throaty roar of the Jeep's engine behind him and realised that they had suddenly become the prey in an obscene manhunt. He also knew that, as in any hunt, the predator would target the straggler of the herd first.

Blood was pumping from the bullet wound in his

arm, but at least he was able to run. And had it been just him and Walker they might have stood a chance. Jouma, though, was already struggling to keep up. Jake could hear the older man's hacking breaths and was aware of his footsteps getting further behind.

'You've got to run, Daniel,' he said. 'You can't stop.'

Jouma could only look at him with desperate eyes; and behind him, cresting the low rise, was the Jeep, its driver silhouetted against the rapidly dipping sun.

'Walker!' Jake shouted. 'How far now?'

'Just beyond the trees,' said the Scotsman, pointing at a stand of flame trees a hundred yards ahead.

It was no distance at all. But Jake looked back again and saw Jouma stumble and fall to his knees – and he knew the inspector was not going to make it.

How sweet, Beye thought, as up ahead Walker and the other white man stopped to grab the little policeman and drag him to his feet. *But how foolish*.

With one hand gripping the steering wheel, Beye reached for his Mauser and, resting its barrel on the frame of the windscreen, fired indiscriminately at the three targets ahead of him. The bullets zipped harmlessly over their heads.

Beye cursed. This was no good. He stopped the vehicle and quickly reloaded. Then he stood and carefully drew a bead on Frank Walker.

He fired, and Walker went down.

Jouma tumbled over the lip of the ravine and down twenty feet of muddy bank. His lungs burned and his legs were weak as feathers, and his only thought was that if he died here in this wilderness Winifred would never know what had happened to him. The thought of her sitting in their apartment day after day, hopefully looking at the door, was more than he could bear.

No – he would not die here. He *could not* die here.

The last thing he'd seen before flinging himself over the edge was Frank Walker lunging forward, seemingly hit by a bullet. Yet when he looked up he saw that Jake and Frank were a few yards away at the edge of a sluggish brown river. The Scotsman's face was twisted in pain as Jake tied a makeshift tourniquet around his thigh.

'He's hit, but he's OK,' Jake called.

'Who is shooting at us?' Jouma demanded.

'Tom Beye,' Walker said through gritted teeth. 'Security Division's resident psycho. He's after me – but the bastard won't stop until he's got all our heads on his office wall.'

They were in a shallow canyon, fifty yards wide, where the fast-moving river had eaten through the plain, leaving jagged earth banks on either side. The only possible advantage it gave them was that it was impossible to get the Jeep down here. But with one of their number lame and being propped up by the other two, and one of those two shot, it was, Jake thought, a perfect shooting gallery for anyone wishing to try their luck on foot.

And there was another problem, one which only became apparent when he looked across to the far bank of the river.

'Walker—' he said.

The Scotsman followed Jake's outstretched finger. 'Oh, shit,' he said.

'What is it? Why have we stopped?' Jouma demanded.

Then he saw them. A dozen fat, malevolent crocs lying in wait on the mud flats, like some ghetto gang waiting for their next victim on a street corner. And Jouma, who still had nightmares about the reptiles he'd come face-to-face with in a croc park near Flamingo Creek recently, realised that in comparison to these monsters the ones in captivity were little more than lizards.

'Come on, Frank,' Jake said. 'We've got to take the chance.'

He reached down and attempted to heave Walker to his feet with his one good arm. But Walker shook his head sadly.

'I'm fucked, Jake. You and Jouma take your chances. It's me he wants.'

'For Christ's sake, Frank!'

But Jake knew Walker was right. Beye had climbed down the ravine and was now sauntering along the riverbank, the Mauser at his hip and Malachi's ancient Winchester slung over one massive shoulder. Jake recognised him now: the Spurling goon who had smashed a baseball bat into the face of one of his own men at Jalawi village. Somehow he suspected he was not the type to let bygones be bygones.

'Go on,' Walker insisted. 'Get the fuck out of here.'

Jake turned to look at Jouma and their eyes met – and in that instant he knew that they were going nowhere. Furthermore, he understood precisely what the inspector planned to do next – and that there was nothing he could do to stop him.

Jouma breathed deeply and marched out in front

of the hulking gunman, who stopped, momentarily nonplussed.

'My name is Inspector Daniel Jouma of Coast Province CID and I order you to put down your weapon,' he said, hand outstretched as if he was stopping traffic on Digo Road.

Beye glared down at him, a huge rhino confronted by a scrawny bird. 'Inspector Jouma?' He smiled. 'I remember you now.'

'And I remember you, Tom Beye. A bully and a reprobate from Chamgamwe.'

'Maybe I will kill you first, then.'

'You are such a big man with your guns and your fine talk,' Jouma said. He moved slightly towards the river – and, as Jake had hoped, Beye followed him with the snout of the Mauser.

'What must your mother think of you?' Jouma was saying, taking another step away from Jake and Frank Walker. 'You could have made her so proud.'

'My mother was a whore who never cared whether I lived or died.'

Jouma took another step away, then walked up to Beye and defiantly jabbed him in the chest with his finger. 'You are a disgrace, Tom Beye. I can sympathise with her.'

With a growl Beye swiped Jouma across the face with the butt of the rifle. The inspector fell backwards and landed by the river's edge. Jake knew that this was the moment of opportunity that Jouma had engineered. But as he tensed himself and prepared to lunge, Frank Walker sprang to his feet. With a roar of pain and anger the Scotsman flung himself at Beye. The bigger man saw him coming and raised the rifle defensively, but he was off balance and facing the wrong way. The two men grappled frantically, Beye's brute strength against Frank Walker's adrenaline-fuelled impetus, and for a moment their eyes met. Then they staggered backwards and into the fast-flowing water.

On the opposite bank the crocs saw the splashing and needed no second invitation. In a sudden, terrible movement the monsters came to life and slid sinuously under the surface. Jake saw and tried to shout a warning, but the crocs had transformed into torpedoes. Crazed by the taste of Walker's blood in the water they reached the two struggling men in a flash. Tom Beye's eyes widened in surprise, then terror, as something snagged his leg and, with one powerful tug, ripped it out of its socket. The jaws of another of the monsters clamped down on his arm, crushing flesh and bone to a pulp. Now the brown water was frothing pink as the frenzied crocs fought each other for what remained of Beye's shredded body. For one horrible moment the limbless torso was tossed in the air as if the crocs were playing with it; then it was gone as the reptiles continued to tear it apart beneath the surface.

Of Frank Walker there was no sign.

Jake sat down on the bank, his heart pounding, his eyes still fixed on that small expanse of water where Walker and Beye had been just a moment ago. Now there was nothing except the swirls of the current.

There was a groan and Jouma picked himself up out of the mud. There was an unsightly gash on the side of his face where Beye had hit him with the rifle.

'Are you all right, Inspector?'

Jouma nodded. 'I am more concerned with what Winifred will say.'

'There are some things a man should keep to himself,' Jake said.

Slowly, painfully, the two men grabbed hold of each other and began hobbling back along the riverbank.

Day Eight

77

They came for Douglas Roarke shortly after eight o'clock in the morning, although the head of the Security Division had been at his desk since five, ever since a police mole had alerted him to the email Cyril Craven had sent to the head of CID the previous day. He was wearing a crisp new suit and a tie with the Spurling Developments insignia. Beside him was an overnight bag packed with a change of clothes and a bag of toiletries – an optimistic touch considering he knew he would be heading first to Kingorani, and then the rat hole of Shimo la Tewa.

The possibility of making a run for it had crossed his mind, of course – but only because he was accustomed to weighing every option. So had the idea of denying everything. But to do that would be to admit that he was wrong, and that was something Douglas Roarke was simply not prepared to do. His job was to protect the interests of Spurling Developments, and for the last five years that was precisely what he had done. Why should he belittle his achievements when so many people in this shithole of a country had achieved absolutely nothing? He would go to prison knowing that he had wielded the sort of power those in positions of authority could only dream about. His time would come, he knew that. In years to come they would speak of Douglas Roarke as a legend.

Indeed, as he stood at the plate-glass window of his office and watched the ant-like police officers running inside from the street far below, Roarke's only concern was that in spilling the beans Cyril Craven had got his story right.

Craven's confession was Roarke's testament.

He would hate to think that the lawyer had left anything out.

The document consisted of ten neatly typewritten pages. As befitted a lawyer of more than thirty years' experience, Cyril Craven had laid out his allegations concisely and accurately.

'Where is he now?' Jouma asked. He too had been up early, mainly to escape from his apartment before Winifred came back from her sister's.

'I have him at a secure location,' Simba said, but did not elaborate. She picked up the document on her desk. 'There is enough here to indict Douglas Roarke for murder and more than a dozen high-ranking Spurling Development executives on conspiracy charges. Not to mention most of the Security Division.'

'And Craven will testify?'

'As long as certain conditions are met. Immunity from prosecution being one of them.'

Jouma smiled to himself despite the pain from the

stitches on the side of his face. It always struck him as perverse that someone inextricably linked to a crime could bargain their way to freedom by ratting out the others. It seemed *unfair* somehow.

'What about Bobby Spurling?'

Simba shook her head. 'Even Craven does not believe there is enough evidence to charge him with anything. Roarke's Security Division worked independently. He always ensured Clay and now Bobby Spurling could never be implicated in any felony.'

'A loyal servant indeed. And so Bobby walks free.'

'We have nothing with which to charge him, Daniel.'

Not yet, Jouma thought. *But somewhere under the city was a secret that would put Bobby Spurling behind bars for the rest of his life.*

78

As he drove south to the tiny village of Majimboni, Mwangi listened again to the interview that he had recorded the previous day with Brother Willem. It was quite extraordinary, he thought, pressing the headphones of his dictaphone into his ears. He had only gone to confront the priest about Sister Gudrun's use of corporal punishment on the young nuns – but once he had started talking, Willem had not stopped.

WILLEM: In just three years at the Lake Victoria mission I raised money for three churches, six schools, and I don't know how many community centres.

MWANGI: And how much money did you raise for yourself?

WILLEM: Nothing too much. Nothing that would raise suspicion.

MWANGI: How much?

WILLEM: A hundred thousand dollars maybe. Believe me, that was nothing compared to the money that was being donated. It almost made me sick to see these rich bastards trying to buy their salvation.

MWANGI: It strikes me you had it made. Why did you move to the coast?

WILLEM: All waterholes run dry eventually, Constable Mwangi. I heard about plans for a mission in Jalawi. It sounded good — a small village, pretty much unexploited, and with untapped wealthy donors in Malindi and Mombasa. Getting the job of running the mission wasn't a problem — I had a good record; the elders back in the Netherlands were impressed with my work out west. But when I got there, I found that grasping old bitch had beaten me to it.

Oh, yes, Mwangi thought, when it came to ripping off the Church, the sainted Sister Gudrun was in a class of her own. She had been raising money for charitable projects — and systematically lining her own pockets — for nearly twenty years. She had worked all over Kenya, but in recent years had settled at a mission outside Majimboni, in the foothills of the Shimbas, conveniently near the money wells of Mombasa in the north and the estates of the rich white landowners along the Tanzanian border.

Mwangi found it hard to suppress a smile when he thought of Willem and Gudrun each racing head-long for the vast unexploited pastures of Jalawi — only to run straight into each other.

WILLEM: Maybe it takes a sinner to recognise a sinner. But we looked at each other and we just knew.

To their credit, the two sinners had quickly decided there was no point fighting over the spoils. Instead, they had entered into an uneasy, but lucrative truce. Together they raised money to build the church – naturally sharing the skim fifty-fifty – and were busy tapping businesses for the funds to build a school when the bombshell dropped.

WILLEM: Gudrun had heard about a Catholic mission near Kisumu that had been bought out by Spurling Developments for over half a million dollars – just because they wanted to build a house for some rich government official. So you can imagine how we felt when we heard they wanted to build a hotel at Jalawi village.

Their optimism was justified. A few days later a representative of Spurling Developments called Cyril Craven offered them a cool million dollars in compensation for the razing of their church and their support in the unlikely event the planning application should experience difficulties.

WILLEM: That day was the first time I ever saw Gudrun smile. But the very next day, half the planning committee were rounded up on corruption charges and the Spurling application was put on ice. I should have known then that God was displeased with us.

For six frustrating weeks, Gudrun and Willem had been forced to carry on as normal while they waited for the jackpot to drop.

Then Gudrun disappeared.

MWANGI: Which means you stand to get all the money.

WILLEM: I know how it must seem, but I swear I didn't kill her. She must have got in with the wrong crowd. They must have found out she was ripping them off.

Poor foolish priest, Mwangi thought. Willem dealt with shady financiers, but clearly didn't understand that if Sister Gudrun *had* upset them her body would *never* have been found.

No, what had happened to her in the sewer went far beyond any money vendetta. It was, as he had suspected, everything to do with the thirty-nine whip marks on the old woman's back, and the fading scars she had inflicted on Sister Florence and God knew how many innocent children over the years.

79

The FBI's Mombasa operation might have been run on a shoestring, but there was always a little Federal capital stashed away for a special occasion. It was in the form of a sound-proofed room in the basement of a rented house next to the airport, and Special Agent Bryson was currently heading there in the back of a taxi cab. He had showered and shaved and changed into a fresh suit and, as he left Room 507 of the Colonial Hotel for what he hoped would be the last time, he caught a glimpse of himself in the wardrobe mirror and concluded that he looked ten years younger.

The house was in a less than salubrious neighbourhood patrolled by gangs of feckless-looking toughs in soccer shirts. Its windows were boarded up and its plasterboard walls shook every time an aircraft took off. Bryson paid the cabbie and rapped on the door. He did not bother to look up at the concealed CCTV camera in the frame.

After a few moments the door was opened by a tall black man in a T-shirt, cargo pants and slippers.

'Afternoon,' Tradecraft drawled.

Bryson followed the surveillance expert across bare floorboards to a steep flight of steps accessed by a trapdoor. This led to a newly installed steel door, which led to a fully enclosed steel box manufactured in the United States and flown to Africa at great expense to the American taxpayer.

Inside was what looked at first glance like a weights bench, except it was six feet long and bolted to a fulcrum that enabled it to be swung up and down like a see-saw. Shackled to this bench was a man. He was naked save for a pair of soiled briefs. His head was pointing at a slight downward angle and his face was covered by a cloth. It was the man they had picked up at the boatyard at Flamingo Creek – and any time now he was about to admit that he was a highly paid assassin called the Ghost.

'Clarence Bryson, as I live and breathe!' exclaimed Agent McCrickerd, who was standing next to the Ghost, holding a two-litre pitcher of water in his hand. 'You going out on a date?' he asked, staring at Bryson's suit.

Bryson smiled. 'One of us has to raise the tone around here, John.'

McCrickerd, who was wearing surfing shorts and sandals, chuckled to himself. Then he slowly poured the water over the face of the man on the bench. The Ghost immediately began to choke and beg for mercy in an accent that struck Bryson as being vaguely Arabic.

'Tell me who you work for and I'll stop,' McCrickerd said reasonably.

'I already tell you!' the man screamed. 'I work for

Spurling Developments. I in security!'

McCrickerd looked across at Bryson and shrugged. Bryson indicated for him to remove the cloth from the prisoner's face. He saw now that the Ghost was in his late twenties, with a straggly goatee beard.

'My name is FBI Special Agent Clarence Bryson. What is your name?'

'Ibrahim. Ibrahim Mohammed.'

'Where do you live, Ibrahim?'

'Mombasa.'

'And what were you doing at Flamingo Creek, Ibrahim?'

'My boss, he tell me to go there. Spy on English boat skipper.'

'I see. And who is your boss?'

'Mr Roarke.'

'Ah-huh. And Mr Roarke works for Spurling Developments, is that right?'

A look of desperate hope flashed across Ibrahim Mohammed's face. 'That's right.' He nodded frantically.

'And did he tell you to go armed with a stiletto knife?'

'Stiletto? That no stiletto! Is *shafra*! Arab knife. I always carry for my own protection.'

'Is that so?' Bryson said. 'Well, let me tell you something, pal: I've made a call to Spurling Developments. Mr Roarke is behind bars and they've never heard of anyone called Ibrahim Mohammed. Which makes me think either they're mistaken or you're not telling us the truth. Are you telling us the truth, Ibrahim?'

'I swear! I swear!'

Bryson looked long and hard into the prisoner's eye. Then he nodded to McCrickerd, who replaced the cloth over his head.

'Let's try again, shall we, Ibrahim?' he said over the sound of muffled screams.

80

The church mission and orphanage at Majimboni had struggled on for a few months after Sister Gudrun left for Jalawi village. But now the white-wash had faded and peeled on the small wooden chapel, the breezeblock bunkhouse was crumbling, and the tiny open-air classroom was overgrown with weeds. It was hard to imagine that this place had once been home to twenty children, Mwangi thought. Even the ghosts had deserted it.

'After she went, we could no longer afford even basic amenities. Food, clothes – even chalk for the blackboard. Sister Gudrun may have had her faults, Detective Constable Mwangi, but she was a bloody miracle worker when it came to squeezing money out of people.'

The speaker was a dumpy, middle-aged white woman called Susan Gillen. She ran a provisions store in Majimboni village, but had taught part-time at the mission.

'What happened to the children?'

'Some of them went to other orphanages. The

younger ones, that is. The others – they just disappeared.'

'You say Sister Gudrun had her faults?'

A look of distaste appeared on Gillen's baggy face. She stopped and stared at the derelict classroom where once she had taught. 'She had a reputation as a disciplinarian.'

'She used to whip the children, didn't she?' Mwangi said.

Gillen nodded sadly, and her eyes moistened. 'The poor children. The younger nuns if she felt they had misbehaved. Gudrun said there was a purpose to it, that it showed how Christ had suffered for our sins. But that was all bullshit, Detective Constable Mwangi. The woman was a sadist.'

'Sister Gudrun is dead,' Mwangi said. 'The pathologist tells me she was whipped – *scourged* – until her heart gave out from shock and blood loss. I believe the person who killed her may have been one of the children she used to beat.'

'One of the children?'

'Mrs Gillen – the person I am looking for has terrible burns over most of their body.'

Susan Gillen blinked, and a tear rolled down one plump, downy cheek.

'Rose,' she said. 'Her name was Rose Oniang'o. Poor little wretch. That bitch made her life intolerable.'

Rose was fourteen years old when she was brought to the orphanage.

That she was still alive, Sister Gudrun said, was nothing less than a miracle.

Why, then, did you treat her as if she was an abomination in the sight of God? Mwangi thought angrily as he drove back towards Mombasa.

'From the very first day she arrived Gudrun treated that child worse than a dog,' Susan Gillen told him. 'Humiliated her in front of the other children, made her out to be some sort of freak of nature. The other nuns were horrified – but there was nothing anyone could do or say. Gudrun ran that mission with a rod of iron.

'What made it worse was that Rose was such an intelligent girl. She was way ahead of the other kids in reading and writing; if you spent time talking to her it was like being with an adult. Yet whenever Gudrun was around she was persecuted. Maybe that was why.

'Can you imagine what it must be like to be whipped on skin that has already been burned? I simply cannot imagine the agony that poor, poor girl must have suffered at the hands of that evil woman. I was pleased she ran away. Everybody was. If she had stayed here, Gudrun would have killed her I am sure.'

81

Brother Willem sat alone in the church at Jalawi, staring at the crucifix on the wall above the altar, praying for some sort of guidance.

But Jesus just stared at the ceiling with blank, wooden eyes – as He always did. Rivulets of blood flowed from His crown of thorns, from the dramatic puncture wound in His side and from the iron nails driven into His feet and hands. Was there any need for so much blood? For so much ostentatious suffering? As usual, He was too self-absorbed to give a shit about anyone else's problems. He preached a good game – but where was He when He was needed?

And Willem needed someone right now. *Some sign*. The police would be here soon. They'd given him twenty-four hours to sort out his affairs in Jalawi, but they were coming for him all right. All he wanted was just one small spiritual intervention, a tiny little miracle to light the darkness.

But no. Nothing. Willem stared at the altar and the font and the crucifix and suddenly all he saw were worthless artefacts and superstitious bric-à-brac. To think that he had wasted his adult life ascribing some sort of higher meaning to this shit when he was nothing but a common crook. Religion was just a cloak he wore to lend legitimacy to his criminal endeavours. He realised now that he had never loved God, or wanted to serve Him. The Church was just something that kept him occupied while he targeted the next person to rip off.

Well, now he was going to hell for his crimes. And not before time, either.

He stood and went across to the altar. He stared up at the crucifix.

'Fuck you,' he said.

Then, with a sudden, uncontrolled rage, he reached up and pulled the heavy wooden cross from the wall and brought it crashing down on the altar. The flimsy structure snapped in half, sending candle-sticks and other items flying. A bottle of chrism oil shattered on the floor and was immediately ignited by the glowing wick of one of the spilled candles. The flame licked at the white ceremonial sheet that had covered the altar and suddenly it was ablaze.

Willem saw the fire and instinctively stamped on it. But it had already taken hold, eating its way through the sheet and setting light to the painted mural of the Gospels that hung on the wall. The priest backed away, his mouth open with horror. But as the flames roamed greedily towards the roof beams he found himself transfixed by the sight.

Yes, he thought. *This was the sign he had been looking for. Here was his redemption – his way out.*

He saw the crucifix on the floor and picked it up. He held Christ's punished body tightly to his own, and his own eyes stared heavenward; and, as a section of the roof fell in exposing the blue sky above, Willem fancied that he could at last see the face of God.

The thick black smoke from the burning village was visible for miles around Flamingo Creek. In the privileged sanctum of the Yacht Club, members watched the spectacle from their balcony and wondered out loud whether the fire might spread along the riverbank. This prompted some to become extremely animated about the lack of a proper fire brigade in the vicinity. What if the fire *did* spread? What would happen to their villas and marinas? Would they have to be evacuated, and if so where would they go? Surely it was time that the Residents Association got together and made provision for an independent fire response unit here at the Creek itself.

The residents of Jalawi sat on the riverbank with what few possessions they had been able to salvage and watched their village burn. The mood was sombre but pragmatic. It was not the first time the village had been razed. Nor would it be the last. When houses were made of wood and thatch, and people cooked on open fires indoors, there was always a strong likelihood that a stray spark would set the whole place ablaze. At least no one had been burned to death. One had to be thankful to God at all times, no matter how small His mercies.

Evie Simenon stood with Sister Constance and felt the heat of the flames against her face.

'How long will it take them to rebuild their houses?' the young nun asked her.

Evie smiled. 'It usually takes about a week. But we'll be lending a hand.'

A hundred yards away, the scorched, skeletal frame of the church collapsed in on itself, sending a plume of sparks into the sky. Such was the intensity of the fire that had destroyed it, it would be several days before investigators would be able to enter the ruins of the building to find the remains of Brother Willem – if indeed there were any left to find.

'*My house shall be called a place of prayer,*' Constance said to herself, gazing at the pulsating embers of the church. '*But you have made it a den of robbers.*'

Day Nine

82

Jake had never been to Fort Jesus. But then he'd never been to the Tower of London or Buckingham Palace either. Tourist attractions were of no interest when you weren't a tourist. He justified his visit today by the fact it was no sightseeing trip.

He passed through the gatehouse and into a broad sunlit compound surrounded by high, fortified walls. What struck him most was how peaceful it was compared to the mayhem of downtown Mombasa. He could see now why Jouma came here to escape the madness of his job.

How ironic that the madness should pursue him here.

The inspector was sitting on a bench facing a row of black-painted cannon as if he was a prisoner about to be executed by firing squad. There was a large white bandage down one side of his face, adding to the sorrowful tableau.

Jake raised the bandage around his left arm. 'If it's any consolation, it hurts like hell.'

'I think we are both lucky to be alive.'

'Amen to that. I just hope it was worth it.'

'The story is complete.' Jouma nodded.

As a small child she was always afraid of the dark.

Now she cannot exist without it. It provides her with succour. It comforts her. It cloaks her disfigurement and helps her to imagine that she is still as beautiful as Jasmine used to say she was.

'Pretty little Rose,' her sister would sing as she teased her hair into plaits and secured them with bone clips. 'As pretty as a sunset.'

But her hair has gone now, and so has Jasmine. Both consumed by fire.

It would have been easy to give in to the grief, to the pain. But when she fled the orphanage and came to the city she knew she had unfinished business. What kept her strong was the memory of the soft, almost childlike face of the man who brutalised her sister; the cruel eyes of the man who burned down the house with Jasmine and her father inside it; and the hate-filled visage of the old nun who tormented her in the name of God.

She knew she would have to wait. But it would give her time to prepare.

And when she was ready for them they were easy to find, because they all thought she was dead.

The nun was first.

All those people thronging the Old Town that day, so many eyes — and yet none of them saw the old woman go into the alleyway, or heard her exclamation of surprise as the needle entered her neck and she collapsed to the ground.

The open drain cover, unused for years and covered in dirt, led directly to a culvert of the main sewer. She knew every inch of this section of the underground system because it had been her home for the last few months. She knew that other people lived down here in the darkness, but she hid away from them. She wanted no one to see her, to know that she was alive.

Her preparations had been thorough. As well as the toxin, she had prepared a rope harness with which she could drag the deadweight of her victims. She had also chosen her location carefully: the pipe was at a slight incline down to the junction with the disused tunnels beneath the Fort. The tunnels themselves were the perfect dimensions for her purposes.

But still it was not easy.

She knew all too well that her strength was ebbing, that the infection that had taken hold in the scorched lining of her lungs was getting worse by the day. She was finding it increasingly hard to draw breath – her time was getting short. But the knowledge that she still had so much to do spurred her on, forcing strength into her tortured body.

It did not surprise her that Sister Gudrun screamed for mercy as the flail turned her back into a mass of bleeding welts, striking deep enough in some places to expose a white nugget of vertebra or a tantalising slash of shoulder blade. A true woman of God would have made her peace and accepted her fate with muttered prayers. But the nun was not a follower. God was, for her, a means to an end.

The scourging continued until Rose's chest burned and she could no longer physically raise the flail. But she had done enough. She would need her strength for the tasks ahead of her. For the sake of her dead sister, her beloved Jasmine, she must remain strong.

'Quarrie was only signed up for one job,' Jouma said, 'and only because he needed the money. But he was determined to do it thoroughly.'

'Not thoroughly enough,' Jake said.

'No – and it would ultimately cost him his life.'

She did not know his name, so she called him the Big Bad Wolf because of the night he had come and burned down their house of wood and straw.

For days she had watched him, learned his routine. She could see that he was a strong man and she knew she should have waited longer, prepared a stronger batch of toxin; but she was getting so weak now. So tired.

She took him by surprise, but he had fought back. Somehow, in the alleyway, she had managed to jab him in the leg. But even as he fell to the ground she knew the effects of the poison would not last.

Dragging his dead weight along that sewer pipe had almost killed her. By the time she finally got him into the tunnel and tied his hands to the hook on the ceiling next to the nun's corpse she was close to collapse. She needed her medication, and she needed to rest for the rigours ahead. Because once her collection was complete, the Big Bad Wolf would know what it was like to burn.

With what little strength remained she crawled through the tunnel to her lair, and there she fell into a feverish sleep.

When she woke, he had gone.

'And Bobby Spurling was the last piece of the jigsaw,' Jake said.

They were walking towards the San Filipe bastion, where a number of uniformed officers and paramedics were gathered around the tunnel access chamber.

'His apartment was near the fort. She must have seen that he was back in Mombasa,' Jouma said. 'All she needed was the opportunity.'

★

The fever was beginning to take hold now. Shivering, sweating, she lay curled in her underground cell and force-fed herself herbs and roots to keep it at bay long enough to complete her task.

As the baby-faced rapist pissed against the orange tree outside his house, just as he had pissed that morning at the roadside, she came up behind him and jabbed the needle into his backside. This time the moringa root solution was much stronger. It paralysed him instantly and she was able to slide him into the connecting sewer pipe easily. By the time the powerful nerve agent wore off, he was in the tunnel, naked and bound by his hands.

'What do you want?' he had asked. 'Money?'

Money was always the solution. They had offered money to Jasmine to keep quiet and she had refused it. So instead they murdered her.

Well, she didn't want his money either.

He was going to die a slow, painful death, just like her beloved, beautiful sister — and she would look forward to hearing his screams.

'I almost wish I had arrived a couple of minutes later,' Jouma said wistfully.

The two men dipped under the police ribbon and stared into the chamber.

'So where was she hiding the last couple of days?'

'I have no idea,' Jouma said. 'The sewer rats say they never saw her, and I believe them. Wherever she was I think she must have come back sometime last night.'

Rose Oniang'o's tiny, wasted body lay curled in a foetal position on the floor of the chamber. Her mouth was slightly open and her lidless eyes stared lifelessly at the wall.

'Fuck,' Jake said.

'She's with her family now,' Jouma said. 'That's the best any of us can hope for.'

Day Ten

83

Bobby Spurling was seven years old when his mother died of cancer. He could remember how beautiful she looked in her casket, her black hair combed and sheened, her lips like rose petals against white skin. He had wanted to reach up and touch her, to see if indeed she was real and not some porcelain reproduction. He could not understand why his father had then closed the casket and buried it under a flame tree in a secluded corner of the ranch. To the little boy, watching the ornate coffin being lowered into the parched earth, it seemed like an act of vandalism to his mother's memory – as if his father was angry with her for dying so young.

But now it was his turn.

Clay Spurling lay in state in the garden in front of the ranch house. With the casket lid open from the chest up he was resplendent in a white suit and pastel-pink tie. On Bobby's instruction the lines in his rugged, weatherbeaten face had been smoothed with dollops of pancake and powder and his cheeks and lips were rouged.

He looked, Bobby thought delightedly, like some ageing faggot.

He couldn't wait to see the expressions on the faces of the mourners as they filed past to pay their last respects to this hard-bitten construction magnate.

He checked his watch. It was nearly midday. The first of the guests would be arriving at the ranch in an hour, and, after the bullshit was concluded, his father's body would be buried beside that of his mother. Were it up to Bobby, the old man's head would be stuffed and mounted above the fireplace; but it would not do to be so disrespectful. Today he must play the role of grieving son, wounded soldier and acceding ruler. He must be both humble and strong.

That would be no mean feat, considering how his wrists were pounding inside their bandages. Painkillers were no good; he needed a stronger pick-me-up before the rigours of the day commenced, and there was only one panacea that would do the job. He tapped a large pile of coke on to the lid of his father's casket, chopped it into two fat lines with his credit card as best he could, and snorted both. Instantly he felt better, and as the narcotic rush sizzled through his veins he looked at his father's face and burst into hysterical laughter.

He turned and looked at the house. He had changed his mind about selling it. Nineteen million dollars was a lot of money – but now that Spurling Developments was his that figure was a drop in the ocean compared to the billions the firm was worth. He had been over the figures with the company accountant and they really were quite staggering.

Yes, he could quite easily see himself living here as *bona fide* Kenyan landed gentry. He looked at the landscaped garden and imagined how it would look filled with the well-heeled élite in their summer finery, Arabian-style marquees gleaming white in the sunshine, liveried footmen ferrying canapés and drinks, and maybe even Coldplay or U2 performing for the guests.

Now that he had ascended to the throne it was time to act like a king – and he couldn't do that in a crappy apartment in downtown Mombasa.

He would, of course, make changes to the place. The old man's staid antique furniture would have to go. He would get the world's finest interior designers in to give the house a much-needed makeover. *But first he would get rid of those fucking desert-rose plants.* Replace that whole area with a Japanese garden of tranquillity. Or how about a garden of remembrance for Clay Spurling? Now that *would* be funny.

His wrists were still aching; his personal physician had told him to expect them to be painful for at least another six weeks or so while they healed. The prospect was depressing, and reminded him that all his grand plans were on hold until his new legal team could sort out the chaos that Douglas Roarke and Cyril Craven had left behind them. The inevitable court case, in which Craven planned to tell all about the nefarious workings of Spurling Developments, would be hugely damaging. The murder charges against Roarke would only make matters worse.

The only ray of light was the fact that he, Bobby Spurling, would emerge unscathed from the whole messy business. He could not be implicated in any of Roarke's schemes, because Roarke had ensured everything was deniable. And as for the matter of the girl from Lukore – well, regrettably, everyone who could have implicated him was now dead.

That included Frank Walker. Dear old do-gooding Frank, last heard of as a crocodile's lunch not five miles from here, according to the reports he had heard. It was just unfortunate that his body would never be found. Bobby would have liked to have given him a good send-off – in a cheap wooden crate back to the Glasgow council estate where he'd come from.

He threw back his head and stretched out his arms and felt the warm sun on his face. A sudden cocaine rush exploded like a firework behind his right eye, and he reached out to steady himself against the casket; but his hand landed on the cold, greasy skin of his dead father's face. It was all too much and he began to laugh again – and this time he couldn't stop himself.

He was still laughing as the high-velocity .300 Winchester Magnum bullet, fired from nearly three-quarters of a mile away, entered his chest at twice the speed of sound and blew his heart out of a hand-sized hole in his back.

84

Normally Harry was loath to share his vintage bottle of Pusser's rum with anybody. But, as he poured out three glasses in the office of Britannia Fishing Trips Ltd, he felt the occasion warranted a little largesse.

'I can't say I'll be sorry to see you leave, gentlemen,' he said.

FBI Special Agents Bryson and McCrickerd laughed and raised their glasses.

'Here's to you, Harry,' Bryson said. 'The feeling is mutual.'

They downed the fiery spirit in one and lined up for a refill.

'So where is our friend now?' Harry asked.

'We've got him downtown in a special lock-up we were keeping warm for him,' McCrickerd said.

'Is he talking?'

'Oh, he's talking, all right,' Bryson said. 'He keeps insisting that he works for the Security Division of Spurling Developments.'

'Yeah,' McCrickerd added. 'He says he was sent to

spy on your partner. Spurling Developments, as you might expect, have never heard of the guy.'

'So what do you plan to do with him?'

The two FBI men exchanged glances. 'Let's just say we have a little facility closer to home that we reserve for people who require more forceful interrogation,' Bryson said.

McCrickerd grunted. 'At least we did last time I voted.'

Harry handed him a topped-up glass. 'Say no more. I'm just pleased it's all over. I don't like assassins and I don't much like being under surveillance either.'

'Believe me, it's been no picnic for us either,' said McCrickerd.

'It's just a pity Jake isn't here to bid you *kwaheri*.'

'I would have liked to have said goodbye,' Bryson admitted. 'From what I hear that sonofabitch has got the makings of a great FBI field agent.'

'Well, keep your hands off him,' Harry said. 'He's spent too long gallivanting around almost getting himself killed. I need him to get back to work.'

'Where is he?'

Harry looked at his watch. 'Right now he will be picking up a client from the Ocean Hotel at Shanzu Beach. A *female* client, I might add,' he said, raising his eyebrows, 'with an exceedingly sexy voice.'

'Lucky bastard,' Bryson said. 'All I've got to look forward to when I get home is my old lady.'

After everything that had happened, Jake thought, he couldn't have asked for a better job to ease him back into the routine. The Ernie's name was Sasha, she was in her late-twenties, she had long copper-coloured hair, and all she wanted for her two hundred bucks was to see humpback whales.

'You don't see many in Belorussia,' she explained.

Well, that could most certainly be arranged. And the fact she didn't want to fish meant he wouldn't need Sammy, either – which was just as well, because right now Jalawi needed every available villager to rebuild it from the ashes of the fire.

They were out beyond the reefs now, and the coastline had slipped beneath the horizon. Apart from a couple of distant freighters heading south towards Mombasa, it was as if they had the entire ocean to themselves.

'You must lead an interesting life,' Sasha said, spinning from side to side in the fighting chair.

Jake handed her a cold beer and cracked one open for himself. 'It has its moments. What about you?'

'Oh, I do a lot of travelling, but I don't see much outside of hotel rooms. After a while I find it kind of defeats the object. You might as well work from the office.'

'So you're here on vacation?'

'Sort of,' she said. 'I have a little work to do while I'm here, but once I'm finished I plan to have a few days to myself.'

'Well, here's to a few days to yourself,' Jake said, and raised his beer bottle. Sasha tapped it with hers, but the bottle slipped through her fingers and smashed on the cockpit deck.

'Jesus, I'm sorry,' she said. 'Let me get that.'

'Sit still.' Jake smiled. 'I'll clean it up.'

He went through to the cabin and got a cloth.

'You never told me what your jetsetting job actually is,' he said as he emerged back into the cockpit.

He barely had time to register the girl was no longer in the fighting chair, when a hand clamped around his mouth.

'I kill people,' a voice said matter-of-factly in his ear.

Jake felt something sharp against the back of his neck and he reacted instantly, smashing backwards with his head. Something crunched on impact and there was a gasp of pain. The grip on his mouth slackened momentarily and he was able to turn. Sasha was standing directly behind him, blood pouring from her nose. There was something strange about her, and it took him a moment to realise that her hair appeared to be squint on her head.

'You're—?' he said in disbelief.

'A woman? How perceptive of you,' the Ghost said, and drove the stiletto blade into his midriff all the way to the hilt. Jake felt no pain at first, just the dull buzz of an impact. He reeled away towards the fighting chair, grasping the warm leather for support.

'You men are all the same,' he heard her say. 'You really do make it easy for me with your preconceptions.'

Jake had been shot once and the sensation was like being kicked by a mule. This was a more insidious sensation; a searing, tearing pain deep inside. It felt like he imagined dying should feel.

'Stupidity helps too, of course,' the Ghost said. 'The FBI must have thought they were so clever to decrypt the transmission – but they didn't think to consider that *you* were the target, not your partner.

Sometimes the simplest deceptions are the best. They assumed, because your partner had been involved in trafficking, you were the very last person they felt they needed to protect.'

'But why me?' Jake gasped. 'I'm just a fishing-boat skipper, for Christ's sake!'

'You destroyed one of their assets, Mr Moore. You *hurt* them. And revenge is often the only motive somebody needs.'

The Ghost closed in for the kill. There was absolutely no expression on her face. The stiletto blade, Jake saw, was wet with his own blood, and he knew that very soon he was going to die for the simple reason that he had killed Patrick Noonan.

'Does it hurt, Mr Moore?' the killer said. 'You should have let me do it my way. It would have been over by now. Painlessly.'

It did hurt. It hurt like hell. Jake staggered backwards against the stern rail. 'Fuck you,' he said, and toppled backwards into the water.

The Ghost peered after him to make sure he was not clinging on to the side, but he had disappeared beneath the surface.

'*Bastard*,' she said, gingerly touching the bridge of her swollen nose and wondering how much a course of intensive rhinoplasty would cost. The last thing she wanted was to look like Rocky Marciano. She may have been a killer, but she was still a woman after all.

The Ghost pulled off her wig and threw it over the side. Underneath, her shaven scalp was hot and itchy and she scratched it with the bloodied tip of the stiletto. Then she went up to the flying bridge and consulted the marine chart. According to her calculations, the Tana river was only sixty miles from here, and the airfield another couple of miles inland. She started *Yellowfin*'s twin engines and brought the boat round on a north-westerly course. In a little under six hours she would be in Somalia. By then she would have a new identity – a prospect which, even after all these years, she still found intensely exciting.

Turn the page for a sneak peek
of Nick Brownlee's gripping new
novel

Machete

coming soon from Piatkus

1

It was Christmas morning in Mombasa, ninety-five degrees and climbing – and what nine-year-old Jonas Yomo had hoped was a gift-wrapped soccer ball under the frosted plastic tree in the living room had turned out to be his father's severed head.

The boy, understandably, was struck dumb with shock. He was now in a bedroom of the first floor apartment in the island's Kwakiziwi district, rocking urgently back and forth on his grandmother's knee while emitting a low, dull moan. His mother, Tabitha, while no longer hysterical, was in no fit state to speak. She wept silently on the sofa with her head on her father's shoulder while he softly stroked her face and made soothing noises.

Paul Yomo's head had been placed in a coolbox and was on its way to the morgue in the back of a police patrol car.

'He was supposed to be on business in Nairobi,' said Commander Charles Wako Chatme. 'What I want to know is what sort of *animal* could do such a thing, Inspector?'

Tabitha Yomo's father was a tall, broad-chested man of sixty-five, with clipped white hair and a neatly trimmed moustache, and in his blazer and tie he still looked every inch the high-ranking naval officer he had been until very recently. His question was addressed in the stentorian tones of a man who expected an immediate answer.

'Be assured I will make it my priority to find out, Commander,' said Detective Inspector Daniel Jouma of Coast Province CID. He snapped on a pair of white latex gloves and prodded a suspicious-looking stain on the carpet next to the polyurethane trunk of the Christmas Tree. 'What was the nature of Mr Yomo's business in Nairobi?'

'You will have to ask his employer,' the Commander said curtly.

Jouma looked at the desolate Tabitha Yomo. 'Perhaps he told his wife.'

'Tabitha has never interfered with her husband's business.'

'Of course.'

Jouma was wearing white latex gloves because his superior, Superintendent Simba, wanted all scene-of-crime sites to be protected from forensic contamination. It was a futile exercise – the stain on the carpet was dog shit that had been dragged in on the soles of the attending uniformed constable's boots.

'According to my officer, the ... *item* was left on the doorstep this morning.'

'That is correct. My daughter found it.'

'There was no message?'

The Commander shook his head. 'It looked like a

football. We assumed it was a gift for Jonas from his father.'

'And you didn't see who delivered it?'

'No. Again, we assumed Paul had arranged for its delivery.'

Jouma nodded. Before being carefully wrapped in silver gift paper, the head had been swaddled in several protective layers of newspaper, presumably to prevent it leaking. It was this that had given it a spherical appearance. Mistaking it for a football would have been easy – especially for an excited young boy on Christmas morning.

He stood up, knees crackling, and looked around. The apartment of Paul and Tabitha Yomo was spacious by the standards of downtown Mombasa, he thought, and certainly bigger than his own in the nearby neighbourhood of Makupa; and he wondered just how much that had to do with the Commander. Paul Yomo was a thirty-year-old credit officer earning nine-hundred shillings a month. His wife, two years younger, was a lab technician on half that. Even combined, Jouma could not imagine their salaries could have afforded a place this size. It also had a well-maintained cleanliness that suggested a maid. The furniture was of a good quality, and there was a modern television in the corner of the living room. Piled under the Christmas tree was a dispro-portionately large number of presents, almost all of them, he had noticed, for the boy, Jonas – and of those all but a few were from his grandparents.

The door opened and the Commander's wife came in. Ellen Wako Chatme was a slim, elegant white woman, as well-preserved as her husband. She wore an ankle-length robe made of turquoise silk, with an understated ruby pendant around her neck.

'He is sleeping,' she said softly, closing the door behind her.

'Mama ...' Tabitha blubbered, and Mrs Chatme hurried across to her daughter's open, needy arms.

The Commander stood up. 'A word, Inspector,' he said.

It was one of those oppressively muggy Mombasa days when the heat was like thick jelly.

Adjoining the apartment block, separating it from a busy main road, was a small walled garden with a lawn of coarse grass and a couple of well-positioned palms offering shade. Jouma and the Commander sat on a wooden bench beneath one of the trees. The Commander had removed his blazer and folded it neatly across his knees. Jouma noted with approval that the creases in his white, short-sleeved cotton shirt were razor sharp.

'What do you need, Inspector?'

Jouma looked at him. 'Pardon?'

'Money? I have money if that is what you need. If manpower is a problem I have people I can call upon who can help.'

'Commander—'

'It is imperative that you catch the person responsible for this heinous crime, Inspector,' he said. 'Now – tell me what you need.'

'I can assure you, Commander Wako Chatme, that I have every confidence in the resources of Coast Province CID. We *will* catch the killer of your son-in-law.'

The Commander smiled sadly and shook his head. 'I was not born yesterday, Inspector Jouma. Nor am I some grief-stricken mother from the slums, prepared to cling to any reassurances the police can give them. No offence to you, Inspector, because I am sure that you are a most diligent fellow – but you and I both know that Kenya Police is an ill-disciplined rabble. So you will forgive me if I do not share your confidence.'

Jouma opened his mouth, then closed it again. He wasn't quite sure how to respond. After all, it wasn't so long ago that his own investigations had exposed endemic corruption in the Mombasa force with the result that a number of its high-ranking officers – including his own superintendent – had been sent to jail.

'Did your son-in-law have any enemies?' he asked eventually, hoping to change the subject by engaging in some relevant detective questioning.

'Not that I know of,' the Commander said diffidently. 'He was a credit officer. Do credit officers have enemies?'

'People who are in debt can sometimes resort to desperate measures.'

'Like cutting off his head and sending it to his son as a Christmas present?' The Commander laughed harshly. 'A person who is that creative should not be in debt.'

His jawline set as he stared over the whitewashed concrete wall at the high rise buildings of the city centre in the distance. It was a look Jouma had seen before, and he did not like it.

'I feel I must warn you, Commander Wako

Chatme,' he said carefully, 'that I will not condone vigilantism under any circumstances. This is an official murder inquiry, and any interference will be dealt with most severely.'

Commander Wako Chatme smoothed the bristles of his moustache with his fingertips. 'Don't worry, Inspector Jouma. I have no intention of interfering in your investigation, if that is what worries you.' He turned and stared at him with the dead eyes of a shark. 'But I *will* be watching. I can assure you of that.'